DOWN BY THE
SALLEY GARDENS

SUSANNA M. NEWSTEAD

PASTMASTERY PRESS

Cover art and design by matthewryanhistoricalillustrator.com/
Photography by Valerie Drew valadrew@yahoo.co.uk
Editing by Gill Whatmough

Published by PastMastery Press
Medlar House
Hanover Drive
Brackley Northants. NN136JS UK
sue@pastmastery.com

DOWN BY THE SALLEY GARDENS

Down by the Salley Gardens
My love and I did meet;
She passed the Salley Gardens
on a flutter of snow white feet.
She bade me take life easy,
as the grass grows on the lea;
But I was young and foolish, a
nd with her did not agree.

In a field down by the river
My love and I did stand,
And on my leaning shoulder,
she placed her snow white hand.
She bade me take life easy,
as grass grows on the weirs;
But I was young and foolish,
and now I am full of tears.

WILLIAM BUTLER YEATS
reconstructed from a fragment
of Old Irish Folk song

Thanks to Rich Price for help with the Latin.

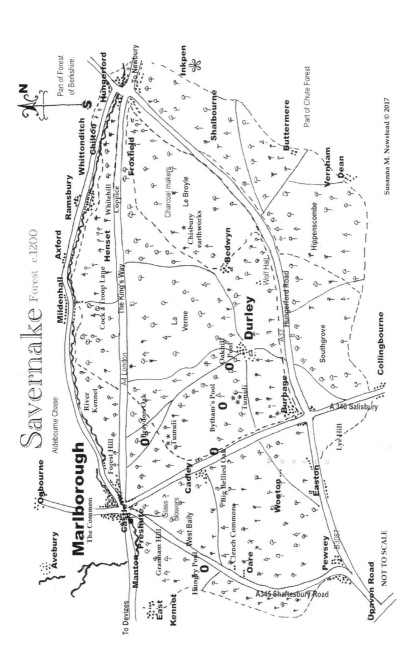

Savernake Forest c.1200

Susanna M. Newstead © 2017

NOT TO SCALE

Marlborough and Savernake Forest c.1200 (1)

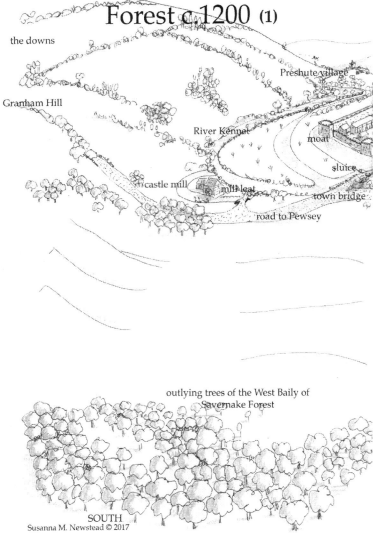

the downs

Preshute village

Gramham Hill

River Kennet

moat

sluice

castle mill

mill leat

town bridge

road to Pewsey

outlying trees of the West Baily of
Savernake Forest

SOUTH

Marlborough Town and the forest c.1200 (2)

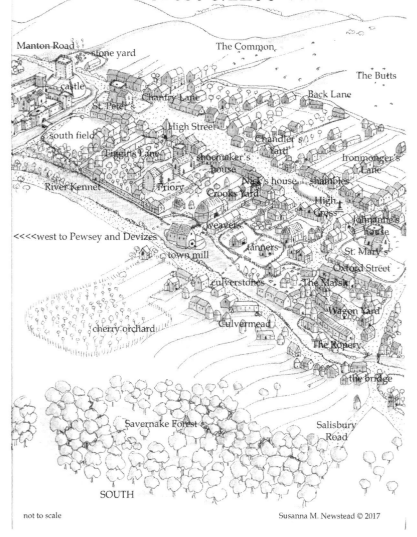

not to scale

Susanna M. Newstead © 2017

Marlborough and the forest
c. 1200 (3)

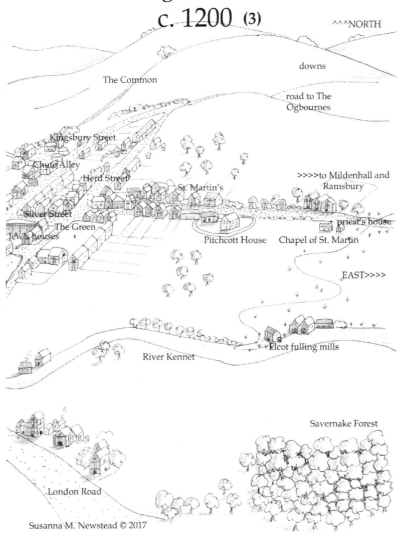

^^^NORTH

downs

road to The
Ogbournes

The Common

Kingsbury Street

Chute Alley

Herd Street

St. Martin's

>>>>to Mildenhall and
Ramsbury

Silver Street

The Green

Jew's houses

Pitchcott House

Chapel of St. Martin

priest's house

EAST>>>>

Elcot fulling mills

River Kennet

Savernake Forest

London Road

Susanna M. Newstead © 2017

Chapter One

I looked down at the body again. At the body of Swithun of Attwood, priest of my maor of Durley. I sighed.

The coroner had come and gone. He had packed his little jury, (for so they were becoming known) of twelve men over fourteen, into the little attic room of the priest's house on my manor and had asked for their verdict on his death.

Some shuffled their feet, I noted whom; some looked aghast, shocked at the ferocity of the attack on a priest, a man of God. Others stared as if they had never seen a naked body before, or perhaps so much blood spill from a human being.

The verdict was delivered quickly. Folk wanted to get back to their dinner, to their homes; or was it that they wanted to go and find their womenfolk and pass on what it was they had seen? Gossip. Oh yes, they loved to gossip. No one seemed surprised that the body they had viewed and had been called to identify was the village priest. The most despised man in Durley. Murder by persons unknown. Let me explain.

"Do you think I should explain, Paul? You are here to write all this down for me because I can no longer hold a pen, so I wonder what you think.

Do you think it important that my reader knows the history of this unfortunate man? How he had been appointed by the bishop of Salisbury, to our little forest village after the death from liver disease of our long serving priest Benedict of Cadley and had turned it upside down with his harsh treatment of the folk living here; free man and unfree villein alike. How he had accidentally caused the death of one young man, turning the village against him. How he had refused burials of the young and the old; had issued penances far in excess of the sins committed and had terrorised the villagers with his nastiness. You do? That's good. Write it down then.

What? What do you mean you can't remember it all? Goodness me boy. I

*can give you fifty years or more and I can remember it. I'm an old man and you
are a young thing. Who is supposed to be the one failing of memory eh?*

*Oh well... yes I suppose so. It did happen to me, Aumary Belvoir, lord of the
manor of Durley and hereditary warden of the king's forest of Savernake. I was
there and you are just here to write it down for me and be my scribe.*

Well, write this then."

Swithun had been the priest of Durley for just about a year. In that time
he had managed to alienate the whole community, including me. I had recently
written to the bishop of Salisbury, who also happened to be my God-father, to
ask if Swithun might be removed from Durley, the little manor of which I was
lord, deep in the Forest of Savernake close by Marlborough town, in the county
of Wiltshire.

Swithun had confessed to me that he never had a wish to become a religious
nor a priest and that he had been happy in his previous life - that of a second
son on a prosperous manor in Hampshire, until he was ten. I well-remembered
the last conversation I'd had with him.

"You were a child oblate then?" I reached for a jug of ale on the table and
found it empty and full of dead flies.

He nodded. "My father gave me to the abbey when I was ten. He had
fallen ill and was like to die. I was a younger son and expendable. My brother
Ralph, the Attwood heir, was there, ready to inherit the manor in Hampshire."

"I know all about the position of the younger son, Swithun. And the
resentments which bubble up under the surface." I think this explained Swithun's
attitude to me for in his eyes, we were of the same class—nobility.

"Go on."

He looked at me under his brows. "You are not the younger son?"

"No, I had a brother once... a half-brother to be exact but that is for another
day." I stretched out my long legs.

"So what happened? I thought that when one reached puberty, there was a possibility of leaving the abbey and making one's own way in the world?"

"My father recovered. He pledged me to Salisbury as a bribe to God, to aid his recovery. For me there was no escape. I was there to pray for his soul and to give thanks for the throwing off of the illness which so consumed him."

"He made a vow then?"

"He did. 'If I recover from this terrible malady, my younger son will become a monk and I will pay the abbey a great sum to have him.' " The bitterness was apparent in his voice.

"Besides, my whole adult life had been spent in the cloister. The world outside was an awesome place. What could I do? Except be a clerk, a lowly scribbler. At least in the abbey I had a chance to rise, perhaps to abbot."

"Yes, I suppose you might. I thought the practice of giving children to the church had been stopped?" I said.

"Some years ago it was still a custom practiced in some places. Money is a very persuasive tool, my lord."

"Ah. But there is a gulf between becoming a monk and taking holy orders and becoming one of the priest-hood. Why did you do that if you...."

"The bishop....not the present one...the last one...."

"Hubert Walter?"

"He wanted men to take the word of the Lord to the people. It is hard to refuse when your whole life has been spent in obedience to your superior."

"Yes, I suppose it is." I looked him straight in the eye.

"You have no calling at all, do you?"

He looked down at his hands. "I have tried. I am the son of a titled lord. I have never lost sight of that fact. I have kept that fact in my heart these fifteen years. It is who I am. That knowledge helps me to come to terms with my life as it is now."

"Hence your disdain for my people. You believe them far beneath you. As your serfs and villeins were on your father's manor"

"Do you not, my lord?"

"No Swithun, I do not."

He stared at me and quoted. "Let every soul be subject to the authority of the great, for there is no authority that is not from the same God, and those authorities who are from God are under orders."

"By the same token must you then accept what has happened to you, for it is God's will. God ordained it."

"It was the will of an unfeeling father."

I shrugged. "I do not feel myself superior to my folk on the manor for we all pull together to make it work. I have a responsibility to them, they look up to me and I do what I can to make their lives bearable. They provide their labour for me and the fruits of those labours, we share."

"But God made you a lord."

"Perhaps he did. He also then, made Hubert Alder a blacksmith. He cannot do my job, though he try and I...well I might make a fist of it, but I don't think I could do his job. No. Not well at all."

Swithun stared at me trying to understand my reasoning.

"You did not wish to be a priest. So why such zealous pursuance of the word of God as you see it?"

"It is the only way I can make sense of what I have been sent here to do. I must teach right from wrong. I must bring the people back to the true way. How else am I to validate my life?"

"Well, for a start by getting the folk on your side and you will not do that by bullying, by being distant and making everyone hate you."

Too late, I thought...far too late.

"Surely you must honour your father's wish...?"

He shrugged.

"I was there, remember when you quoted the commandments at Harry Glazer, Swithun. 'Honour thy father and thy mother: that thy days may be long upon the land which the Lord thy God giveth thee.' One rule for Harry and another for Swithun? Hardly fair."

"He is a tradesman's son."

"He is. You do not see the similarity do you?"

In his mind, he was still nobility. Far above those around him. He must have found obedience the hardest of the rules by which he had had to live at the Abbey in Salisbury. I can imagine he had been flogged often for the sin of pride.

And now he was dead.

***

When he was found by Old Joan, one of the village women, Swithun lay on his back in his bed, one arm flung out. He was dressed in his dark brown robe and the front of it was covered in blood. His arms too were lacerated as if he had tried to defend himself from blows which had rained down on him from above. The wounds which he bore were many. A frenzied attack. Some had pierced his throat, others had gone down as far as his belly.

When I had first seen him, I could not tell one wound from another. Blood lay everywhere, splattered up the wall beside him, spreading out on the mattress beneath him, sprayed onto the floor by him.

Now he had been stripped of his clothes. His robe had had to be cut from him, for the blood had melded it to his body and the blows, in some cases, had driven the material into the knife wounds.

He now lay under a thick hempen cloth supplied by my blacksmith.

The coroner had measured and counted the wounds. Twenty.

Twenty major wounds and some little scratches.

"Are you all right lad? You do love the tale of a gruesome murder but your stomach seems to rebel at the writing down of it. What? Something you ate last night? Oh I see.

Shall we carry on Paul my scribe, or do you wish to avail yourself of the pot situated just over there, behind that screen? No? Good."

I lifted the hempen cloth. Yes, possibly twenty wounds. Some much deeper than others. Two to the throat.

"Johannes, come look at this."

My friend and the doctor-surgeon from Marlborough town, Johannes of Salerno, had been staring out of the small window at the back of the cottage.

He had come by my request from his duties in the town last evening, when the body had been discovered and had stayed with us at Durley so that when the coroner had done his work, we might get to work also. We had a history of looking at dead bodies, Johannes and I. I did not know it then, but we would gain quite a reputation for the solving of mysterious deaths, in time. It was now our turn to look at the body and see what we could fathom. Bodies do speak to you after death. They do - but not with the voice.

For example, the first thing we both noticed was that Swithun had been tied. There were rope marks around his wrists. As he twisted in his agony, the ropes which had held him to the bed had scored deep red lines on his flesh.

"He was not tied at first. Asleep perhaps."

"He was lately relying on the flagon to rid him of his memories, Johannes. He may have been insensible with alcohol." I said.

"He woke with the first blow and defended himself. See his arms and hands."

"Then he was tied to the bed. Why would someone do that? Surely they would just keep knifing him till he was dead."

"I don't know," said my friend, "but we cannot tell which was the first blow. My guess is it was one which missed its mark somehow. Then the murderer decided to overpower him no mean feat, he was a young man - and tie him so he could not evade the blows."

"That would be hard to do. Do you think he was tortured?"

He shook his head. "I don't think so. The wounds are nearly all to the chest. One or two lower down." He peered carefully at the corpse. "The lower ones are not delivered with quite so much venom. See how they don't pierce as far as those in the upper body? Almost half-hearted."

Johannes reached for a straw from the floor; a sturdy piece of chaff and inserted it into the wound.

"A few inches only." He threw it away. "Even though the target is softer here and the upper body is protected by ribs."

"Aye...I see it."

"He was not killed immediately, for he bled a great deal and you and I both know that, upon death when, the heart stills, the bleeding stops."

"And the position of the sprayed blood upon the floor and wall indicates that he was still alive after many of the blows."

"Yes indeed," said the doctor.

I cupped my hand around my chin, my elbow leaning on the heel of my hand and scrutinised the body of Swithun the priest.

"Poor man. Shall we let the women have him, Johannes? Then once he is cleaned we shall look at the wounds once more and try to decide which killed him."

***

"Did the coroner look for the weapon?"

"Aye, he did."

We were crossing the courtyard of my little walled manor.

"It was a large knife of some two inch blade and a twelve inches long. The hilt was wound with silver wires. It was thrown in the rushes by the bed and bore Swithun's blood up to the hilt."

"Did you know it?"

"No. I had never seen it before." The coroner had it now.

"I will make a drawing from memory, when I get back to my office. We might need to remember it."

"A good thought," said Johannes.

In my office, a small room off the screens passage of the hall, we sat and fiddled with our wine cups. I got up and shut the door.

No prying eyes, no flapping ears would look or listen to our conversation. Then I closed the shutter to one of the small windows and lit a lamp. We were one floor up but I would have no eavesdropping.

I reached for parchment and a piece of charcoal and drew the knife, as best I could from memory. I was no limner but I could make a drawing of a knife. Johannes watched me.

"It looks a finely made knife to me, one such as a noble man might own."

"Yes, it was."

I finished my drawing with a flourish.

"No gems. Serviceable but fine. Not a cheap one. And made for defence. For fighting."

"A wide blade, pointed and sharp on two edges. Yes, just the type to have made those wounds," said Johannes. "We shall know better when we see the body once more.

Tell me again, what you found when you reached the scene." I sat back on my chair and folded my arms.

"Swithun on his back. Blood everywhere. Knife on the floor. I did not touch it. Left that for the coroner. No light. All candles and lamps extinguished. All shutters closed. Door to the upper floor open. Downstairs door closed—so Old Joan tells me. She had to put the pottage she was carrying to Swithun on the floor to open the outer door."

I looked up at the ceiling and pictured the scene.

"His right arm flung out. No sign of any rope with which he might have been restrained that I could see but I did not search every corner then."

"Any other item nearby?"

"Nothing."

"No wine cup?

"Ah yes. On the floor. Turned up and empty."

"We might find that."

"It was, I think, kicked under the bed by the jury crammed into the space."

"Good."

We sat in silence for a moment.

"Then I called for Hal of Potterne to go and see if Margaret and Henry were all right."

Johannes' eyes grew wide.

"You suspected them above all?"

"I did. For Henry had cursed the man in my hearing and was the one in my mind who had the best motive, the death of his little brother Piers by the priest's hand and the anger to carry out the murder."

"You told me of it. Piers had a lung disease and Swithun locked him in the priest's robing room, an airless and dusty place..."

"To 'think about his sins'." I tutted. "For Heaven's sake, the boy was fourteen... just."

"And he died of asphyxiation?"

"You told me it was possible."

"It is. It is most possible. One can die of an asthmatic attack... yes."

"The boy was asthmatic. I wondered if Henry had taken the law into his own hands for, naturally the priest would plead 'Benefit of Clergy', had we accused him of murder."

"He did not mean to do murder?"

"No. Swithun didn't know that Piers' asthma could kill him. He did not know the boy well at all. It was a surprise to him that he was Henry's brother."

I took a sharp in-breath. "Henry cursed him... wait!" I held my breath as I remembered what Henry, my young manor steward, had said to Swithun.

" 'I hope you go blind and mad. I hope your heart swells and bursts within you. I curse you twenty times with twenty knife blows.' "

Johannes leaned forward on the table.

"I know the coroner has done it, but we must count those blows very carefully, Aumary."

***

Swithun had now been moved in the parish coffin to the altar in the church in which he had officiated for twelve months. Count we did. There were exactly twenty blows. Each one was delivered with the wide bladed knife now in the coroner's possession. Two to the lower throat.

"Missing all major blood lines and the spine," said Johannes, upon close investigation.

"Amazing. Two to the belly, very weak. Almost as if they were an afterthought."

"The rest frenzied attacks on the major part of the torso," I said, replacing the shroud.

Johannes stepped back.

"No....I think we are meant to see that."

"What?"

"Sixteen blows. All in the area of the chest. Only two are in the area of the heart. See...?"

He lifted the shroud once more.

I held my lantern higher. "I do see."

"If you were going to kill a man, wouldn't you try to plunge the knife into his heart, his black wicked heart, as you see it? Here we have blows all over. Some to the left, some to the right. Then there is this one." He pointed with one of his doctor's tools, a thin metal item about six inches long.

"This is the blow which killed him, followed by another one close by. The first is driven up..." he inserted his probe. "See the angle. Into the heart. Under the ribs."

"And the next?"

"Following the pattern of the first but not so strong. Just a blow to make sure, I think. How was he lying when he was found? Which side was to the room side of the bed, which to the wall?"

"He was lying with his head to the back window and his feet to the door. Left side to the wall. Why?"

"It might be significant. It means the wounds to the heart were inflicted with someone bending right over the body. The others were mostly to his right side. You could be more upright when dealing the blows."

Johannes stared at me.

"I did not dare ask you what Hal of Potterne found when he got to Henry and Margaret, his mother's house."

"Nothing. They were not splattered with blood. They had no clothes around the house which were bloodied. They were calm and unruffled. I do not think Margaret could be so if she had just committed murder, even if she did think it was justice for her younger and much loved son."

"No indeed."

When in the room, Johannes had looked under the bed. There amongst the soiled rushes was Swithun's wooden cup. He'd picked it up carefully and smelled it.

"Yes, you are right. Wine. Strong red wine. No water with it, I think"

The flagon, in which the wine had been held, was missing. I had looked round. It too had been kicked away from the bed. I stooped and lifted it by the string loop. The empty leather bottle with some string, wound around the handle, which was used to hang it from a peg on the wall by the bed. I undid the stopper.

"Empty"

"Now we know he was insensible when he was first attacked," Johannes said.

***

We replaced the shroud around Swithun the priest and left him in front of the altar on his bier. We should have to look elsewhere, we thought, for our murderer.

"Is that a good enough description of the murder Paul, my scribe? By the way you are nodding, you think it's an adequate explanation. Then we shall continue.

We shall carry on and you shall write and you will be the first to know the story of how Doctor Johannes of Salerno and I, Aumary Belvoir, warden of the forest of Savernake in my thirtieth year, in the autumn of 1204, solved the murder of Swithun of Attwood, priest of Durley manor."

I was crossing the courtyard when I caught sight of my wheelwright, Phillip. His father, my senior wheelwright, was laid up with a bad back at that moment and though Phil was only 18, he was more than capable of doing the thing I asked of him. Could he please, along with Alfred Woodsmith, make good the old cart which was lying in the threshing barn. I wanted it to carry the body of Swithun of Attwood to his spiritual home at the Abbey of Salisbury and I wanted it quickly.

Phil knuckled his forehead in obeisance. "Right you are sir. Just needs a little tickling—be as right as night."

I wrote to the manor of Stockbridge, asking one of the carters who trundled the road to the castle at Marlborough to entrust my letter to my friend Andrew Merriman, one of the senior men there. He would see that it went out in the royal post with other missives for Hampshire. I had hopes that my letter telling the lord of the manor of Stockbridge that his brother was dead by another's hand and that his body was being returned to Salisbury Abbey, would be read by Swithun's sibling.

Now, I must tell you all what has been happening in my manor of Durley whilst Swithun was being murdered in his little house by the church.

On one of my trips into the town of Marlborough, some miles away, nestling in the downs and at the foot of the forest where I had been born and raised, I had met Johannes' niece, Lydia of Wolvercote. She had come to look after him when his housekeeper was killed in an accident.

Lydia was a widow of a nobleman of Oxford, an arranged but good marriage. We had, we have to say, fallen instantly in love and I had asked her to be my wife on the same day we discovered Swithun's body.

"No. Not really very romantic was it, Paul? You're quite right. But Lydia was not a shallow girl falling into a faint at the very mention of murder. So we were not so put out."

Lydia had come to Durley to stay until we could be married. Do not worry, we were housed apart and had many chaperones to keep us chaste, not least my little five year old daughter, Hawise, a child by my first and much beloved wife Cecily, murdered in 1200.

We had that very day decided to ask the priest of Bedwyn to perform the marriage ceremony for us. The joy of it all had been rather eclipsed by the death of Swithun.

Joy it was. There was much to plan and I left it all to the women, for they excel at such things and would brook no interference. Henry, my steward, would oversee it all.

Coming up to the hall steps, twelve stone blocks rising steeply up to a sturdy door of seasoned oak studded with hard nails, I met my daughter Hawise hovering at the top, the edge of the outer door in her hands.

"Oh Dada! Is it right...? Is he d- d -dead?"

I turned her round and marched her back into the screens passage and the hall again.

"Yes, the gossip you have heard is correct."

She ran on a few steps and then gave a little dance.

"Oh....I am happy about that."

A sharp voice rang out in the rafters. "Hawise Belvoir...that is not a nice thing to say."

I had never heard Lydia speak so to my daughter but she was quite correct to do so and I supported her with...

"The priest was not a good man, Hawise but he was a human being and one of God's creatures. He was flawed and foolish but did not deserve to die in the manner he did."

Lydia came down the solar steps from the second storey of the mezzanine, where the private quarters were situated.

"Your father is quite right. Murder is wrong, Hawise...however and to whomsoever it is done, despite the circumstances."

"But I did not like him madam."

"You may not have liked him, but that does not mean you may murder him, Hawise."

I decided to play with her a little. "Did you murder him, daughter?"

Hawise's face flushed and her eyes grew large.

Hal of Potterne, my senior man at arms who was sitting at the long table in the hall, at a pot of ale, got up and came up to Hawise. He put his hand on her shoulder. To him, my daughter could do no wrong. I was surprised when he said, "Oh m'lord...shall I go for the irons? We shall need to keep 'er confined if she is a murderess…" He winked at me behind Hawise's back.

"Noooo Nooo!" cried Hawise. "I did not kill him...why would I kill him?"

"Because you just said you disliked him."

"Well, there are a lot of people on the manor who did not like him. Some people even hated him," she said, her chin jutting. "You dada, you did not like him at all."

My daughter was, if nothing else, a feisty Belvoir girl.

"Like you Hawise, I disliked him, but not enough to murder him."

"There then..." she said.

"Well, we shall say no more. Though I would like to know Hawise who it is you think hated him so much, enough to kill him, and how you have learned this?"

She smiled then, knowing at last that we were all playing with her.

"Come and sit down and I will tell you," she said moving to the big oak table.

Hal of Potterne chuckled.

***

Firstly, said Hawise, there was Meg the poultry woman. Her mother had been poorly and Swithun had refused to come to her bothy to minister to her when it was thought she might die. I remembered this in a vacant sort of way for had not Edmund Brooker, one of my villeins, told me that his sister Edith had been looking after Meg senior, some while ago?

Yes, it sounded like Swithun.

There was poor Ralf and Edwina who had lost their baby and Swithun had refused to baptise the infant. I knew about this too, for I had had cause to speak to Swithun about his dereliction and was angry myself about his failure to do his job.

Then, said Hawise, there was Joan the laundress. Swithun had been seen staring at her through the bushes when she was down at the stream doing the washing.

Some of the other women had challenged him. It was not simply the fact that he was watching them working. He also watched them if they went to relieve themselves in the bushes and that was not very nice, thought Hawise.

I could see Hal of Potterne trying desperately not to laugh and Lydia turned away too at this information, so Hawise would not see her smile.

Swithun had fallen foul of Mat Fisher too. Mat was one of my villeins who owed me his labour in my fields. He worked for me three days and for the rest of the week for himself on his small plot of land. He also fished the local rivers and pools and was a useful chap to know, when fish Friday came along. Swithun had stupidly disturbed the fish by stomping up and down the bank when Mat was trying to catch trout and a fierce argument had ensued, which boiled over when Swithun accused Mat of not being married to his wife with whom he lived in a bothy close by the reeve's house. He had called Mat's wife awful names, said Hawise. Naturally their children were called bastards by Swithun. My daughter delivered this information with a natural tale telling flair and again we had to smile.

"And then, Sir Swithun...." Hawise always gave the priest this title, "he went to town and started to argue with Harry the cordwainer's man. You know him dada...he's the one with...."

"Yes, I know him. What did they argue about?"

"I don't know, but Harry was pretty angry. My friend Petronilla was in the shop at the time and she said...."

"Thank you Hawise, I shall ask him."

More of my manor folk, it seemed, hated Swithun. Hawise wriggled in her seat.

Peter Brenthall hated Swithun. Peter was the son of my head woodward, the man responsible for the work which went on in the forest itself and my right hand man. One day Peter would take over from his father. I knew all about the hatred between Swithun and Peter, for Swithun had tried to unfairly discipline the thirteen year old for some transgression and I had been called in to arbitrate.

Swithun had claimed Peter's bees. They had been the property of the previous priest and had been willed to Peter, who was a capable apiarist. In anger, Swithun had kicked over a bee skep causing damage to the hive and difficulty to Peter and the priest was stung in the process.

Hawise liked this part of the story and made much of Swithun's leaping about and slapping himself, for the bees had taken their own revenge.

I remembered well the priest's attempt to flog Peter in the church and Hal of Potterne's intervention.

He spoke up now.

"You remember that m'lord.... Peter was proper angry but I don't think the anger went so deep as to stab the priest time and again and with such venom...as we saw on that corpse. No, I don't."

"And neither do I, Hal."

Peter's father was a quiet man, with his temper very much under control. I did not think that John was responsible either.

"How do you know all these things, Hawise?" I asked, perplexed.

She sat up straight and put her hands in between her knees. "Well, when I go for a walk around the village with Felice sometimes, people talk to her and I talk to them too. And they tell us things."

Felice was Hawise's nurse and I could just imagine the gossiping that went on between the women of the village and one who was privy to the goings on in the manor house itself.

Matthew was my cook. He too had argued with Swithun, apparently. Hawise was unsure of the exact nature of the falling out but it had resulted in Matthew chasing Swithun from the kitchen with a meat cleaver and standing in the courtyard shouting that he would kill him. Well, if every man who uttered those words actually put into practice his threat, the village would be denuded of every second man and a few women to boot.

Hawise did not mention the people I had first thought the culprits, namely Henry Steward and Margaret of Manton. Even though I was loath to think it, they were still, despite the lack of evidence, the most likely to have killed Swithun. Their hatred ran the deepest.

"So you see....lots of people hated him, so lots of people could have killed him."

I shook my head.

"No Hawise. I don't think it was any of them. Whoever did this, was very, very angry. None of these people of the manor could be angry enough to kill Swithun in such a way."

Hawise tutted.

"Dada...you have never seen Matthew when he is in a bad mood? He is really scary with his meat axe!"

Hal of Potterne guffawed.

***

I decided that I would go and have a look at Swithun's domain once more. I started with his church. He was still there, of course, before the altar in the parish coffin.

The church was an oblong of stone, flag floored, with a Bath stone altar at the eastern end and one long bench against the northern side of the nave, for elderly or infirm worshippers to rest upon. Ours was a simple little church. No fancy stone work, no carved re-redos but we did have a colourful painting over the west door. I remembered it being done when I was a small lad. Many-hued devils were prodding sinners into the flames with sharp pitchforks. Above, standing on clouds, were pale silvery angels receiving the virtuous into heaven. I now know that it wasn't really very well painted. I have seen much finer work elsewhere. As a child, though, it had terrified me.

The place was swept and clean. Nothing here.

I took the key to the priest's room from my scrip and fiddled to open the door to the small storeroom where Swithun and all the priests before him, had stored the holy vessels and the vestments. It was already open.

Along the back wall a large oak chest, iron bound, housed the community's rolls, sometimes called descent books. These were records on rolled and stitched parchment, of all the marriages, births and deaths of the people of the village and wider forest. Who was related to whom, where they came from if they were not local. Here too were records of the weather and events in the village and forest.

These has been begun by my Belvoir ancestor two hundred years ago and was as far as I knew it, unique, for I had never heard of any other place recording such things.

The rolls were still piled haphazardly, some open, on the small table in the middle of the tiny room. The last time I had been in this room, I had discovered the body of Piers Pierson lying behind the door. The young man; son to Margaret and brother to Henry, who had died of asphyxiation after being locked in this small space by Swithun the priest.

The room however had not yet been swept and dusted; the dust motes flew around with every movement. It smelled shut up and the air was stale but it was better than it had been when I opened it to find Piers lying on the floor. Old Joan no doubt, as I had instructed her, would soon pay a visit to clean.

She came now, down the nave, bustling up after me, in her black gown and blinding white headdress. I now realised, of course, that Joan must have another key to the priest's room.

"Oh sir...I saw you comin' in 'ere and I wondered if I might ask you to 'elp."

"Help you, mother...?" I asked.

"As you know m'lord, I canna read an' the rolls, well he's gotta go back ' ow he was. Could you jus' see your way to puttin' he's in order for me, on the table like, so I can store he's away right?"

I smiled. "Could you not have asked John or Peter, perhaps Henry...?" No maybe not Henry, "or one of the others who can read Joan?"

"John and Peter are out in the forest sir and Henry...well sir...I don't want him to have to come in here for quite a while, if you see what I mean. The reeve has gone close to Bedwyn and won't be back till sunset. Young Giffard and Gervase are working out at West Baily and Hamon is...well I don't know sir."

I realised how few people on my manor could read or write. Some could sign their name, others might be able to make a mark that was their own but few could read. I must try to remedy that by setting up a school and getting my new priest to teach what he might be able, to those who had the opportunity.

My eyes raked the table. I picked up one roll.

"You dust them of mould and I will stack them in order, then together we shall put them in the chest."

So we began our task.

We coughed and we spluttered, wiped our eyes on our sleeves and went in and out of the small room as the need took us, when we were unable to breathe freely any longer. We left the door open and I opened the shutters of the tiny window in the north wall. No wonder poor Piers had found this room deadly.

The rolls began in 1086 when my great grandfather had built the church, the manor and had extended the village. Naturally then the church and manor house had been built in wood and as time passed, each generation had added to it and rebuilt much of it in stone.

I had completed more work on Durley Manor than any of my previous ancestors; I had rebuilt parts of the wall and had caused the gatehouse to be rebuilt in stone. I had added some new buildings to the courtyard structures. I had put flagstones and cobbles in the courtyard and all upper floors of the hall were now of good solid oakwood. There was no longer a beaten earth floor in my ground floor rooms. They were all finished in good stone. I'd installed those newly invented things, the chimney piece, the sort which funnels away the fumes from the fire and had rebuilt the kitchen fire with a fine chimney and new ovens and joined the stone building to the hall. And recently I had put glass in the windows of my private rooms.

The early rolls were stacked together and had not been separated. The dates, ten years at a time - not much happened in a small place like Durley that we needed a roll for every year, still ran consecutively.

Then we reached the rolls for the end of the reign of old King Henry, our present King's father.

As we handled the rolls I realised that some of them had markers attached at various places; flattened stalks of dried straw were split and inserted over the edge. The nearer we came to the present date the more markers there were. What had Swithun been doing with our descent rolls?

"There are only a few to put back now, Joan. Go and rest your old back. I'll do the rest."

She curtsied and thanked me profusely for the help and waddled back down the nave, her white wimple not quite as white as it had been when she arrived.

I sat at the small table and pulled the rolls with the straw stalks towards me.

I unrolled the first, the roller to the top and scanned first part of each page.

Here were five markers.

I looked at the first marked page.

The first date on the page was 1173, a year before I was born.

I scrutinised the page carefully.

Nothing here seemed important. The priest before Benedict had kept the records meticulously, at this time. His hand writing was firm and strong and his ink good quality. He recorded famine and flood, storms and heat waves in the margins with little asides, and this had been kept up by Benedict when he took over in 1174. There were also small letters here and there, with which I was unfamiliar.

I could see the change in the handwriting style. Benedict's writing was smaller and more compact but still easy to read.

However the light was not good in the priest's room and I wondered if it might be best to remove just these four last rolls to my office, to look at in a better light and a less dusty atmosphere.

I gathered up the rolls, put them under my arm and locked the priest's room.

***

Lydia, my affianced, beautiful in a lavender blue bliaut, caught me as I entered the manor courtyard.

"Ah, Aumary...there you are." Looking round to make sure no one was looking, I kissed her forehead. Such intimacy in public was frowned upon.

My, what have you been doing? You are full of dust."

"Aye, I shall shake out my shirt and it will be fine again."

I balanced the books on top of a convenient cart and pulled the tunic and shirt over my head, ruffling my curly black hair as I went. Lydia watched me, smiling appreciatively. She caught sight of the scar on my shoulder, made by a crossbow bolt, the previous year.

"One day I will tell you the story," I said.

Her eyes raked my torso.

"Save those thoughts for our wedding night," I said cheekily, as I shook out the shirt and donned it again. "We have work to do."

Back in the office, we sat side by side and scanned the rolls.

I read them and Lydia wrote a synopsis so that we might tease out whatever it was in these little rolls that Swithun had found so compelling. Did they have anything to do with his death?

February the twenty fifth — Hamon Black died of the cold. Aged fifty one. Buried seventh of March. Terrible snow storm was written in the margin.

"I suppose he could not be buried sooner because the ground was so frozen," I said.

March the first. Born of Godiva and Arnulf Brooker. A son - Benedict.

"Oh how kind to name the child after the new priest."

"But he did not last...look," said Lydia. There under her finger was a reference to his death four days later and his interment on the seventh March 1187.

March sixth Godiva Brooker died of a fever. Aged twenty five. Buried seventh of March.

"Oh how sad," said Lydia. "She followed her little son not long after."

"They were busy on March the seventh," I said.

There were more references to such events and I could see no reason why Swithun would mark them especially.

We looked through all the rolls.

All the children born on the manor were detailed here. Peter Brenthall, Henry and Piers Pierson, Phil Wheelwright, the four children of Mat Fisher, who was a little older than myself, Gytha, David, Stephen and Alfred. Only three were alive now for David had died in the winter of 1202. And here was his sad entry too.

I leaned back and scratched my unruly curls.

"What can this mean, that he had a marker to every fifth page or so? I can see nothing unusual about the entries at all."

Lydia laid aside her pen.

"It may become apparent at a later time, when perhaps we know a little more about the man Swithun of Attwood."

"Yes. Yes I'm sure you are right."

I closed the last roll.

"Meanwhile the last set of rolls stays here with me, in the office."

I stood. "I must speak with Henry."

***

Henry was in his own office, counting out the money which was paid by tenants who were freemen and who hired their labour to the manor in return for land and housing, for it was Michaelmas when such things were due. Likewise Henry paid those who worked for the manor. We did not have so many of them, but they had to be paid every week.

Before him he had a chequered board rather like a chess board and he had piled coins on several of the squares.

Men were coming in and out of his little room all afternoon. Some stayed to chat a little, others were in and out like a ferret down a rabbit hole.

The piles diminished and there were only two when I entered Henry's office.

He stood quickly and in his haste he knocked the table. The last two piles of coins teetered and fell.

"Sir." I saw his Adam's apple bob as he swallowed.

"Afternoon Henry."

"I looked round the little room. This was the place my half-brother Robert had lived in before his trip to Rouen and his demise there. I sat on the stool in front of my steward.

"Please...carry on with the payment."

"The last two will be in later sir...when they return from West Baily."

"Ah." I looked up at him. He was almost as tall as me. Fair of hair and skin. As fair as I was dark. He would grow thin on top, I thought, as had his father. His hair was worn at shoulder length and like Johannes, he took to catching it back in a queue sometimes. Today it hung free and it shone like sunshine on silken fibres.

"Please sit."

I gestured to his hair.

"You have washed your hair I see.....it looks good. Mine is hopeless when I wash it....just goes curlier," I smiled, "and when the weather is damp... aw! It is a devil to keep tangle free."

He smiled but did not reply and he did not sit. He began to pile up the coins again and stopped as I said,

"Henry, I would talk with you, for it will become open knowledge soon and I would it be told to you now, rather than later when things could be.....a little....difficult."

Henry took a deep breath through his nose. "Swithun?"

"Aye." I leaned forward.

"I was there you remember, when Swithun came back into the church after we had found Piers so I heard you curse him."

"I did," he said. "I did, I will not deny it. 'I cannot kill you, Swithun the priest, but I can curse you,' I said. 'I hope you go blind and mad. I hope your heart swells and bursts within you. I curse you twenty times with twenty knife blows.' "

"You sounded then as if you meant it. Twenty knife blows. What made you say that, Henry? Twenty knife blows."

He looked into my eyes. "I do not know. I was so angry and wanted him to suffer. Twenty knife blows seemed a small number for the hurt he had caused my brother and the grief he gave to mother and myself."

"You know that when we examined the body of Swithun, we found he had been pierced by twenty knife blows?"

"Yes. I have been told it was so."

"A coincidence then?"

"A fulfillment of the curse?" he said glibly.

"You know I don't believe that."

"If you are going to ask me if I caused the priest's death, then I will tell you under oath that I did not."

I blinked. "All right."

From my scrip I took out the little drawing I had made from memory, of the knife which killed Swithun. "Do you know who this belongs to, Henry?"

I felt him jolt and blink but in a heartbeat the hesitation was gone.

"No, I do not know who it belonged to." I noticed the change in tense.

I nodded. "Very well then. I must tell you that of all the folk on the manor, it seems that you are the person with the most urgent need of revenge on Swithun the priest."

He was going to deny it again but I forestalled him with, "There are others, who would have liked to see him dead, it seems and I am going to investigate and question them too. You, however are the person most will suspect. I will get to the bottom of it, Henry, whether you are guilty or not."

"Does he deserve your efforts, sir?"

"Maybe not. But I am a man who likes to know the truth, Henry. What I do with that truth is up to me. But I do like to know it."

"The truth is many things to many people m'lord. I hope you find your version of it."

He sat and began to rebuild the coins again. His hand shook a little.

"My truth, is that I loved my little brother Piers with all my heart and it is the truth that I am glad that the man who sent him to his grave is now awaiting burial in his own pit."

Chapter Two

The forest was a beautiful sight. I stood on the steps of the manor house and gazed out. The sun was lowering, casting the trees with a rusty glow. The stately oaks were already showing their autumn colour of a saffron yellow tinged with rust. The beeches were yellow and rust-brown. The birches were turning a bright green-yellow. There were trees which stayed green all year of course; the hollies and some of the holm oaks and sweet chestnuts which were scattered through the glades, but the hollies had few berries this year and so were not their usual bright colour. A sign of the dryness.

It had indeed been a very dry summer, the recent rain had done nothing to prevent an early leaf death. October was two days old. It was darkening early in these days.

I sat at the oak table with those of my staff who ate with us here in the hall and toyed with my food.

Lydia watched me carefully and Hawise watched Lydia watching me. Felice watched Hawise watching Lydia and told her to sit up and eat properly. Hawise pouted.

The food was good. Matthew was a fine cook and could be relied upon to serve up tasty fare and lots of it, in a season of plenty. There was partridge with roast autumn vegetables and a goose farced with grape, onions and eggs. And good bread and plenty of it to sop up the gravy. Those on the lesser benches ate well but not of the fare provided for me, my family and upper staff.

I would have enjoyed this fare were my mind not elsewhere.

Hal of Potterne, Hubert Alder and Phillip Wheelwright senior, Phil's father, were calling on the various merits of certain foods against illnesses and Phillip was absolutely sure that goose was good for the back. I was so engrossed in their conversation and with toying with my own goose, that I did not at first hear the clamour outside the gates.

Hal was up in a moment and unlocking the hall door. He was about to draw his sword but realised he had left it on the bench in the passage, for no one bore arms at meals in times of peace.

He did not need to, for we heard plainly the chant of, "Fire, FIRE! FIRE!"

Fire was the most dreaded thing in a place like ours, for most buildings were thatched and those of the village lay close to each other and a stray spark could mean ruin for not one family, but dozens.

I ran down the steps followed by all the diners except the women. Lydia craned her neck.

"The church, Aumary...the flames are by the church."

Several people were by the south door of the church and smoke could be seen coming from the small priest's room window on the other side.

I pushed my way through. "Form a chain of buckets...anything...from the manor pond and the stream," I shouted. "Everyone to help. Men, women and older children."

I danced round the people in the doorway. The priest's room was alight but the body of the church was as yet, safe.

"Drag the big bench away....right away," I shouted, for that item was as old and as dry as bones and would add fuel to any fire licking under the door. Some of the women took that task in hand.

Smoke was pouring from the little room. The door looked positively ghostly with its halo of silver smoke in the darkness.

"Phil, ring the bell, those who are further away may not know we have fire." He bolted to the western end of the church, to do my bidding, ran up one flight of steps and pulled on the bell rope.

"Hal, can you organise some lanterns so we might see what we are doing and not by firelight?"

I turned to the village blacksmith. "Hubert, can you get Swithun's body out into the open air. I would not have him roasting here as well as in Hell."

The man laughed at that and signalled some of his friends to help him push on the coffin lid securely and then hoist it to trot out of the door.

I noticed how many people gave the men with their burden a wide berth.

"Everyone... I am going to open the door. Stand back and throw in your water when the main surge of flame is over. No one get too close until I say throw."

I put my hand out to the door. From six inches away I could feel the heat from the black iron ring which acted as the handle. I tore off my cotte, wrapped it round my hand, grabbed the metal and pushed with my foot. It was locked. I had locked it. I felt for the key in my scrip. No time and I could not get near with the hand, it was too fierce a heat.

"Stand back!" I yelled and I kicked the door as hard as I could.

Phil had now joined me and on the count of three we kicked together. The door sprang open. I jumped back as quickly as I could. I knew that when a fire is fed with new air, it surges like a wild beast and becomes hungry. As it was, I swear my eyebrows were singed by the fierce flames which licked out of the door like a pouncing cat.

I patted Phil on the back as he coughed with the smoke.

"THROW! Throw. Keep going. Doesn't matter what you soak...just throw."

I ran around the back of the building. Luckily the shutters were still open from my work of the afternoon with the manor rolls. Smoke poured out of it. I could see nothing inside. However, on the stone cill I did see a darker stain. I put my hand to it. I smelled it. Oil.

I ran back again to the south door. I grabbed a few folk by the arms, careless of whom I caught. "Go round to the window and pour your water there.... be careful. We shall attack this beast from two sides."

The buildings in most danger were the priest's thatched house close by, two bothies by the manor wall, one of them Old Joan's, also thatched and the thatched roof of the stables to the manor over the stone wall, for the wind was coming from the north west. The bothies on the other side of the church were not in as much danger but a stray spark, fluttering up into the night sky and descending again, might ignite them

John had now arrived from his house a little beyond the orchard.

"John! Can you organise water to be thrown on the house roofs? Joan's, Philbert's, The Priest's, Bevis' house and Dysig's bothy and Hamon's. Then the stable roof." He nodded and was off, Peter his son, close behind him.

I then applied myself to throwing water from the bucket chain on the fire in the body of the church and priest's room, from the front of the line.

Suddenly I realised that the person behind me had changed. Small white hands, handed me the next bucket. I coughed.

"Lydia...?"

"You did not think I was going to stay in the hall, with you in danger out here?" she said.

"You are a fine, brave lass," I answered.

"This is my home now," she replied.

***

After quite a while, I gave the bucket to Walter the reeve and stepped back from the priest's room door. I picked up my discarded cotte.

Lydia and I came out into the open and breathed in the clean air of the night.

The bucket chain was still operating but it was less urgent now.

I caught Lydia's arm and we went down the line congratulating and thanking every participant, young and old. I walked right to the manor pond where we bred fish for the eating.

There on the first bucket was the youngest son of my reeve, Johnathan. I clapped him on the back and said my thanks.

I then walked to the stream's edge close by the carpenter's workshop and thanked the chain beginning there. Henry was on the first bucket here.

We had saved our church.

To be truthful, we had practiced this manoeuvre before. I had wanted us to be competent should a fire break out anywhere on the manor and so had devised a way of protecting ourselves by drilling the folk to form bucket chains from the pond and the stream. Depending on the location of the fire, they knew to mass in one place or another and await instructions from the reeve, Henry, Hal, myself or John. It worked. They were all very proud of themselves.

It was very late when we eventually dampened the last of the embers and a couple of the younger lads offered to stay awake and make sure none rose up again, whilst we slept. Dawn was not too far away when I fell exhausted onto my daybed in my office and poor Lydia, her face black with smuts, wearily climbed the solar steps to lie in my good four poster bed. We both stank like a bonfire.

***

Next day, cleaned and with new clothes which smelled of rosemary, from being stored in my clothes chest, I made another trip to the back of the little priest's room wall.

Now, in the daylight I could see what I had peered at in the unreliable flickering light of the flames.

On the cill, oil, a spill of some drops. I stood on tip-toe and looked through the window into the room. Further in, there were more oil marks but these were irregular. The old oak shutters on the inside were charred and black and would collapse in cinders if they were touched.

My guess was that the fire had started here, that something... a rag perhaps, had been doused in oil and pushed through the window. Then the end had been set alight and it had been pushed in further until it fell onto the floor and ignited the rushes lying there. Maybe oil had also been poured through the window onto the floor.

Someone had wanted to destroy the priest's room.

I walked round to the main door. Walter was already there, his trusty staff in hand, poking at the ashes. Everything was sodden. That which wasn't sodden was charred and that which wasn't charred was gone to ash and beyond retrieval.

"We are lucky this was all we lost sir," he said. He turned to look at me. "Oh m'lord...your eyebrows!"

I smiled. "Just eyebrows, Walt. We lost no lives, no homes, no stock, no real possessions...we are lucky, Walter."

"No little thanks to you sir. Your clever thought that we must prepare ourselves for fire saved us I think."

"I'm glad it did, Walter, but we all pulled together and that is what makes it work."

What did we have left?

The silver chalice in its box was saved. The priest's garments were ruined. The pyx, used to carry the host to the sick, was buckled but serviceable. The silver candlesticks had been on the altar and so were saved a scorching. All the linen cloths used at the mass were gone, including the spare altar cloths sewn by my mother. The paten was buckled too and would need some work from the silversmith in the town.

The descent rolls were beyond recall.

The smell from the little room was overpowering. Smoke, ash, old and burnt parchment.

The ancient chest, which had stood on the back wall almost under the window, had borne the fiercest of the fire. I had left the lid open and in it I had replaced most of the rolls. Whoever had done this thing had made sure that an oiled rag had dropped into the chest for there was hardly anything left of it.

"When everything has cooled and settled, get some of the men to clear the room and then ask the women to clean... but make sure it is all safe, Walter."

"Yes sir."

"Any of the rolls still readable, even a tiny amount, bring them to my office."

He looked round at me then...."We have long memories in this village but... now we shall have little idea who was related to whom. It will make life difficult if we have close families who wish to marry for example, or if we have to prove the legal birth of a child say, for the right of heredity."

"I know and I think this is what the fire was all about. I saved four of the rolls, Walter; the most recent. What made me take them I don't know."

And I told him about the rags which I thought had been pushed through the window.

"To destroy the rolls. Who would want to do that?"

"Someone who had something to lose should they be freely available to read, Walter."

My reeve scratched his chin, with a rasping sound. "But hardly anyone can read, sir."

"I know. Swithun could. I think he had seen something in those pages and was killed for it."

Walter crossed himself. "Deus adiuva me," he said. "God help me, I have read those rolls many a time."

"I know," I said. "Watch yourself old friend, watch your back."

***

Phil Wheelwright came to me the next day to tell me the cart was ready.

He pulled it up to the church door for me and I looked it over. It hadn't needed much attention to make it roadworthy, worthy to carry the corpse of an unmourned priest to his last resting place. I asked for volunteers to take it to Salisbury Abbey.

No one came forward.

I raised my eyes to Heaven.

"I will not compel any man," I said, "but I will not forget the slight."

" 'Tis no slight to you, m'lord," piped up Mat Fisher. " 'Tis just that no man wants to be doing a man like him a good turn. 'Twill not get us into Heaven."

" T'won't keep us outta Hell neither," said another and there was a ripple of nervous laughter.

"If you were to command us....now that's a different thing, for we'd be doing your will and that we are pleased to do," said Will Deerleap.

In the end, I asked Hal of Potterne to fetch my two men at arms, whom I kept at the castle of Marlborough at my own expense, against the time when I might be called to muster for my king and country, or simply to accompany me when I travelled; for the country was not safe everywhere. The presence of a couple of armed men was usually more than enough to keep even the most tenacious brigands and lawless men at bay. They were attached to the garrison at the castle and had nothing special to do at present. Let them take him. They were my paid men; they would do as I asked.

Stephen Dunn and Peter Devizes jogged in on their rounceys a little later that day. They would set off for Salisbury, some twenty eight miles away, at first light. We lodged them in the hall with some of those who worked in the manor and who slept there each night.

I was up early to see the cart and its sad burden off on the Salisbury road. I strode up the slight incline towards the church. The cart waited with its pony. One would drive it, the other would ride and tow a horse behind so that a speedy return might be made to Durley by them both. The cart would return next time anyone went to Salisbury. The two horses were ready and waiting.

No one had as yet moved the coffin to the back of the cart. I heard raised voices coming from the church.

"God's teeth, who would do such a thing....?"

"We had better fetch the Lord Belvoir and the carpenter too."

"I'll go."

Stephen had turned to come down the nave as I turned in at the south door.

"Ah m'lord," he said, taking off his coif and screwing it up in a ball.

"We has a slight problem."

"Oh...and what is that?" I asked, keeping on walking but as I passed him, I could see what the problem was.

Someone had taken a crow bar to the coffin and had prised off the lid which had been closed so carefully after the fire by our village carpenter. It lay skewed along the top of the coffin.

The body had been searched for it lay in an uneasy jumble; the shroud disturbed and the head turned.

Stephen crossed himself as he came back to stare down at the body. Peter was frowning and catching his bottom lip in his teeth. "Why, m'lord?" he asked.

I shook my head. "Someone is very worried that Swithun, even unto death, has concealed about him a piece of parchment perhaps, upon which is written some information they would rather the world did not know."

"But the man was sealed in his coffin for goodness sake. Even if the writing was there, who is going to read it? 'Cept God and all his angels perhaps."

"It is very important to the murderer, for I suspect it is he who is so keen to commit such a blasphemy. Setting fire to the records in the priest's room was not enough, it seems."

"Yeah. We 'eard about that. Can smell the damage too," said Stephen and he crossed himself again. "I'll go for the carpenter, shall I?"

***

Alfred Woodsmith came in later and stopped at the church door. He bowed to me and came up the nave.

His face showed such bemusement that I had to say something.

"Yes, Alfred...we know you closed it. But now it needs to be done again."

"How?" he swallowed. "Is he still alive and trying to get out? I have heard of cases where..."

"No, Alfred. He is dead, very dead. Someone saw fit to search him that is all."

"After he was closed in his coffin, m'lord?"

"Aye. We know that it is a blasphemy of the greatest order but we will make enquiries to discover who we can apprehend for the crime, never fear."

"Good and just God," said Alfred, crossing himself, his hammer in his hand, "I didn't like the man but I wouldn't wish this on him."

"No." I answered, "it is taking the death a little too much beyond the death, isn't it?"

***

The coffin was closed. It was loaded onto the back of the cart and I watched as it trundled up the road from the church, turned round the bend by the priest's house and up on the lane through the forest to the Salisbury Road. I moved off to the path by the manor to follow its progress.

A few people watched it go. Hamon Deerman turned in the action of filling a bucket from a larger barrel, with which to douse his head. He circled away, poured the water over his head and watched, dripping, as the cart passed him. He caught sight of his neighbour and waved.

Dysig too had come out of his bothy to watch the cart pass. He waved back at Hamon, spat on the grass as the cart passed him and disappeared inside again. I would not take this action too seriously, for Dysig was a simpleton, born with a skewed head; damaged at birth, I suppose and a body too big for it. We found him jobs around the manor. He could settle to nothing for long but he was harmless and we all watched out for him, especially Old Joan who was his great aunt. Edmund Brooker too seemed a good friend to him.

Peter Brenthall was outside his house, the last one in the village on the road to the forest. He watched the cart go past in silence and then loped off in the direction of the manor fields.

And that was the end of Swithun the priest.

***

I decided to go up to my office and hide the now only surviving and whole, descent rolls for the manor of Durley. I must protect them carefully and no one must know that they had been rescued. In these little rolls might rest the answer to the questions thrown up by Swithun's murder. I locked them in with the Belvoir regalia, These were items given to the first warden by William the first to add some weight to his office and consisted of a saddle ,bridle, sword and belt, and a beautiful ivory, silver decorated, hunting horn, which it is said should be blown when the sovereign was hunting in Savernake.

These badges of office and symbols of power were already one hundred and thirty years old when I came to the wardenship. The horn in particular was a beautiful item with a silver mouthpiece and a small silver edge with engravings of the animals of the forest: deer, boar and wolf, in small roundels. The leather strap also had silver roundels, of the heads of men but we never could distinguish what these were, they had become so polished away.

These were kept in a chest which was iron bound and fixed to the oaken floor of my room. The hanglock key was always with me on a chain around my neck and Henry had the only duplicate. They would be safe there.

The rest of the morning was taken up with manor business. I owned some sheep which I farmed out on the downs; the gentle chalk hills which surrounded the town and framed the forest. In my father's time many of the fleeces were sent right out of the area to be carded and spun, (I also owned a spinning industry in Collingbourne, out on the Salisbury Road).

Newbury town, nineteen miles further east, was the centre for the collection of the wool packs and laden mules plodding along the Ramsbury Road through the forest were a common sight. At Newbury the merchants would gather, coming from all over the country and even abroad, to get their hands on our good English wool, which was prized throughout Europe. Lately, my wool factor Tom Herder and I had negotiated to keep some of our spun wool in the town and now it was woven into cloth, fulled and dyed right there in Marlborough. Although Tom was a capable worker, I personally had papers to sign and bills to organise for the sale of wool to the weavers, fullers and dyers.

This job done, I sought a beaker of ale and a hunk of bread for my morning meal.

The next thing I wanted to do was talk to those people whom it was thought had a grievance against Swithun of Attwood and I could not do that on an empty stomach. I'd start with Matthew.

Since I was in the manor house, I ran down the back stair which connected the kitchen, one of the new stone buildings I had caused to be raised in 1197, to the first floor hall. A wall of heat hit me as I opened the door.

Matthew the cook was leaning over his largest iron pot daintily tasting from a ladle. He smacked his lips and spun on his heel to lean for a pinch of salt. He saw me standing by the door, wiped his hands on his apron and bowed.

"Master, sir, what can I get for you?" He was off into his larder looking for choice pieces for me...

"No Matthew truly, nothing. I just want to chat with you."

He came out of his cold store holding a large pot of onions. "Chat to me?"

This seemed to confuse him. No one ever, it seemed, just came to talk to him.

He gestured to the table, the only one not in use for food preparation, in the corner, flicked his head at a small lad who was given the task, poor boy, of peeling and chopping the onions and pulled out a stool for me.

Matthew had been my cook since the murder of Colmar, his senior, in 1197, and had not failed me. He had been young, everyone said, to be promoted to such a role but he had proved his worth. He worked magic with food and could conjure a meal from very little, if very little was what we had.

The years had been kind to us lately though, for food had been plentiful on our manor and surpluses could now be sold at the new twice weekly market in Marlborough town, granted by the monarch that very August, of 1204. Some of my more enterprising workers went, with my permission, to sell the produce from their plots. Others sold to Matthew my cook.

I sat and as if by magic a beaker of ale appeared in front of me.

"Matthew. I am told by some that you and Swithun the priest argued. You were heard threatening to murder him. Can you tell me what that was all about?"

Matthew paused, a cup half way to his lips.

"Aye...we argued. He was a bad man, that Swithun. A priest he may have been but his soul was as black as the bottom of my skillet."

"Why do you say that?"

Matthew sighed. " 'Tis all about the time I came here from Marlborough."

"That was..." I blew air from between my lips "eight years ago perhaps?"

"Aye. That it was."

"You were hired, I remember, for the castle kitchen."

"Yes, m'lord you recall rightly. I had come in from the country up round Gloucester way. Up in the Dean Forest a couple of years before and was helping out with Master Philbert in the High Street."

"I remember. You and Colmar my cook, struck up a friendship, didn't you."

"We did, both of us being Gloucester men, and then you decided that Colmar needed help in the kitchen and there I was."

"So what did Swithun think was so awful about that, Matthew?"

Matthew wriggled a little on his stool. Then he started to pick at a small snag in the front of his apron.

"It were all about me being a year and a day in the town. Before I came here."

I shook my head, confused.

"A year and a day. He said that I was a felon, running away from the Forest of Dean. That I'd fled to Marlborough and disappeared there and that after a year and a day I was a free man and could be cleared of my crime."

"Well, that is the law."

I looked at him under my eyebrows.

"Is it true?"

Matthew decided that dissimulation was not a good idea.

"Aye m'lord. It is."

"How did he know this?"

"The priest at the time, old Father Benedict, had made a note in the margins of the manor rolls, the rolls that records stuff that goes on at Durley, to say when I arrived at the manor and how long I had been in Marlborough. I suppose the rest was guess-work. Clever guess-work. I told him that he could tell who he liked, for I was a free man now and had worked out my year...more than my year." Matthew proudly lifted his chin. "I don't mind who knows now. I can't be held to account. I wasn't a runaway serf!"

"What was your crime, Matthew?"

He looked down at the floor suddenly.

" 'Twas a crime of my passions m'lord. I found my wife in bed with my brother and I killed him for it. With my bare hands I did. I squeezed the life out of him. 'Twas not something I planned...it just happened." Matthew was a large man.

"And then you fled into the Forest of Dean...to become a masterless man?"

"There was a hue and cry but they didn't catch me—well they didn't really try see, 'cos, my brother's perfidy was well known. 'Cept to me. I ran and I walked for miles up in the forest and then fetched up at a place where I could swim the river. Then I walked south ways in just the clothes in which I stood. I got to Gloucester thinking that I'd go abroad, flee the realm, work my way on a ship. Somehow, I couldn't do that. I stood on the docks for ages and looked at the river and I just couldn't go. So I turned round and I walked in an easterly direction."

"You confessed this sin?"

"I did ,my lord, as soon as I could find a priest who would listen."

I nodded. "Why did you threaten to kill Swithun if, as you say, the crime is long past and you are free of it and don't mind who knows?"

"Ah well sir... I wouldn't like it that well known. And it's a little complicated."

"It is?"

"Aye sir you see. 'Twas my brother I killed. I left my wife back in Lydney. Alive and screaming, she was."

My brow flew up. "Ah....I see."

I pictured the descent roll and the page for 1200 and the entry for May of that year, popped into my mind's eye.

1200 May the second Matthew Cook of Lydney Gloucestershire and Edgiva of Savernake spinster of Durley married in Durley. Fine weather for a week.

"Ah... I do see...you are a bigamist, my friend."

"So it seems, sir. Swithun was threatening to tell my Edgiva."

I closed my eyes. What other sins were lurking under the surface of my simple and quiet Manor of Durley?

"We must make inquiries, Matthew. We might find that your first wife is no longer alive. Yes, I feel sure that we shall find that she is no longer in this world. You were a widower, my friend."

The look of relief on the man's face was tangible. "You would do that, sir? Just forget it all...just like that? Tell no one?"

"I will not forget, Matthew. The law says you are a free man, even if you have murdered. I can see that finding a beloved wife with a trusted brother would be enough to try any man's passions to the limit. Marrying again is another matter. I will however, keep quiet about it. Unless I have cause to think that it must come into the open. I am after all, the law in the forest."

"Yes, sir."

I fiddled in my scrip. "Have you ever seen this before, Matthew?"

He stretched his neck to look at the drawing of the knife.

"No sir...I haven't."

"And where were you at about the time of vespers last night?"

"At vespers? Here dealing with supper and all the comings and goings of feeding people, sir, where I always am at that time of day."

"Look me in the eye Matthew, did you cause the death of Swithun Attwood....at peril of losing your immortal soul now?"

"No sir, I did not. I told him to his face that I would. But I did not." His gaze did not waver.

I stood. "Thank you Matthew. You may carry on. Good cooks are very hard to find, I'm told."

"What's that Paul? You think that was kind of me. Nah....what use would it serve to have it raked up? The man had been on the manor eight years. The wife had not tried to come and find him. How many others thought themselves free to marry; a husband lost at sea or not returned from the wars? It was quite common for folk to start over again, begin a new life, with a new spouse, in a new place. It can all come out now. No one is alive who will be hurt by knowing the facts. I have even outlived Matthew's children... God rest them."

***

I knew that Joan the laundress would be somewhere near her house on the edge of the village green, close by the river. She had a work-place in amongst the willows which grew there, where she pounded the village and manor washing in a tub and laid out the linens to dry on the riverside bushes. We laughingly called this the Salley Gardens after the old name for the willow tree - sallow. These trees formed their own little wood here, where they leaned over the river, almost touching those on the other side. They were large, old trees, some of which had fallen over and lodged on their companions. I could well imagine Swithun lurking here when the trees were in full leaf; the interlacing branches would provide good cover. One might even sit or lie by the trees and be completely hidden from view by the dense canopies.

Now though, the trees were losing their leaves. The bright yellow drop-pings carpeted the grass by the stream and through the branches I could see Joan working at her tub which was placed between two stout levelled tree trunks for ease of reach, her hands up to her elbows in the soapy water.

"Ho Joan," I cried so as not to startle her.

She was not alone. Three other women, wives of the field workers or foresters, were here with her, all washing in the stream, wringing or laying out the linens to dry.

She lifted her head and peered through the trees. A stray lock of hair had come adrift of her head cloth and she wiped it back across her head with the back of her wrist.

"M'lord. What brings you out here on washing day?"

"I'd like to have a word please, if I may," I smiled.

She wiped her hands on her apron, a large piece of sacking and came over to me.

"You did not need to walk out here to find me, merely send me word and I would come to the hall."

"No, Joan, I wanted to see the place where the thing I have been told about, happened."

She looked puzzled.

"Swithun the priest?" I said. "I hear that he was pestering you. I looked around, "here in the Salley Gardens?"

She put both hands on her hips. "Man of God. Why I am more a man of God than he ever was. Or for that matter Mariel here. God rest him. I should not speak ill of the dead," and she made the sign against evil with her fingers.

I smiled. "I take it he did make a nuisance of himself?"

"He did, though the girls and I sent him packing."

"What was he doing?"

"Doing? Why... watching, secretly from behind the branches," she replied.

"Was he watching all the girls or just you in particular?"

"Well at first, I'd catch a glimpse of him facing upstream from the trees just there, by my house," and she pointed towards the village green.

"Then lately, I saw him further in, staring towards the stream up by the Brookers place. Just where those big old trees fell over in the storm last year."

"So you can't say for sure that he was watching you in particular, or everyone?"

"Well, I told me husband Robin — you know him, sir,"

"Yes, he is a forester, is he not?"

"Aye and he said he'd have a word with him, if he needed it, in the form of a fist, if you know what I mean. So he thought he was looking at me."

"But was he, Joan? It's really important that I know." Joan was a very good looking woman.

"He could'a bin."

One of the other women had been eavesdropping and now piped up, "He was, Joan...he followed you home one day, didn't he?"

"Aye, he did that."

"And what happened?"

"Me man stepped out of the cottage and the priest made a quick move to avoid him and went up the road by the reeve's house instead' a coming past our home, though that way were a quicker route to the church house."

"Hmmm. He never spoke?"

"No, it mighta bin better if he's just said 'evenin' Joan' or summat, but he said nothing, Said nothing."

"Did your husband have a word with him, Joan? It's a grave sin to strike a priest."

She realised what was implied in the question and looked down quickly searching the ground with flickering eyes, as if the answer to the question would be found in the grass. She wet her lips.

"No sir. Someone got to him before Robin could say anything to him."

"With fists or anything else."

"Aye sir."

"Thank you Joan."

I began to walk away.

"Have you any idea who might'a done it, sir?"

"No, none at all Joan."

***

I wandered round the trees, trying to imagine Swithun concealed here. I looked back towards the village green. Nothing to see there. I looked over towards the road and up the hill to the west. Five dwellings were in view before the hill began to rise. Two of them were freemen's houses, two were larger family houses of manor villeins and the last was the Brooker's small cottage. I moved through the trees, keeping the houses in sight.

Edith and Edmund Brooker were two of my villeins and were twins, brother and sister. This meant that unlike Margaret and Henry, they were not free and were feudal tenants entirely subject to me as their lord, to whom they paid dues and services in return for land. Their house was a small one and they lived together after the death of their family some while ago.

The side of the Brooker's cottage came into view with its small garden. Hmmm. Swithun had been caught here, watching Edith, hadn't he? I had come upon her brother Edmund, up by the church warning the priest to stay away. I searched my memory for the exact words of their conversation. Edmund had accused the priest of spying on Edith through the cottage window, as she was washing and dressing.

Swithun had assured me that this had been an untruth and that he was merely walking from one part of my demesne to another through the outlying trees of the forest. Coming from spying on Joan and her friends, I suspect.

I crossed the grassy bank and jumped onto the road, hardly more than a track here, but leading to a wider road a couple of furlongs along, which meandered on through the forest on its way to Ramsbury. I was unsure if either of the Brooker siblings were in the house but I would chance it. They might be up in my fields; they might be working their own plot.

The little garden was well tended, if going to seed now. There was kale still to be cut; I saw some leek tops and a few turnips poked up from the soil. They would soon be harvested and laid down for winter in the loft of the house. A pig rooted around at the back of the house, penned in, not realising that it had but weeks to do so before it was turned into ham.

There was a low wattle fence around the garden which prevented the depredations of the neighbours' chickens and other small animals. I opened a diminutive hurdle gate and a little bell rang. I turned to fasten the gate.

A shrieking voice almost lifted the thatch from the rafters.

"You will have to do it now. I can't have the beast roaming around much longer! Oh get out you good for nothing piss pot. You've as many holes in your brain as your fishing net!"

Edmund came bowling out of the suddenly opened door, almost falling over and tucking his shirt into his braies and smoothing down his hair, his tunic under his arm.

"Good day my lord," he said. "The baggage won't let me have a minute's rest. I thought to lie down for a while to catch up with sleep lost the night of the fire and she must have me kill the pig....now."

"And will you?"

"Nah... not just yet m'lord." He threw a look back into the house. "Women have no patience," he shouted.

We ducked as what I recognised as their old and holed pot came cartwheeling out of the door.

"Her temper has not improved then, with the purchase of a new pot?" I had been at the market in Marlborough, when the new pan was sought out.

"No. Nor her tongue, sir."

Edith was noted for her shrewish behaviour and her sharp tongue, particularly to her brother.

"Edmund, shall we walk awhile? I want to ask you about Swithun."

Edmund's body stiffened beside me. We wandered over to the stream again.

"Joan the laundress tells me that Swithun was seen here by the Salley

Gardens, watching them as they worked and also staring into your plot from the concealed space there under the big trees. When they were in full leaf of course."

"Aye... we saw him."

"Even after I told him to stay away?"

"When did that one ever do what anyone told him, sir?"

"I would hope that he did, for I was his lord. I know that if I told you to do something, you would do it."

Edmund shook his long black curls.

"He was besotted with Edith. He followed her around. Up to the fields if she went to work there, down to the river when she went for water. No sir, he did not do as you told him."

"I see."

I held him back with my hand. "Edmund, I am talking to everyone who had reason to dislike, even hate the priest. Though I already know you did not like him and it was no secret, can you tell me when you last saw him?"

Edmund looked up at the white clouds scudding past. He folded his arms defensively across his chest.

"The day he died."

"When?"

"In the afternoon."

"And he was...where?"

He turned to face me. "He was walking fast across the village green in his long brown cotte. That damnable black cloak of his flowing out like a crow's wings behind him."

"Where was he going at such a fast pace?"

He shrugged. "Home?"

"Where had he been do you think?"

"Well sir, that is an easy one to answer."

"It is?"

"Aye. He had been here. In the cottage. I was coming down the hill from our strip out the back and I saw him cross the green from the path."

"What was he doing here? I had forbidden him to come anywhere near."

"That too is easy to answer sir."

"Tell me."

"He had been raping my sister, sir."

Chapter Three

His words struck me like a blow, I reeled back. "Rape?"

"Aye. I came into the cottage to find Edith weeping on the floor, her clothes all awry, all torn from her body."

"Why did you not tell me?"

"I would have done, sir but I had a devil of a time getting Edith settled and then I found a woman to be with her and then by the time I thought to come up to the manor and rouse you, it was dark and past curfew. The gate was shut....it could wait till the morrow."

"Edmund... I am so sorry."

"Aye well...we knew he was a wrong 'un, we just didn't know how wrong, sir."

"So why have you not come to tell me of this since his death?"

Edmund put his head on one side; it made him look like a small animal. "I come and tell you this and you think...right...here is his murderer. Let's put him in irons.

The man is dead. Best keep quiet."

"And what about Edith? How does she feel about keeping quiet?"

"She'll do what's best for us."

I shook my head. "Who was the woman who came to help you with her, Edmund?"

He twisted his mouth awry, as he wondered if he might keep this a secret from me.

" 'Twas the poultry girl, Meg. Meg Pouter. They are special friends."

"I know her." I looked him straight in the eyes.

"You know that this does indeed give you a very good motive for murder, Edmund?"

"Yes sir. I know it does. And I was damn angry, I can tell you. Had he been in front of me then...well... I can't say as I would just have given him the time of day and passed on."

"No. So you saw him alive when...?"

" 'Twas coming up to an evening glow but still light. The sun was just going down over the trees yonder," he pointed to the west, up behind his cottage and beyond the villagers' fields.

"And Old Joan found him not long past the vespers hour - we have supper a little before that. When you saw him on the green, was he weaving about at all...? Did he seem as if he had been drinking?"

"Aye...he'd been drinking. To work up his passions for Edith I think, or to give him courage for what he was about to do. She said he smelled of wine when he was......"

"Not so much that he was incapable?"

"No, obviously."

"Hmm. So you were with your sister at all times after that?"

"Yes...and with Meg. We gave Edith a draught in some ale to calm her and she slept the rest of the night quite steady."

"You were with Meg till...?"

"'Till dawn sir." Edmund's expression almost dared me to work out what this meant.

"Meg was in your cottage with you all night, from the time that you called her to look after Edith, until she went off to tend her chickens at...?"

"Dawn sir."

"I shall speak to her. And Edith was sound asleep all this time...whilst you...and Meg..."

He nodded.

"Right." I turned to go, "Oh....yes..." I fished the drawing I had made, from the front of my cotte. "Have you seen this before, Edmund?"

He took the paper, upon which was the likeness of the knife which killed

Swithun.

He turned it this way and that. "No sir. I've never seen it before."

***

The poultry bothy was on the way back to the hall. It was a small one roomed house with a thatched roof and a beaten earth floor. A piece of land had been set out around it and fenced off with torn up bushes and thorns. The ground was strewn with hay and rushes. The manor's chickens roamed in this space, grubbed up the ground and laid eggs where they willed. It was Meg's job to collect the eggs, see to the chickens and once every so often she would tear up the thorn hedge and move it around the bothy, so that the fowl had new ground to scratch.

A blackthorn bush had been uprooted to act as a gate. I wasn't going to chance my fingers on the nasty long spikes so I called for Meg over the fence. She came out, in the act of tying a long hessian apron around her waist.

"How is your mother?" I asked. I knew that she had been ill and that she had been refused Last Rites by Swithun.

"She rallied sir," said Meg, curtseying. "But in truth I do not think it will be long."

"I'm so sorry," I said. "Is there anything we might do? I can ask Doctor Johannes to..."

"We have no money to pay him, sir and if truth were known, the canker has eaten her so much that I doubt even he could save her now."

"I will ask him to bring her some pain killing draught then, and I will pay for it, Meg," I said.

Her eyes grew large.

"Aye... I'll tell her then." There was no denial of the gift or thanks and she turned to go back into the house but I forestalled her with,

"Meg I would speak with you about the night of Swithun's death."

Meg blinked then, many times and she looked fearful.

"It's all right Meg, I know about you staying with Edmund Brooker all night and about the problem Edith had with the priest." I was not going to say the word rape for I think this would have sent the girl into a frenzy.

She was already shaking.

"Edith had been raped then, Meg?"

She looked away then... "Well, I think that were true. She was bloodied all right. As you are when..."

"You believed this to be the truth?"

She twisted her apron in her hands.

"How else was she to....oh sir. I don' like to say no more."

"Why?"

"Well, the priest an' all. He was a priest after all. I can't say no more, sir."

"Is it true? That you stayed with Edmund and Edith all night?"

"Aye, I did. Old Joan was here with mam."

"So you left your mother with a trusted friend and went to help Edith in her need?"

"I did so. And...."

"Yes....and...."

"And I stayed, as I sometimes do with, Edmund."

I smiled at her.

"That's fine. Do you like Edmund Brooker, Meg?"

Her face lit up like a Beltane bonfire. "Oh I do sir. He's a bonny man."

"Are you thinking that you and he might be wed some day?"

She looked a little coy at that. "Well, sir....I know he likes me, so maybe......"

"Good." I remembered the time when the lass had been but thirteen and, passing the bothy, I had stumbled upon and foiled the rape of this simple girl by my over-eager half-brother Robert, or so it had seemed. I also remembered the words I had said to her at the time.

"You have been a good girl then, Meg? Like your mother wished you to be, and like I asked you to be, all those years ago?"

Her eyes grew round as mushroom caps.

"I only done it with Edmund...no-body else."

I nodded. "I shall have a word with him then."

She beamed. "Oh sir....."

Neither of them could marry without my permission.

"What does your mother think?"

Meg shook her head.

"She can't think nothing now....just lies and moans and sleeps."

"Talk to her, Meg. Even if you think she can't hear. Tell her that you are in love with Edmund Brooker and that the Lord Aumary will see what we can do, for after she passes on to God, you will be all alone in your little house there."

Her mouth formed an 'O'. She blinked again and she curtsied.

I passed on.

One of my main suspects had an alibi! Damn!

I would need to confirm it all with Edith but I needed to go very softly with her. Suddenly I knew what I would do. I would ask Agnes Brenthall to have a word with her. She was a sensible woman who could be guaranteed to keep silent. She was a freewoman and had known Edith all her life. And she was canny. All this could be achieved with a woman to woman conversation the like of which I would never be able to construct.

Agnes I knew, would be in the hall at her various jobs, for she acted as housekeeper to the manor house. I tracked her down to the undercroft where she was measuring the amount of flour and the state of the weevil in the bins, and estimating how long this would last us, with or without them. I told her about Edmund's assertion that Swithun had raped Edith.

Her hand flew to her mouth. "Oh poor child."

"Child? She is about twenty eight, I think."

Agnes chided me, "Oh, sir...'tis a turn of phrase as they say."

"Will you ask her about it please, Agnes, for I think it would be better coming from a woman."

"I will... I will..." Her face took on a hard, determined look.

"Oh that man. That... beast!"

"I always think it odd, Paul my scribe, that whenever we talk about behaviour in man which is awful and beyond belief, that we call it 'beastly'. Beasts do not do to each other those things we call beastly. I have never seen a horse rape another, nor a cow stick a knife twenty times into another's body. Most certainly beasts would never devise some of the punishments men have designed for each other. We are the true beasts I think.

No, no, there is no need to write that down Paul...it's just a bemused old man wondering what on earth God was thinking when he made men."

***

I took a little food at the afternoon meal, when some of the lads came in from the forest after a half day's work. Supper is much later and a smaller repast. After this most folk go straight to bed, for many are up at dawn the next day.

Sitting in my office, I took a piece of birch bark paper and a stick of charcoal and scribbled, as I was wont to do, an aid to my memory—all the facts I had discovered that day.

I stared at it.

We had an ex-felon and bigamist loose in the kitchen.

We had a furious laundress by the river and a disgruntled husband loose in the forest.

We had an angry young tied villein loose about the manor, with an alibi.

We had Henry the Steward, loose about the manor, very angry and without an alibi.

I had yet to speak to the Sylvestre family. What bones might be buried under their hearth?

***

I rubbed my eyes. I was tired and could have given in to sleep but, no, I must press on. I poked my head through the hall door and called, "Out again."

Lydia looked up from her work of teaching Hawise her letters.

"Dada...can I come with you?"

"No," I said and instantly regretted my stern tone.

"This is..." I puffed up my chest and struck a pose. "Man's work!"

That was guaranteed to make Hawise giggle. Lydia chuckled too. Hal of Potterne who was watching the reading and writing lesson with great concentration, guffawed.

Off I went, down the manor steps, through the gate, past the bothies which clung to the manor wall, past the back of the reeve's house and through a small stand of trees to Ralf and Edwina's bothy at the back of the church fields. Edwina was out at the rear, milking the goat. Ralf was out in the forest with his father Fulke. They were both skilled at making wattle hurdles. Ann, her mother-in-law was in the manor kitchen with Matthew. The parents-in-law lived in the little house next door. The door was open and chickens were running in and out.

"No...do not get up, Edwina." I leaned on the bothy wall, after first testing it to make sure it would bear my weight. Most of my manor folk cared for their houses well; just a few were a little lax and would not whitewash against insects or repair holes in thatch. For that they'd be fined. This little house was splinter new, as they say.

"Edwina...how are you now? Are you and Ralf getting over your loss?"

"Bless you m'lord," she said, still squirting the milk into her pail. "We are... children come and go, don't they? They are a gift from God and if God sees fit to take them back, well, who are we to argue?"

"Er... yes"

She seemed to be extremely settled about the loss of her daughter.

Susanna M. Newstead

"She were five hours sir...you can't get fond at five hours, can you?"

"Er well... yes I suppose you haven't had the time to..." This wasn't really what I had expected. "Are you happy that she is lying in the churchyard at Bedwyn?"

"Well, when Sir Swithun the Durley priest wouldn't let her be buried here, I was worried sir, that she would have to be stuck out there..." She motioned to the forest, "With all the beasts and the monsters and witches and the like but that was very kind of you to arrange her burial there."

The poor little scrap had lasted a mere five hours and it was said that Swithun had refused her baptism. She had been baptised, as was allowed, in extreme cases, by the midwife Aolfe Midwyf and so had been taken into the church community. Swithun refused to bury her for he did not recognise such baptisms. Edwina's original home was in Bedwyn, a village just three miles away. She had come to Durley on her marriage. Her family was there and were close to little Mariota's grave.

"Edwina... Ralf was very angry, was he not, when Swithun would not come to baptise Mariota?" Edwina ceased to pump the goat's udder.

"Aye sir...but my father-in-law was angrier."

"Angry enough to kill him?"

Edwina picked up her pail and stood. I noticed it was not even half full. I had the feeling if I had not asked my question, the bucket would have continued being filled.

"At the time maybe."

"But not later in cold blood?"

"No."

"Where was he when Swithun was being killed?"

"That was when, sir?"

I smiled to myself. I could not catch her out. "Around vespers. Not long after full dark."

"Ralf was with me. We were...ahem...." she hefted her bucket and the milk splashed and sploshed in the pail, "trying to make some more little Sylvestres, if you catch my drift, sir."

A smile passed her lips and was instantly gone. "And Fulke was at Widow Giffard's, sir. She had brewed some new ale and many of the men were there that night. Ask anyone."

The towns were beginning to get ale houses. Buildings solely designed for the brewing and drinking of ale. Marlborough had one, The Green Man. In the rural areas, a woman would brew some ale and would hang a bush on a stick from her eaves to tell everyone that the ale could be bought from her. Each man would take his pot, or a jug and either have it filled and walk home with it, or in the summer months stay close by and chat to others who had decided on the same thing. It made for a cosy and convivial evening. As long as there wasn't too much ale drunk and tempers flared. When the ale was gone, the bush would be taken down.

"Will you ask Ralf and Fulke to come to me at the manor please, when they return, so that they may account for themselves personally?"

Her eyes widened momentarily. "You don't believe me, sir?"

I felt the little frisson of fear which ran through her. "No, not at all. I just want to hear it from them."

She watched me all the way past the reeve's house and out of sight.

I trotted back to my office and added the names of the Sylvestre men to my list.

An angry father and an angry father-in -aw loose in the forest with alibis. I asked Walter the reeve if it was truly the case that the Widow Giffard had brewed ale recently?

"Aye and I tasted it. She's a damn fine brewster, no arguments. Everyone flocks to her house when she has new ale."

"Ah... next time she brews, Walter, let me know. I'll come with you," I joked.

***

The next day dawned grey and cloudy with an east wind. Gone were the sunny days which had lit up the forest. The sky lay heavy above and seemed ready to drop rain on us.

I had decided to go into Marlborough to speak with Johannes and to put all my findings before him. He could be relied upon to find something I had hitherto overlooked.

I was fetching my things and organising the day for Walter, Henry and John, when through the gate, followed by a few of the younger manor children, came four horses and riders, with a fine beast trailing behind.

I had seen this animal before. What was the fine racehorse which I had last seen a while ago, trotting down Marlborough High Street with its companions, doing here on my manor?

"Good day m'lord." The senior groom threw his legs over his horse's head and jumped down. He bowed. "I have a letter for you, my lord Belvoir." I recognised him as one of the palfreymen who looked after Guy de Saye's horses.

He fished in a pannier on the side of his horse and then handed it to me over the gap between us. I moved nearer to accept it.

The fine bay horse with his high stepping gait and his proud head, sidled.

"Whoa there Fitz... easy boy." The groom holding him patted him on the neck.

I broke the seal of the letter, three lions rampant. I recognised it as that of Guillaume de Saye.

In the late summer, Johannes of Salerno and I had solved the murder in a locked room at the very top of the tower keep in Marlborough castle, of Guillaume de Saye's son Guy.

The young man had been besotted with race horses and had a string of them with him at the castle where he was lodging prior to being married to Matilda de Neville, Hugh's daughter and Marlborough castle's constable.

Not only Savernake's warden, the king had seen fit to appoint me under constable of the castle at Marlborough. (It does not pay to be childhood friends of the monarch) and I had been asked to solve the murder by the family. Solve it I had, with Johannes' help.

According to this letter, this was my payment and thanks. The groom bowed low when he saw I had finished reading the letter.

"The master Lord de Saye wanted us to bring the horse to you sir, directly from the Baydon stable. Here is a letter transferring the right of ownership to you... Sir Aumary Belvoir."

I took the proffered letter, in a bit of a daze. "Yes, um, thank you."

What does one say when someone gives you an unexpected present worth many, many pounds? Naturally I knew what the present really represented. Silence.

De Saye was buying my silence about the death of his son.

My own grooms had come out from the stable to gawp at the beautiful beast, who was tossing his head and pawing the ground.

"May I offer you the hospitality of the manor hall—please do go up and take ale and bread, before you return to Baydon."

The four men bowed and thanked me for my care. I nodded to Henry who was at my elbow. "Henry, can you look to our guests? My steward will take care of you."

Henry was as staggered at the appearance of such a fine horse at Durley as I had been and I had to dig him in the ribs before he could say, "This way please."

I shouted to Richard Marshall, my chief groom and he came running and took the horse from the de Saye men.

The whole courtyard was now full of people watching the arrival of such a rare piece of horse flesh. The blacksmith, the wheelwright, Hal of Potterne who had been lounging by the door of his little room, Wyot the gatekeeper, even some of the women had stopped in the middle of their tasks to stare.

What was I going to do with the beast? I did not race. I had no interest in racing.

Once someone had given me a hawking glove as a name day present. I rarely hawked. I had no birds at Durley and never felt the need to acquire any. My father-in-law, Cecily's father, had a mews of fine birds which he indulged as if they were his children, and I hunted with him now and again. The glove had eventually gone to Toruld Congyre.

What was I going to do with... I looked up at the receding backs of the grooms stepping up my manor stairs…. "His name is...?"

The last man turned, "Fitz... sir... Fitzroy."

What was I going to do with Fitzroy? The son of a king, for that is what his name meant. Fitz was Norman and was applied to the landless sons of nobles.

Richard was walking him round, just to settle him before taking him into the stable building. I caught hold of the bridle just as the horse passed me, patted the noble head and ran my fingers through his silky black mane.

"Welcome to Durley, Fitzroy," I said.

The hubbub died down. Bayard, my roan gelding was brought out to me for my journey to Marlborough. His eye looked furious and he tossed his head and blew through his nose.

"No, my old friend" I said as I mounted and turned his head to the gate. "He is a race horse. What use is one of those eh? He is fast and temperamental no doubt. He could not save my life, as you have done, many times. Have no fear, you are still my best friend," and we set off at a trot.

***

Johannes of Salerno and I had been friends since 1194. He had been called then to look to my wife Cecily when she had received a mysterious wound to her temple and was near to death. He was now in his forty second year, I believe. He was a tall man, muscular, for one who was not a fighting man, though I know he had once wielded a sword, for he had been out in the Holy Land on the crusade with our last king, Richard Plantagenet. He had shoulder length brown hair, now greying a little at the temples, scrupulously clean and shining, which he often wore tied back in a queue. He was clean shaven, unlike myself who went with the current fashion for a small clipped beard. His eyes were an amber brown, clear and direct of gaze and he had a fierce intellect. I liked that.

He lived in a small house which doubled as his workplace at the top of the High Street in Marlborough, directly behind the High Cross and in front of the church of St. Mary. All in the town, wealthy and poor, knew that he would open his doors to them and would do his utmost to help them. He was a wealthy man, having made his fortune in The Holy Lands. That fortune he now deployed for the good of the poor and sick of Marlborough.

He was now helping, a small man with a very bent back put on his shirt again. I put my head round the door. He saw me and nodded. I trotted off down the passage-way to find his housekeeper, a tiny dwarf of a woman who had once been lady's maid to Matilda de Neville, before that poor girl had been murdered at the top of the tower at the castle along with her fiancé, Guy de Saye.

Agnes, also known as the Pixie, beamed when she saw me and signalled that I should sit and take a beaker of wine. Happily I did, for Johannes kept some good wines in his cellar. Agnes had no speech at all, though she did have a bright brain and a cheerful disposition and when we needed to communicate, we did so by signs or by writing. She had taught herself to read and write whilst living with her mistress at Amesbury Abbey and it was this skill, amongst others, which now came to good use in the doctor's business.

Agnes busied herself.

"How are you liking it here with Johannes, Agnes?"

Agnes turned and beamed again, nodding. She put her hands to her heart, tilted her head and looked to Heaven.

"He is a good man, yes."

She drew a large heart in the air with her fore-fingers.

"Ha ha, you have grown to love him, have you, in so short a time?"

She giggled silently and poured the wine.

"You are content?"

I was partly responsible for Agnes' position here for I had stolen Johannes' previous housekeeper from him and was about to make her my wife. Johannes was Lydia's uncle.

As if for an answer, Agnes tripped around the table on her small, light feet and kissed me quickly on the cheek, looking a little embarrassed for she had just kissed a landed lord.

"I take it that you are happy?"

She smiled as Johannes came through the door wiping his hands on a towel.

He had learned his doctoring in Salerno in Sicily, the best school of learning in the world for doctoring, he assured me, and though he had some odd ideas as far as the rest of the profession believed, he lost fewer patients and cured more people than they could ever hope to find to send their bills to. Cleanliness was paramount to Johannes.

"So, the busy bridegroom returns to town," said Johannes nodding kindly to Agnes as she poured him wine. "How goes it with the hunt for the priest's killer?"

I brought him up to date with the news so far and what I had done to gather information.

"Hmmm. He was certainly unpopular."

Then I told him about the rape of Edith. His face grew grave.

" 'Tis one thing to bully and punish villagers for perceived transgressions, or fail in one's duty to God, Aumary, but a man of the cloth rape one of his flock?"

"Sadly, Swithun did not really see himself as a man of the cloth and it will not be the first time this kind of thing has happened somewhere in an English village. A priest is a figure of authority, one whom villagers would normally revere, as they did our old Father Benedict, God rest him." Both Johannes and I crossed ourselves.

"Swithun was a young man with no experience of life at all. A young man thrown into the priesthood by, as he told me himself, an uncaring father. You know as well as I, that many young men of birth think that their demesne has been created solely for their pleasures and lusts. Perhaps, to Swithun Attwood, Durley had become his playing ground."

Johannes was shaking his head. "Did he have a history of bad behaviour in this way, do we know, elsewhere?"

I stretched out my legs. "I am about to find out. I have written to both his brother on his demesne in Hampshire and to the Bishop in Salisbury. Swithun's body is on its way there now. More information should be forthcoming shortly." I paused, the cup half to my lips. "And there is more." I sipped.

"More?"

"Someone - our murderer no doubt, set fire to the descent rolls in that little room in the church and then opened Swithun's coffin and searched it."

Johannes sat up, his brow furrowed. "You have more here than simply the murder of an unpleasant and reviled priest. Hated he was surely, but there is more to his death than we at first thought," he said shaking his head.

"Aye. We have someone who would kill to keep something a secret. A secret so awful that murder, blasphemy and arson are but pin pricks to the person's conscience. Something so secret that it takes twenty knife blows to purge."

We chatted further and then, before I took my leave, I told Johannes about the Poulter woman and her need for relief from her pain.

"Might I buy something from you Johannes, to aid the poor woman in her last days?"

"Better than that my friend. I shall come and see her myself. This way I can decide exactly what medicine is needed and I can, at the same time, satisfy my insatiable curiosity as to the murder of Swithun Attwood. You know how I love a puzzle."

And that is how Johannes and I discovered the next body.

***

We were laughing and joking as we approached the priest's house on the manor, having ridden at a stately pace along the Salisbury Road and through the forest. We saw John Brenthall, my senior forester, in the distance raise his arm in greeting as he trudged along the hillside, coming down over the manor fields, a large long handled wooden sledgehammer over his shoulder. We passed Old Joan's bothy and clattered in through the manor gatehouse just as Phil Wheelwright was rolling and checking a new wheel up and down the flagstones of the courtyard. Cedric ran to take our horses.

"You must come and look at my new beast Johannes," I said. "You'll be surprised, I warrant, when you see him."

"Later, I think. Shall we take our medicine to your sick poulterer? Let me stow my pack in the guest room."

We left the manor again and walked the short distance to the bothy surrounded by the thorny hedge. I took my riding gloves from my belt and donned the right one, and went to lift up the thorn gate but as we rounded the fence, I saw that it was open and pushed to the side. As a result some of the chickens had escaped. Johannes mustered all the strays he could find and they fluttered and ran into the enclosure again, clucking in displeasure. I replaced the gate behind me.

"Ho Meg!" I shouted. There was no answer.

"It's odd that she has left the gate open, she never does that, unless she is out with the fowl."

I shouted once more, "Joan, are you there?" Just in case Meg had left her mother with Old Joan again.

Johannes dipped his head under the lintel.

The inside was very dark. The bothy had but one tiny window, just a sliver of wood divided the space, covered with a curtain of hessian. I entered the bothy and pulled back the curtain so that we might have more light; it made very little difference.

Johannes looked round. "God, that people are forced to live so."

"Aye," I said, "We are gradually replacing the old bothies with cruck houses but some people hang on to the old ways and it's hard to shift them."

"We shan't be shifting this one anyway." Johannes was on his haunches by a pallet and a pile of bedclothes close by the side wall. Meg's mother, also called Meg, was lying on her back. Her eyes stared at the thatch of the roof and her jaw was slack. She was thin and gaunt and her chest did not rise and fall. Johannes felt for a throb in her neck.

"No, she has gone. The illness has eventually claimed her. I'm sorry I could do nothing to ease her passing." He closed her eyelids and stood.

"We have no priest to give unction, though I know that she had that some time ago from Father Godfrey when he was over from Bedwyn, after Swithun refused to come out to her."

"A matter of a few hundred yards?" said Johannes with distaste.

"Aye, and Godfrey walks from Bedwyn, three miles."

We stared down and each of us said a silent prayer. Johannes genuflected.

"So where is her daughter?"

"Perhaps she ran off when her mother passed. There are two places she might be."

I loped off up to Joan's bothy by the manor wall and just across the grass, and Johannes made off at a fast pace to the river and Edmund's house.

Old Joan was not at home. I ran after Johannes' receding back and had almost caught up with him when the squealing began. At the place where the stream widened a little and the willow trees leaned out over the water, Joan the laundress and another woman were yelling and pointing. Joan the washerwoman came running up the bank.

"M'lord, there's a body floating in the stream."

Johannes was already there and wading in. The water came up to his waist. He grabbed the sodden clothing of the woman floating there and pulled her to the bank. I caught up and slid down the bank to grab the cloth of her dress and pull.

Johannes picked her up in one movement and laid her on the grass on her front. He turned her head to the side, opened her mouth and began to push rhythmically on her torso. I saw the two women glance at each other.

"It helps to get the water from her lungs," I said.

"Ah..."

Very little water was coming out of the drowned girl's mouth. At last Johannes gave up and sat back on his knees, dripping and muddy and full of weed.

"She's dead," he said.

I gently pulled the hair from the girl's face. Meg Poulter. I knew that by her clothes anyway. A dull mud coloured tunic, a supertunic of almost black faded with washing to brown-purple. Her coif was gone but that had only been a small head cloth to contain her hair whilst working, and would fall off easily into the water; her apron was missing too. I scanned the bank and the stream. They might have fetched up a little further along, in the plants.

Johannes was turning the body on its back and searching for clues. Why had this innocuous, not very bright eighteen year old girl ended up in the stream? I watched as he examined her head. No blows here. He turned her, looking at her neck.

The watching women were now getting quite agitated and so I chivvied them along and told them to go back to work. Meg had obviously slipped and banged her head and drowned. They obeyed with a few sneaky looks over their shoulders.

"Johannes?"

"She drowned, yes but I think she was almost dead before she got into the water."

"What do you mean?"

He stood up. "Her lungs were not as full of water as those of a person who takes it in when they breathe. The water was not deep, she could have recovered and stood in it. It would have reached only to her bosom even if she were in the very middle. She is not a tall person but nevertheless, she could have waded out had she slipped in."

"I see."

"And see here," he rolled up her loose sleeves, and lifted the arms to show the backs, "the marks of a hand holding her. One on each arm."

I leaned over the body of Meg. I noticed something else.

"And a boot print on her back, plain as day. Mud."

We looked at each other and both said at once. "We shall look at her in the mortuary."

Meg was turned on her back. I was just off to organise a blanket to carry her to the manor when Edmund Brooker came slipping and sliding along the bank. He ducked under the nearest willow, a large branch of which was leaning over the water.

"Meg…no!" He slid to a halt by the body and fell down on his knees and stared. In his hand he held a few fish suspended in a small net. They were all dead.

He put down the net and carefully lifted Meg's head with both hands.

"I'm sorry Edmund," I said, "I know you were very fond of Meg."

He began to weep silently. "She had just been to tell me that you had said we might, if we wanted, be married."

"She had just left you then?"

"Yes. I was up over there, where the pool widens out netting some fish for supper and she ran up to tell me that her mother had just gone. Died. That now we were free and with your permission we could….." He sobbed into his hands.

My eyes glanced at his shoe soles, turned up to face me as he knelt over the body. Mud.

I mentally measured the size and type of the print on Meg's back. No, too large. Edmund's soles would be muddy; he had been fishing on a muddy bank and had just walked all along it, but it was not those which had made the print.

"We shall take her to the mortuary, Edmund," I said. "Then once more I shall send to poor Father Godfrey in Bedwyn to come and be our priest again."

This time I would send a cart for the poor man.

Word had gone on before. The manor courtyard was lined with folk. All had known poor Meg, both mother and daughter.

As we passed, Hal, Johannes, Wyot the gatekeeper and I with our burden, the manor folk took off their caps, bowed their heads and genuflected.

I saw Hawise and Lydia on the top step of the manor stairs. Henry was half way down and had stopped to watch, then he came bustling up, through the crowd.

"Henry, find Walter Reeve and ask him to fetch the body of Meg Poulter senior from her bothy. She too has died."

"Aye sir." He ran off.

Our little mortuary, a tiny round stone building at the corner of the stables and by the privy was just big enough for our body and for four grown men to stand. Here the parish coffin stood upright in a corner, ready and waiting for any who needed it. The last one had been used for Swithun. One of my carpenters, Alfred Woodsmith, had made another. Now we'd need one more, though they would go into the ground in nothing but their shrouds.

We manhandled young Meg onto the trestle table and I asked for another to be brought in for her mother.

It wasn't long before they were lying side by side. I dismissed the men and soon it was just Johannes and I in that small gloomy building.

We opened the windows, one to each side, north and south for more light.

Johannes ran out to the guest rooms, for he had deposited his pannier there in which he kept his doctoring equipment. He also changed his clothes, for he was beginning to shiver.

Then, Old Joan stripped the poor unfortunate girl of her sodden clothes and covered her decently with a linen cloth. She left and we looked at the body.

"Lesions to the arms, we have seen. Water - some in the lungs. Held down by a foot to the back. No blows to the head or neck."

Johannes fished for his metal probe. I had seen him use this before.

"Ah..." he bent at his work, his knees flexed. "She did not drown. She was suffocated in mud."

The probe had been inserted into her nose. It came out full of smelly black muck. "And in her mouth too. The water washed the surface stuff away as she floated along in the deeper parts of the stream. She was almost dead with the mud when she was thrown in, I think."

"Thrown in? Surely that would have been heard?"

"Eased into the water then. There is no chance, Aumary, that in her grief for her mother she drowned herself?"

"You just heard the lad. Edmund. She was looking forward to a new life."

"Aye, she was."

I looked down at the poor mouse of a girl.

"Why?"

"Hmmm?"

"Why would anyone want to kill her?"

Johannes was wiping his probe on a rag, before inserting it tidily into a roll of such things.

"What did she know eh?" he asked.

"I think she knew very little, Johannes, but maybe the killer thought she knew more than she did. She was certainly worried about something when I spoke to her about the night Swithun died. She was shaking like a palsied man."

I sighed. Yet again I would have to inform the coroner.

***

Agnes Brenthall waylaid me as I walked up to the manor steps. Her head popped out of the undercroft.

"M'lord... pssst."

I smiled, Agnes could always be relied upon to be direct and discreet.

"I will follow you, Johannes." I fished the key to my office from my scrip. "Go ahead. Here's the key."

Agnes came out of the shadow of the steps.

"Well, look at the state of you both and your boots Dr. Johannes? Joan will not be pleased to have to wash all that mud off sir."

"Joan was there when the mud was acquired, Agnes, I doubt she'll mind." Her eyebrows flew up into the band of her head cloth.

"Ah... poor wee Meg."

"Aye." Johannes went off up the steps. I slid into the darkness of the undercroft.

"So, what did you find out about Swithun and Edith?"

"It was very hard to get her to talk about it at all. She insisted that she was all right and that, yes, he had surprised her alone in her own cottage." Agnes was whispering and her words were susurrating like wind around the stone crypt.

"She did not cry out?"

"I asked her about that."

I smiled. "He pushed her onto the bed upon which Edmund sleeps, which is on the ground floor. Her own bed is up a ladder in the space in the eaves made by the animal pen in the corner."

"Yes, I know what you mean."

"She said he had a big knife and he was going to use it on her if she did not comply."

"That is interesting."

"She could not cry out sir, for her face was pushed into the material of the bed. And she was almost suffocated as he held her down on her front and... she said he was strong... and he...and ...."

"Come now Mistress Brenthall, you are a wife, a mother and an experienced woman of the world... what did he do?"

Agnes patted her headdress and looked away as she said,

"He took her like a beast does sir. From the back."

"Did he rid himself of his clothes? Can't have been easy performing that kind of act with a robe wrapped round your loins."

Agnes tried not to laugh at the image this conjured up. "Oh sir I never thought to ask...but yes. It would."

"Her brother said the robe was back on and the cloak and was flapping like bat's wings as he crossed the green moments later."

"Perhaps he did not take it off then."

"No. Did she look to you like a woman who has been raped by the village priest, Agnes?"

"There was certainly something. She was jumpy and uncertain. I've never seen Edith like that. She is always so confident and well a bit—too much, if you see what I mean. She's a bossy, hard kind of woman. Not much flusters her. I think the day of Judgement could arrive and she'd say... 'sorry God, I haven't milked the goat yet'...and send him packing!"

I laughed at this image.

"So, she bears no scars from this little episode then."

"Oh no sir...I didn't say that."

"No?"

"No mental scars I think, She seems to have accepted it and squirrelled it away... got on with life."

"AH...but?"

"I think in about seven months' time m'lord, you will have another little villein on the manor. And it will resemble Swithun the priest."

My eyes grew round as moons. "But surely that's a bit early?"

"Aye it is...but some women are like that, sir. They take just like a willow twig does when you stick it in the ground. Easy. Others take ages to conceive, no matter what."

"Well!" I was so surprised I just stood staring into space.

"I'll keep my eye on it, sir... never you fear."

"I know you will Agnes... I know you will."

***

Back in my little office, Johannes was warming his toes by the brazier I kept here, year long. "Hope you don't mind. I lit your fire and am trying to dry my boots."

I fished under my table and brought out some newly re-soled indoor shoes which Gilbert Cordwainer's apprentice, Harry Glazer, had mended for me. I threw them at Johannes.

"Here we are."

Harry was another person who had fallen foul of Swithun the priest. I pulled the aide memoir to me, which had been lying on my table and scribbled

Harry Glazer - angry in the town. Alibi?

Johannes pulled them on. "I must get some of these. Very useful."

Gilbert Cordwainer, far end of the High Street. By the priory gates."

"I know the man you mean."

I reached for the jug of wine sitting on my pot board.

"More information." I said.

"The redoubtable Agnes?"

"Aye." I laughed. "I set her to find out about the rape incident and she tells me that she believes that Swithun did indeed assault Edith. Little Meg was also convinced that the thing had happened."

"Hmm."

"You are not convinced?"

"I might be if I thought that Swithun had a history of such attacks, or even if I thought that he was one who like to watch women, at their ablutions."

"God, Johannes, are there such men?"

"Sadly there are some such men. They seem to become aroused by such activities. In France they have a word for it. Voyeur."

"A watcher?"

"Some men secretly like to watch sexual congress, others nakedness, some another sordidness of a different kind."

"We must try to find out about his past then and see if he has been reprimanded at Salisbury Abbey for such sins, or something like."

"That would help us, yes."

"And another thing.... Agnes is convinced that Edith is with child."

Johannes sat up then... "Well, well."

"I asked her if this knowledge was a little premature and she said that some women are just made so. What do you think?"

Slowly, Johannes sat back again on my cushioned back chair.

"Did I mention, Paul, that Johannes had made himself comfortable on the best chair in the room and that I was relegated to the stool? No? Well, we need to write that somewhere."

"Well, I think it might happen but it is very unlikely. I don't think a woman would know this early that she was with child. Where are we....a few days? Swithun dies on the evening of the ninth. Here we are on the eighteenth. The rape took place, so Edith and Edmund say, on the 9th. No...it's too early to know."

"Well, Agnes is convinced. She thinks she is two or three months."

"Does Edith have another beau around the village?"

I laughed out loud.

"You don't know our Edith, do you?"

"No...never met her."

"She is a pretty thing. Blue eyes, fair hair. Curvaceous. And there the good-ness ceases. She is a shrew, my friend. A Gorgon. Medusa herself would quail at her look. She has a temper to rival Poseidon and she stirs the waters just as fiercely. No one would want or has wanted her. Besides, I doubt they could get anywhere near her. She has a fearsome reputation and a vocabulary to shame a sailor. Her sweet looks belie her nature. A beau? Poor man if she has."

"So it is not likely she is with child by another village man?"

I chuckled and chuckled.

"No indeed."

"So we shall just have to see if Agnes is correct."

"If she is...then I shall move her from her role as housekeeper and promote her to House Seer and pay her on results, for the woman will be able to tell me what will happen every day before it has happened."

"Do not mock, my friend," said Johannes. "There are some, I have heard, who can do just that."

And we laughed both long and hard.

***

The rain settled in to a wetting drizzle all that late afternoon. Folk who didn't need to be out sought the dry of their homes and the warmth of their fires. Johannes and I, shut up in my office until supper, discussed this latest death of Meg the poulterer, over a beaker or two of spiced wine.

"Can I have a look at the manor rolls?" asked my friend, "There may be something there which you have missed because you are so familiar with the place."

I pulled the key from the front of my cotte and opened the chest where I had hidden the descent rolls.

The four rolls came out in order. The latest first.

1190 to 1204, the present year. My beloved Cecily's death was recorded here, in this roll as was my son Geoffrey's. My father's too was recorded here.

1180 to 1190 and 1170 to 1180 -twenty-fifth of March of that year. The New Year. Here was my own birth recorded.

"Of course, I do not know the people. You will have to help me there."

"Lydia and I have been through them all and we cannot see anything amiss."

Johannes made a moue. "Maybe not but it does no harm to look again. It would also pay us to take particular note of those folk who had a grudge against

Swithun—anything to do with their families."

We began with 1170. The people mentioned in this decade who were embroiled in this present matter were the Brookers; their births being recorded here. Edmund and Edith in 1180. Their father was noted as being Arnulf. The mother's name was not recorded. Matthew Cook was here in the latest roll, as having first come to the manor in an aside, just as he had described, in 1196. A small note in the margin said, "Matthew Lydney came to Durley from Marlborough town. He had been a year and a day there, serving with Master Philbert Fleshmonger, who vouched for him. Colmar Coke also vouched for him. His age was recorded then, as twenty-two. A little while along, there was the record of his marriage to Edgiva. Joan the Laundress was in her late thirties as was her husband Robin, and the rolls recording their births were now lost. However, two children were born to them. One died in infancy and the other, Warren, was now about four. Henry Manton was here, as was poor Piers junior who was recorded as having been born in 1189. His death was recorded by Father Godfrey's hand in 1204. Henry was given life in 1181. The senior Sylvestres, Fulke and Ann were both missing for they were in their late thirties and the rolls recording them were gone but their children were there. Ralf was now 19. His birth was recorded in 1185 along with his brother two years later, who had not survived beyond birth. Two further children were entered: Aldwin who was one of my foresters born in 1189 and Alysoun, in 1192.

"It all looks so innocent."

"But there is something here that should tell us something, if we could but tease it out," said Johannes.

We rolled up the parchments and went to our supper.

***

On the next day Hal and I served on the jury of twelve men for the coroner. The doctor told the king's man that in his professional opinion, Little Meg had been murdered by someone who had held her down in the mud at the edge of the stream and had forced her head into the sludge. She had asphyxiated. The first finder, Joan, gave her tale of seeing the young girl floating in the middle of the shallow stream and the coroner was content. The verdict was murder by person or persons unknown.

We would bury both the Megs, on the morrow, if Godfrey could be persuaded to stay with us and officiate.

I had kept the dress which young Meg had worn, even though much of the mud of the footprint on her back had dried and disappeared. It might prove useful. This too, I locked away in the chest in my office. Johannes had gone home to Marlborough.

***

I had neglected Lydia and my daughter Hawise over the past few days and felt guilty, so spent the evening playing fox and geese with them in the hall. I was particularly good at this game; in fact I had been village champion, but my mind was elsewhere.

My foxes all had the faces of my suspects and the geese had faces of the folk I had known over the past few years who had been murdered, either here or in the town. Eventually Hawise was packed off to bed and Lydia and I could sit together on a bench in front of the dwindling fire. Others, who slept in the hall, were bedding down around us. Hal of Potterne said goodnight and went on his last round of the manor, making sure that Wyot the gateman had locked up, before settling in his own bed, in the south range of rooms, though sometimes he slept in the hall.

Lydia and I spoke quietly and I told her of the day's developments.

"Do you think that Young Meg knew who the killer is?"

"Perhaps. I cannot think how she knew though."

"Maybe she saw them?"

"Her home was close to the church, but the manor wall screens it from the priest's house. Unless she saw someone hurrying away, covered in blood. No, that cannot be, for it was pitch black when the deed was done. She might have seen a shadow but nothing more."

"Some people are recognisable, even by their outline shape, Aumary. Old Joan could be mistaken for no one else, for example. Others have a peculiar gait or way of moving."

I leaned away from her to look at my wise almost-wife.

"Do you know... you are right. I must ask everyone who was still out and about that night, if they recognised anyone else skulking around."

"And you might also make a search for any clothing which is blood-stained. Someone will have been covered in gore. Someone else may have noticed this but has not made a connection to Swithun's murder," she said, yawning.

I hugged her close.

"You are amazing. Why didn't I think of that?"

"I'm sure you did, it's just that it slipped your mind."

I harrumphed. "Well, I did get Hal to search Henry's place but...nothing."

"So, which house is the closest to the priest's and who lives there that they may have seen someone going in or coming out?"

"Close to Swithun's house? Old Joan's bothy is on the east wall of the manor, close but the wall screens her too. Dysig's bothy is the closest as it's opposite the priest's house and Hamon Deerman has a house next door."

"Then start with them and ask them....if they saw anything."

I too yawned. "I shall. But that is for another day."

"You too my dear scribe, look as if you should be for your bed. The light is fading now. Yes, I suppose it is difficult getting up in the middle of the night for Matins. A growing lad like you needs his sleep. Off you go then...I shall see you tomorrow. Give my thanks to the prior for letting you come to me."

***

"Hello Paul I hope you slept well and managed to get through Matins without snoring.

    Do you know, we shall start today with a report of the weather and it was just the same as it is today. Miserable. I shall need two rugs over my knees today, I expect."

The day was as gloomy as the day before had been. I woke and wondered what time it was, for the light was so poor filtering through my shuttered window. I stretched and yawned, threw off the coverlet and stepped onto the wooden floor.

Alceste, my old wolf hound, was sleeping right by me on the floor and I stepped over her to retrieve my clothes from the chair. I had relaxed the rule about dogs being allowed to stay overnight in the hall and in the manor house, especially for Alceste, who was old, blind and deaf. I could not let her arthritic bones seize up, by banishing her to the stables, in the cold with the other younger dogs. I am sure she was grateful. I reached down and let her smell my hand. She licked it and knew then, that it was I who had patted her and ruffled her noble head. She often slept with Peter Brenthall in their house, as she was very fond of the lad. Today she stood shakily and loped off into the hall to find Hal of Potterne who always gave her some of his morning ham.

My fast broken with bread, ham and ale, (not everyone broke their fast as we did sometimes but waited until the meal of dinner, mid-morning). I tidied my unruly hair as best I could, with a large toothed comb, rubbed my teeth with salt and quickly shaped my beard with a small pair of shears, whilst staring into a piece of highly polished metal, kept for the purpose in my office. I would do.

I needed to be up early, for my forest folk rose early and were out before it was fully light.

The reeve too was up early for I saw him leaning on his stick, two hands, gnarled now with age, over the top of it, giving instructions to some of the villeins, over by the manor fish pond. I jogged over to the house opposite the priest's door and scratched. It was a chilly morning but no frost yet.

There was general scurrying inside and a voice shouted, "Gerald...the door." I remembered that Hamon's eldest son was a Gerald. The lad was about ten. His face was grubby and he was stuffing a piece of rough bread into his mouth as he swung open the door. His eyes opened wide as he saw who it was and he retreated, coughing.

"Ma, Pa, Ma, Pa!" he eventually managed to shout.

I entered the house and called out. "God's greeting to you. It's Lord Belvoir, Hamon. I have come to talk to you, if I may."

Hamon's wife, a small creature with a round nose like an acorn and hair the colour of a mouse's back, who came from Overton, I remember, bobbed a curtsey and ushered the three children out into the back room.

Hamon rose slowly from his morning ale.

He nodded. "G'mornin', sir." He was wary and was not quite sure what to do. I had never been in his house before. I was not surprised he was a little unsure. He stood nervously and then put down his ale cup. "Can I offer you..."

"No thank you, I have broken my fast. Can I sit?"

Hamon gave me his stool. Then he found another for himself which was not quite as big.

"Are we going out to Le Broyle today, sir? Are you coming with us?"

Le Broyle was one of the balliwicks of Savernake forest, out towards Ramsbury where much forestry work was needed to be done at the moment.

"No, I have no time today Hamon. I have come to ask you a little about the night of the death of Swithun the priest."

The man went deathly white. He stammered, "I...I..I don't know anything about that, sir."

"No... I'm sure you don't, but I just thought, since your house is the nearest to Swithun's home, you might have seen something. Something you maybe don't realise could be important."

He said, far too quickly, "No sir, I saw nothing."

I looked at him squarely.

"Nothing?"

"No sir, see, when I go to bed, what with the youngsters and all, I make sure I sleep like the dead." He realised what he had said and blushed to the roots of his hair.

"I mean, I don't wake, I sleep sure and deep. Otherwise I'd be tired all the time, see, the noise they make. I learned to fall fast asleep in a thunder-storm sir, so I could get me rest."

"You were fast asleep at that early an hour, Hamon?"

"I do sleep early sir and that's a fact. The wife makes me my meal and I eat it and I often fall asleep over me ale."

A voice joined in. "He does sir, silly man. I often find him snorin' on his bench, his head on the table and his hair in his pottage, or what's left of it." His wife had returned and was standing in the doorway, her arms across her bosom.

"It was a dark night I remember, with no moon or stars, not easy to see anything."

"No sir."

"About the time of vespers?"

"No sir."

"But you might have heard something. Did, for example, Swithun cry out? Surely you would've heard that, being so close and on the side where one of the windows to the loft is situated."

"No sir...like I say..."

"Hamon sleeps like a tree trunk sir. He don't hear anything."

"And did you, mistress?" I asked.

Her eyes narrowed.

"Hear anything?"

Her eyes flicked to her husband. "No, nothing. None of us heard anything."

"Do you too, sleep like a tree trunk mistress?" I asked.

"Sleep? There's a fancy! I sleep very little m'lord. I've too much to do to sleep. I was up and mending much of the evening...by the light of the fire."

"And you, when you were at your mending, heard and saw nothing, by the light of your fire?"

"No m'lord...nothing."

I knew they were both lying but could not, I felt shake them. Not just yet.

"Very well." I turned to leave, the edge of the door in my hand.

"If you remember anything, call in at the manor house and speak to Henry the steward, or tell the reeve, if I am elsewhere."

"Yes, sir."

The smallest child had crept up to her mother's side and was holding onto her apron. The next one was still standing in the doorway of the other room. The eldest had recovered his poise and had crossed the room to the loft ladder and was sitting on the step half way up. His father got up and fetched him down.

"Was there a lot of blood like they says, m'lord, like when they stick the pig and it squeals and thrashes at Christ's mass?" Hamon cuffed him around the head, but lightly.

"Aye, young'un, there was. It was everywhere," I said.

"Awww..." his eyes widened.

"And the person who murdered him would have been covered in blood," I added for good measure.

"Cor..." said the boy and he looked up at his father.

"Good day all."

Well. What was that all about?

They would most certainly need a further visit. Once they had been left to stew like an old laying chick in a pot.

I then called in at the next house. The bothy where the lackwit young man, Dysig lived. He lived alone but could not look after himself. I did not quite remember but I thought his parents had died in the outbreak of fever, like those of the Brooker's. A succession of women came and went to feed him, make sure he was washed now and again, his clothes, such as they were, were darned and laundered and his little bothy swept and kept clean.

I called out Dysig's name. There was no answer.

I pushed on the wattle made door.

The young man was still snoring in his bed.

I left and trotted up to the Brenthall house just a few houses away from Dysig's cott.

I know that Agnes often looked after Dysig and he might feel better if she were there. She readily agreed to come and wake him and help me talk to him. Agnes was much more familiar with the lad than I, and once she had plaited her hair and pinned it, donned a new clean veil and her outdoor pattens, she came with me back down the lane. John was long gone to his work in the forest, she said.

Dysig came to slowly. He smacked his lips, shook his head, blinked at the light coming in through the door and squealed when he saw me. There was no window. He backed up against the bothy wall.

Agnes reassured him that I was not an ogre and that I would do nothing but talk to him. I squatted on my haunches, smiling as best I could, so as not to present such a daunting tall figure.

There was a fearsome smell in the bothy and Agnes scouted around to find the piss pot full and brimming and dashed outside to throw it on the field behind.

"So Dysig...how are you?"

He nodded.

"Good, I'm glad. You are a lucky man, aren't you, for so many nice women to look after you so kindly?"

He grinned and I noticed that many of his teeth were gone.

"I don't have so many nice women to look after me."

"Aw go on, sir," said Agnes returning to the bothy, laughing.

"Dysig," she said, coming straight to the point, which I had not. "The master would like to know a few things about Swithun the priest."

The reaction was out of all proportion to the question.

Dysig yelled out....something unintelligible and buried his head in his arms, screaming as if someone were belabouring him over the head with a stick.

Agnes went down on her knees. "Now, now, my brave boy. There's no reason to do that."

She took both his hands from his head. "We aren't going to hit you."

Eventually he calmed down.

"Listen Dysig, at the big house, you know my daughter Hawise don't you?" Dysig loved my daughter and Hawise was fiercely protective of the young man and would hear nothing bad said of him.

"Aye... Hawisy... Dysig love Hawisy."

"I know, and that is very nice. It really is. Well, Hawise has some lovely marchpane pigs. How would you like to come and fetch one to eat. I know that she has shared them with you before." The man nodded.

"I think she has some honeyed plums too, given to her by her Uncle Johannes."

"Ahhhhhh."

"I know that Hawise would like you to help her eat them."

Dysig nodded as if his head would fall from his neck.

"All I would like you to do, if you can, is tell me what you heard the night the priest was... the night he died."

Dysig's face creased up as if he were about to cry but he said,

"Dysig not tell."

"Not even for marchpane pigs and honey plums?"

He shook his head violently.

"Who has asked you not to say anything Dysig?"

Agnes took his hand. The nails were black and ingrained with dirt. The palms were black also with what looked like soil.

"Dysig, the master just wants you to help him. You know that the priest was murdered don't you?"

Agnes looked up at me and nodded. I left it to her.

Dysig assented, this time a little less disturbed.

"The master is in need of help Dysig. You like to help don't you?"

"Aye… help. Dysig likes to help. Dysig is good."

"Oh we know you are, my lad," said Agnes.

"So, what did you see that night? Your house is right opposite, right across from the house where the priest lived. Surely you heard or saw something. You can tell us."

Dysig coughed and spluttered as if the words were stuck in his throat. "Dysig loved Father Benedict."

"We all did Dysig," I said, standing up at last. "We miss him terribly."

"Benedict's gone with God."

"Yes, he has." Agnes' brow was furrowed.

Where was this leading?

"The big black crow."

"Which crow was this?" asked Agnes

"The crow in the house."

I whispered to Agnes. "I think he means Swithun in his black robe and cloak."

"AH…yes…"

"He hit Dysig."

Agnes stood up. "I have seen Swithun hit Dysig once or twice with his stick. That's true."

"He hurt Dysig."

"He can hurt you no longer Dysig," I said appalled at the behaviour of this so called man of God.

"He killed Father Benedict."

"No…I…"

Agnes put out her hand to stop me.

"Why do you say that, Dysig?"

"They all sayed it."

"Who?"

"All the demons."

I caught a lock of my hair, in exasperation.

"Ah we are in the realm of fairies and demons now."

"No...listen..." said Agnes. "So you heard some demons."

"They speaked to me."

"Well, that is very unusual my lad," said Agnes, "I don't think a demon has ever spoken to me. Were they unkind these demons?"

Dysig thought a little, "Nah...they were quiet and black and knowed my name."

"Goodness me, demons that know your name. Was that not frightening?"

Dysig smiled at that, "Nah... coz Dysig's brave."

"Yes...you are...I don't think if a demon was to talk to me I could be so brave. Could you m'lord?"

"Ooh no, certainly not," I said "I would run away screaming." It was said if the devil's minions knew your name that was the end of you.

I looked at Agnes, trying not to smile. She was very good at this sort of thing.

"So how many demons were there?" I asked.

"He cannot count sir," said Agnes. No of course he couldn't.

"Were there a lot of them, Dysig?" she asked.

He nodded.

"And they told you that Swithun the priest had killed Father Benedict?"

"Yes."

"Well... that is the trouble with demons Dysig...they tell lies. They do it all the time. They come from the devil you see, and the devil is bad."

"They dowun't lie."

"Demons are the bad ones, angels are the good ones. Angels never lie."

Dysig laughed.

"There was an angel with the demons."

Oh this was getting ridiculous.

"Agnes...I think we are being led into......"

"No sir... Dysig never lies...he cannot."

"No?"

"We just have to tease out what he says and try to make sense of it."

"So Dysig, there was an angel too?"

"Aye, a very bright one."

"Do you know him?"

"Dysig don't know no angels, Dysig aren't bin to Heaven. But Father Benedict said Dysig can." He smiled, "one day."

"Yes, I'm sure."

Even the redoubtable Agnes was flagging. "Why do you say it was an angel?"

"It were all white."

"White?" said both Agnes and myself together.

"Like the angels in church."

Ah, my wall painting of the silvery white angels.

"So who told you that you must keep quiet about the demons....and the angel?"

"The angel."

"Ah."

"The demons took his soul. I heared it."

"You heard Swithun cry out?" I asked.

"Then the angel took him to Heaven."

"Hmmm." I was even more confused now. "Thank you Dysig. Come up to the hall and I will give you some marchpane."

He shook his head.

"I'll get it for you Dysig," said Agnes, moving to the door. "And I'll bring it to you. Together, before you eat it, we shall wash you."

"Nooooooo."

"Yes, my lad... you stink like a midden!"

I laughed. I recalled that I had known this man, whose name meant foolish in English, nearly all my life. This 'lad' was well over twenty!

Chapter Four

"I have no idea what on earth that was all about," I said to Agnes as we went back down towards the hall.

"Oh I'm sure if we keep talking to him we shall learn what it's really about," Agnes said.

"Agnes, you are a treasure."

"Aw, go on sir..." she replied.

We parted at the manor steps. "I'll keep on at him, sir. See if I can get some more. There's no doubt he saw something but his confused mind doesn't understand what it was."

"No, that's for certain," I agreed.

"Now I am off to see if I can organise a search of the village for a blood-stained....." What was I looking for?

"Sir?"

"Well, a blood stained something....I'm not sure what. All I do know is, whoever did the deed will have been drenched in blood. You don't get rid of that easily."

"AH! no....don't we women know it."

"Agnes?"

"Oh blood is such a hard thing to get out of cloth sir. Unless you have quickly put it in cold water, you have a devil of a job with it. That is why I have not as yet cut the throat of John, my husband, sir."

"I beg your pardon Agnes?"

Her face was quite serious "Oh. There's many a time when I could strangle him, you know. But I think cutting his throat whilst he sleeps would be easier. Except...all the blood on the sheets. Too hard a job to get clean. So...I let him live."

"Agnes...you are a wicked woman," I spluttered, laughing.

She tittered, "Oh I know."

"You love John dearly."

"Aye I do. You're right."

I chuckled.

"Maybe I'll just have to put up with him then," she said.

***

I left Agnes and chuckled all the way to the stream where I hoped to search for Meg's lost apron and coif. I wondered if the position in which Ifound them might indicate where she had gone into the water.

I broke a piece from a decayed branch, long enough for me to poke about in the plants by the banks and began at the easternmost edge of the stand of willows. I walked by the bank, occasionally slipping into the mud where the water was shallow and where branches overhung the stream and I could not pass without ducking under them. I lost my footing several times but righted myself with the aid of the stick. My eye raked the ground for footprints and signs of a scuffle. Leaves were falling into the stream and onto the grass bank, all around me making a soggy, yellow mess underfoot.

Eventually I grew level with the Brookers' cottage. Here it was that I found Meg's coif. It was in a tangled mess of willowherb, meadowsweet and comfrey, now over and beginning to rot down. I held onto the overhanging branch of one of the older sallows and fished with my stick. Little minnows, dozens of them, darted out further into the water, frightened by my sudden appearance and movement. The coif came up dirty and dripping green sludge. I scrambled up the bank and wrung out the material.

Yes, I recalled her wearing this on the day I spoke to her about Edmund. I searched again but I could not find her hessian apron which was still missing.

Coming out from the trees onto the bank by the road I looked south and north up and down the Salley Gardens.

There were two pools on this stretch of the stream, where the water bellied out and the bank became undercut. Here the water was a little deeper than in other places and was where the larger fish could be found. I thought back to my young and carefree days when I had come to this stretch of the stream with my line and net and pieces of rotten meat as bait. I had learned to swim with other boys of the manor too, here in this pool.

When the weather was dry, the stream shrank and the pools lowered. August and September had been very dry. Though there had been some good days, October made up for it and the pools were full once more. These pools were full of rudd and roach, barbel, and gudgeon; yes, especially gudgeon, for they gathered together in the deeper parts when the vegetation was beginning to rot. Edmund had been fishing for gudgeon here when he found Johannes and I with Meg.

Meg had been found floating further along, where the laundresses plied their trade. Our little stream ran east-west, in the main. Edmund had been fishing at the most easterly pool, quite a way from his cottage. Yet, Meg had come to him to tell him the news of her mother's death. She had then been found floating back at the western end of the willows.

Her coif was found in the middle. Did that piece of clothing float away at a quicker pace than its owner and then become stuck? Had Meg run back towards the poultry bothy and been waylaid on her way back?

I looked down at my boots. Again, they would need cleaning. I set off up the lane, crossed the village green, went up past the reeve's house and jogged into the courtyard.

I resolved to find Peter Brenthall, and ask him to clean my boots.

Two horses were being held by my grooms at the bottom of the manor steps. I didn't recognise either of them. I propped my stick up against the undercroft wall, left Meg's coif on the bottom step and rose up the stair with an ear open for voices which might give me a clue as to the nature of the riders of these two horses. They were good horses, with expensive leather works. Perhaps one of my noble neighbours was paying me a visit.

Henry was taking care of the two men as I entered.

"Gentlemen, I am so sorry I was not at home to welcome you."

Both men had been seated and stood as I entered.

"Please sit again whilst I make myself presentable." I lifted my hands from my sides, "I have been about manor work around and about the river."

The elder man wrinkled his nose as if he thought that sort of work was beneath him and was best left to his inferiors. The younger man, dressed all in black, smiled and looked me up and down as if I were a villein myself.

I hastened to the office, drew off my filthy boots and donned a pair of ankle boots. I quickly washed my hands in the bowl by the window, smoothed down my hair as well as I could and fished a couple of dry leaves from it.

"Welcome to Durley," I said as I re-entered. I now knew who one of the men was, for he resembled his brother in colouring, stance and build. "My Lord Attwood."

I bowed.

***

Sir Ralph of Attwood, Swithun's brother, was a man of middling height, thickening around the belly with too much rich food and too little exercise. His clothes were expensive and fashionable. His beard was perfectly cut into a 'v' at his chin with a thin moustache. His hair was long and dark, almost to his shoulder blades, wispy at the ends and the whole man screamed, 'vanity.'

He bowed his head. "My Lord Belvoir. We must thank you for your letter telling us of my brother Swithun's demise. Since the distance is not so great from our demesne to your own, we thought to pause here on our journey to Oxford where we shall reside for a while."

"You are most welcome. Please, we shall make a room available to you for as long as you wish to stay. Henry, can we see to that please?" Henry bowed and went off on silent feet.

Wine had already been poured for the pair; we sat and I poured some for myself.

"This is Audemar of Ascot, my lawyer," said Ralph of Attwood. I nodded to the man.

"We are off to Oxford to discuss a wretched boundary dispute with one of the new colleges there. So tedious but necessary I'm afraid, and we thought we'd stop off here." His eyes raked the hall. His look said 'basic'. "To break our journey and to hear further about my poor brother Swithun."

"There is little more to tell, sadly, than the facts I set down in my letter. I am investigating his death personally. I have some experience of looking into murders. In my role as deputy constable of the castle at Marlborough, I have confronted murder before and my Lord the King has more than once relied upon me to dig out the truth."

It sounded pompous, but I felt that this was what was needed with these two men. They looked at each other blinking as if they had just come out into the light from a dark room.

"We had thought you the warden of this forest of Savernake?"

"Oh yes," I said leaning back confidently and crossing my ankles. "That too."

They stared at me.

"I can tell you very little except that it has come to light in the course of my investigations, that Swithun had discovered some fact, some secret in our manor rolls which, I believe, led to his death. I am going through the rolls and rest assured, I will find what is hidden in them." I was not going to tell them that most of the rolls had been destroyed by fire.

"You have not arrested a felon, one of your manor villeins, for this crime?"

"No sir. As yet I have not. It is but a few days since Swithun died.

Almost every waking hour has been spent since uncovering facts and establishing alibis. I have suspects but, in truth I cannot yet, with certainty, call one man the murderer of your brother."

Ralph nodded, "You are most thorough."

"And yet..." said the man of law.

I turned my head to him. "There must be seen to be some retribution. Justice must be seen to be served, to protect society."

I smiled. "I will not hang a man for a crime just because he happened to be in the wrong place at the wrong time, sir. Here on my manor and in my forest at large, I require evidence. Evidence which stands a severe testing."

Audemar bowed his head. "I hope that the - ahem - authorities do not deem you too lax or lenient in carrying out sentences, Sir Aumary, in your manor court. I should hate to think that you suffer harsh criticisms because of your - ahem - squeamishness...."

I stopped him. "Here Audemar, I am the authorities. I have no fear of criticism."

The man sniffed. That sniff conveyed a thousand words. I ignored him.

"As I told you in my letter, Sir Ralph, Swithun was killed by repeatedly being stabbed with a large bladed knife. The coroner has the weapon now. However, I have a drawing I made from memory. No one here in Durley seems to know the weapon. I wonder if you would be so good as to look at it and see if you recognise it." I fished in my cotte once more.

"Why would I recognise a churl's knife? Really Belvoir, I hardly think..." He stopped and there was a sharp intake of breath. "How?"

"You know this knife?"

He took the drawing from me, "I do."

"How do you know it? Did it belong to Swithun?"

"My brother was a monk, Belvoir...what need had he of a nobleman's knife? He relinquished all property when he became a religious. This is not his knife, but mine."

"Yours?"

"I have not seen it this fifteen years."

"Swithun somehow managed to take it with him when he left Stockbridge at the age of ten and has kept it hidden all this time?"

"It would seem so," he answered angrily.

"A young lad of ten, taking something of his old home with him, something of his nobility."

"Little pilfering rat," said Attwood quietly. "He was always secretive."

"I'm afraid I must say that Swithun was not well liked here on the manor. He was a harsh and hard spiritual master. He had little feeling for his flock as weak and flawed human beings. He was acquisitive, lazy and more than once in dereliction of his duty."

Ralph stood up quickly.

"Sir, have a care. This is my brother of whom you speak. My brother whose life has been foully cut short."

"Aw come Sir Ralph. I doubt you have given him much of a thought in all the years he has been at Salisbury. He has been out of your hair." I looked with undisguised disapproval at the man's hair under his scarlet bonnet. "I do not think that you could truly have been the best of friends."

Ralph of Attwood sat and scowled at me. "Aye well, he was always a difficult child."

"A difficult child? In what way?"

"Petty jealousies, imagined slights and long held grudges...and like I say secretive."

"Did he have a temper?"

He watched me carefully, then. "Not as such, he was more the kind who would keep silent, fester and plan revenge," he said.

"Ah... I see," I answered.

"I know that he was but ten when he went to the abbey at Salisbury and I know that you are his senior by some five years but can you tell me if he had any, unnatural predilections... any...?"

"Sir... I protest," said Ralph,

"No hear me out. I have a reason for asking. If you cannot supply me with the information then I must apply to the bishop at Salisbury." I did not tell him I had already written.

Sir Ralph of Attwood folded one leg over another and flicked an imaginary speck of lint from his scarlet cotte.

"It has been said that Swithun had an unnatural desire to watch women whilst they were dressing, or bathing. That he had a barely suppressed lust for the female body which resulted in him committing rape here on my estate. It is said he raped one of my villeins."

Ralph of Attwood's face became suffused with blood and his lawyer stood and pointed at me.

"That, sir, is a slight on the family of Attwood. A foul calumny and if you persist we shall have no hesitation in drawing up...."

"Draw up what you like sir. Litigation will get you nowhere. Once I have put my facts before the King... and be certain, I shall, for he is a childhood friend, your court case will avail you nothing. I will have the truth. I am the lord of this place lord of this place - it is my right."

"This is a slander and malicious..."

"Then answer my question and we shall all be able to move on to more genial matters." I smiled.

I could see from the corner of my eye that Henry had come back through the hall door. He stopped as he saw the conflict going on at the high table.

"No; my brother, as far as I know, had no such likings," said Attwood grudgingly.

"Thank you."

"If he developed such ways after he left my manor, I know nothing about them."

"I will check with the bishop, then to see if he had been disciplined for any sexual transgressions whilst in the abbey but somehow, I do not think the answer will come back in the affirmative."

"Then why do you...?"

"I am, as you said, sir, thorough."

Attwood stood as if he had been slapped and wrapped his cloak around him like armour.

"I do not know why you are so concerned for Swithun's character. It is obvious he was killed by someone on your manor who was offended by his strictness in passing judgements. Some petty and violent peasant who did not like being held up to scorn. Rape indeed? Why should you be concerned by the rape of a peasant girl?"

"Rape is an offence against the King's peace sir and on this manor I take it very seriously."

"You, sir, are a fool."

I saw Henry stiffen at Attwood's words.

The lawyer scoffed. "Such women have no power to call upon the law, Sir Aumary - you waste your time. Time better spent in pressing your churls for the truth."

"On my lands, all my folk have rights, sir. All; without exception."

"Then you sir, are a fool and your manor populated by idiots. You will hear more from us," said Attwood.

And he stormed out followed by his black garbed friend.

Henry watched them go, a steaming ewer of water in his hands.

I shouted after them. "I was going to say that I am sure the priory in the town will accommodate you this night, Sir Ralph."

We heard the horses clop away through the gatehouse.

Henry laughed. "Nastiness sir.....runs in the family, doesn't it?"

"Aye...I'm afraid it does, Henry."

We never heard from them again.

I sat down heavily and downed my wine in one, not something I was used to doing.

Henry came up and planted the ewer on the table.

"Not wanting to waste the water, sir....would you like to wash?"

"Aye, I'll take it to my office and Henry, could you find Peter and ask him to clean my boots for me? Oh, and might you run down to the bottom of the steps and retrieve a coif—its wet and muddy and belonged to young Meg, and bring it back to me?"

He was almost out of the room when I called after him. "Where are Hawise and Mistress Lydia, Henry?"

He turned back and his face lit up. "They have gone out to pick blackberries sir. Up at the bushes by the stream, at the Salley Gardens."

***

My next task was to organise a search of the manor for a garment, any kind of garment or cloth, which was bloodstained enough to have been the clothing worn by Swithun's murderer.

I asked Walter to find me a group of people to comb the stream bank, the gardens and plots of the houses, of those of freemen and tied folk. Then I wanted them to spread out and look in the middens, bonfires, the pig houses, the barns and stables, all the public buildings. If this failed, we should need to invade the very houses themselves and I would use only well trusted men for that job. I would lead those searches myself.

I settled down to look through the descent rolls again. Some while later, Lydia and Hawise returned. Lydia was flushed and seemed a little put out.

"Look dada, what Lydia and I managed to pick."

There in her hand was an enormous bowl of blackberries.

"Why don't you take them down to Matthew Cook, Hawise?" said Lydia. "He will be so pleased and will make something delicious from them, I warrant."

Hawise ate a blackberry. From the purple state of her mouth, she had eaten quite a few already.

"Yes, I will. I shall tell him that we shall go and look again tomorrow and fetch him more," and she skipped off, carefully holding her bowl. When she had gone up into the hall I asked Lydia,

"What's the matter?"

"Oh...'tis nothing really. We were down at the bushes, engrossed in our task and we came across a pair of your villeins at their pleasures."

"Oh, in the open air?"

"Yes. I quickly managed to get Hawise away so she didn't see what they were up to. 'Oh Look Hawise, there are some really juicy and fat berries - just - over - there."

I chortled. "She has seen the coupling of the pigs and the goats on the demesne but I think at the age of five, seeing people might be a little more difficult for her to cope with. Who was it...? So that I might reprimand them. If they want to take their husband and wife pleasures in the open air, then they can go out further into the forest."

"Oh I don't know. I don't know many of your folk yet. The village is so strung out, there are so many people."

I laughed at that. "Marlborough has many more people."

"Yes, but they are all living cheek by jowl and it's easier to get to know them."

"So you really have no idea who they were?"

"The girl had her back to me. All I could tell you about her was that she was blonde. The man was lying on the grass; he was dark haired."

My eyebrow flew up. If they were coupling then it was not in the way Holy Mother Church dictated.

"No words spoken so that you might catch a name or...."

It was Lydia's turn to laugh. "No, no words...just delighted crescendos of sighing." She began to giggle. "I started to sing so that Hawise was not so interested in the, erm, other noises."

"Well done," I chuckled.

"No harm done. We were nearly at the end of our blackberrying anyway. We'd no more space in the bowl."

"So that is why you both had to eat some, is it?"

I wiped away a purple blackberry seed from her chin.

"Aw, Aumary!" she chided and smacked my hand lightly.

***

We buried Young Meg between her mother and her father in our little churchyard. The rain began to fall again. It almost seemed right that the heavens should weep at the tragic loss of two of our own folk. The Poulters had no remaining family, for all the men: father, brothers, uncles, and aunts too, had died in the outbreak of dock fever years ago.

There was also no one to look to the chickens and I needed someone to take on that responsibility quickly. One of the younger girls offered to take on the role as poultry keeper. I would not allow her to live in the old bothy. I left it as shelter for the birds, for it was fit for nothing else and decreed that the girl should still live in her parental home, which was close by.

We would build a new cruck house when the time came for her to move out.

On a day when the geese were flying overhead on their way south and the pigs were being driven from the village into the forest to gorge on the mast and the acorns, I set off on Bayard to Le Broyle to look at the forestry work being undertaken there and the management of the deer in the park. This was Hamon Deerman's principal role. The early morning had been foggy and I heard the geese but could not see them as I looked up to the heavens. There was something slightly eerie and otherworldly about staring up at the sky and hearing the geese honking and passing overhead unseen, shielded by the cloud.

Some of the men crossed themselves. I asked them why.

" 'Tis the souls of the dead sir, going home to their rest."

"Ah." It seemed appropriate.

John and I rode together, side by side where we could and he would lead the way where the path became too narrow. Here he would point out to me the trees which needed thinning to maintain the lane and I would give assent for the work to be carried out.

Felling overgrown areas further in the forest was another job with which the men were busy and there was a constant sawing and crunching as branches fell from trees. Hazel stools, which would be coppiced in the late winter or early spring before the rise in the sap, were marked and other trees were pollarded above the browse line to prevent deer from grazing the new shoots. We rode out into the little glades between the forest trees to oversee this work, for most pollarding was done in the wooded pastures.

I swivelled in the saddle to look round. "This all looks very tidy, John. Well done. Shall we go and see our deerpark and see how they are faring?"

It was after the rutting season for our fallow and roe deer, which had mated in August and September. In the early summer we kept a good watch on our does for this was when the forest was in 'defence' to allow the deer to give birth in peace and quiet. Winter was a time when the deer roamed free. Late autumn meant watching and counting to see the state of our herds and the health of the fawns. The fact we could regularly send thirty bucks or does to the king for his table, wherever in the south of England he may be residing, was a proof that the forest was very well stocked and managed indeed. We did not feel the loss.

We rode gently through the tracks and lanes of Le Broyle and into the land farmed and owned by my erstwhile father-in-law, Torold Congyre. Although Bedwyn was a separate village, it lay in the middle of the forest and was under my control. I would never interfere with Torold's management of it. He was a good man and lately, in his advancing years, increasing work had been undertaken there by my foresters. He had no living son and it would eventually pass to me, as his son-in-law.

We clattered down the main street and out onto the principal road to Hungerford. We crossed it and found ourselves on the edge of the Bailiwick of Hippenscombe. Here there was a long section of deer fence being mended. I recognised Fulke and his son, Ralf Sylvestre. They were erecting new hurdles and inspecting the ditches which were dug in front of them. This had the effect of making a five foot fence, eight feet tall, for the ditch was deep and right up against the wattle. The deer could not leap up over it.

Hamon was there supervising the work in the area. One or two deer had been netted and he was checking their health before letting them go. They bounded quickly out of the area, with large frightened eyes and white bobbing tails. He gave me a report on how many bucks and does there were in this area and how many does were likely to be in fawn.

We toured the deer fence, checking and liaising with the foresters about overhanging branches and fallen trees.

Hamon and I were deep in conversation. We wandered a little further from the group of workers.

"And so in May—June next year, we can expect a good nursery of babies then?"

Hamon smiled. "Aye this year the roe especially, have been busy. There are two or three really sturdy bucks around. They have mated... for you know, sir, that they do not stay with one doe..."

"Yes. The red deer do not thrive here do they, Deerman?"

"No sir. Savernake is best for roe and...." There was a whining sound and a woosh of air.

Hamon dived to his right and I, a little slow to react, dropped where I stood, to the forest floor. I heard the thud and the thrumming of an arrow as it hit a tree trunk.

A second arrow followed soon after; this one was angled into the ground close by Hamon Deerman but luckily it did not pierce him.

He scrambled on his hands and knees behind a tree. "Holy Mother of God!" he said.

I followed him. There was silence in the wood.

Several voices then rose together and we heard a thrashing of bushes as men plunged into the forest underbrush.

Then John came running up, checked that I was in one piece; he gave no thought to Hamon at first and hauled me up from the back of the tree trunk.

Cautiously I peered around the broad oak which had given me succour.

"Gone sir," said John. "I heard the footsteps running back towards the road. He's gone through the denser undergrowth and horses can't follow."

"Thank you John."

"Some of the men have given chase. Hard to catch him though." He nodded to Hamon at last. "You all right Deerman?"

"Aye… aye I'll do sir." Hamon was shaking and we both looked back to the tree in which the arrow had become embedded.

"So what was that about eh?" I asked, brushing the leaves and twigs from my chausses and padded gambeson.

John strode to the tree and tried to pull out the arrow but it was so deeply embedded, he could not at first. "Meant business," he said gritting his teeth and wriggling the point up and down. At last the barb came free. He gave it into my hand. He picked up the one which was sticking in the leaf mould.

"Manor stock," I said. "Some we've laid down in case of trouble again."

"Aye," said John. "One of Master Fletschier's, in town."

"So we shall not tell who drew the bow and loosed the arrow. Did the man leave his bow or did it go with him?"

John yelled, "Hungerford, Ackerman, Bird! Search the area for a bow, now!"

"Hamon, sit," I said "you look deathly… as well you might, for someone has just tried to kill you."

John shook his head, "Or maybe… sir…they have just tried to kill *you*."

Chapter Five

My brow rose in surprise. "No, I think this was meant for Master Deerman."
"You were both standing so close together, sir. It's hard to know who was the target exactly."

"Why me?"

"Asking too many questions sir?"

I turned to Hamon Deerman. "*Am* I asking too many questions?"

Deerman licked his lips. "I couldn't say, sir."

"Won't say."

"What nonsense is this, Hamon?" asked John his fingers thrust into the belt at his waist.

"Answer the lord...what do you know?"

"I can't...I can't. I don't know anything."

"Whoever loosed that arrow, thought that you and I were talking too intimately, Hamon," I said, "and had no thought that we were simply exchanging information about the deer."

"So you don't think it was meant to injure or kill...simply warn, sir?" asked John.

Bird the forester came up with a bow in his hand. He bowed to me and to John.

"Sir, found by the road." He gave it to John.

"No good I'm afraid," I said. "Another manor weapon. Nothing that can tell us of ownership."

"No."

Hamon was trying to slip away quietly.

"Go Hamon," I said. "Go home....and think on this carefully. Next time... the arrow might find its mark."

Hamon staggered off. John watched him go. "A warning to keep silent, sir?"

"Aye, I think so."

"Was he near to telling you anything at all?"

"Nothing. However, whomsoever loosed that arrow thinks Hamon is not to be trusted. That he *might* tell me something.

Something very useful. He believes Hamon to be weak. That might work in our favour. If he is weak, then we can bend and shake him like a walnut tree and eventually something interesting might fall out."

I chewed my lip a while.

"Can we watch him, John...for a time? See who comes and goes. What Hamon does."

"Aye, we can do that during the day."

"And keep him from harm if we can?"

I tapped my lips with my glove, thinking hard.

"Another thing... who has access to the weapons and ammunition from the manor store?"

"It's locked, sir, and the key is kept by Henry and you yourself have one."

"I will check mine. We need to ask Henry."

"Again and again...it comes back to Henry, sir," said John.

"Yes, I know. I really don't want to think about it, but Henry is still the man that leaps to mind when I think of the murders."

"Even that of the little poulterer. Surely...."

"Aye, that rankles. It's not like him is it, John?"

"No sir." John dabbled his foot in some of the leaf mould.

"Sir... have you thought that maybe we have two murderers?"

"Two? Ah, I see...one for Swithun and another for Meg?"

"Nah.. sir... doesn't hold together does it?"

I simply shook my head.

***

The key to the weapons store which was at the southern end of the undercroft, was still in place in my office and I locked that room every time I left it; the office key being kept in my scrip. I trotted over to Henry's room.

The door was open. He wasn't there. Where did he keep his key?

There were a few keys on the ledge of the window facing out into the courtyard. I took out my key and compared it. There was the weapons store key; the third from the end. Henry had tied a piece of twine around it with three knots. Two other keys had twine, one with two and one with four knots. One was the key to the undercroft, rarely locked and the other, the key to the tiny lock up, where we put malefactors to cool down. It was our little prison, right by the privy. There was one without any knots. This was the key to this little room, which was rarely locked, except when there was money stored in it, or at night when Henry left it to go home to his house. He had a place to sleep here too, should he feel the need to stay in the manor all night. I know he kept the key to the manor gate in his scrip and the key to the manor hall door around his neck on a string.

He was very tidy with his keys. However, anyone could have stolen in here and taken the key for a while, replacing it without Henry's knowledge.

Or he could have been in the store himself. I knew too, that Henry was a good shot with a bow.

I sighed.

***

Walter Reeve caught me just as I was exiting the office.

"Ah sir....news of the search."

"Yes Walt. Find anything?"

"Not a scrap sir."

"Then it's a search of the village houses and the manor buildings."

"Yes, sir. Shall I leave the choice of men to you?"

"Yes, you can. Oh and Walter, can you send Peter Brenthall to Marlborough for Dr. Johannes and get him to bring Peter Devizes and Stephen Dunn back here from the castle. Tell Peter to ride there."

It was going to be quite a task to search all the houses. I thought carefully about it. Where should I begin and how could I prevent anyone from removing incriminating evidence whilst the search was underway? I could manage it, if I ordered all the manor folk to leave their houses and stay in the courtyard. I would then lock the gate. As the houses were searched I would allow the folk out, one at a time. If they were out in the fields or forest, they could stay there until after the search was complete. Laborious but thorough.

Johannes came in that evening and the next day he helped me search.

One by one we searched every house. The only bloodstained item we found was the butcher's long apron which he used to protect himself when slaughtering the beasts. It reached from his upper chest to his ankles and when not in use was hung on a peg in a small outhouse by his cottage.

John Kellog farmed his small plot amongst the villagers' fields and in addition, when needed, he slaughtered the sheep, cows and pigs we required for our food supplies on the manor, a service for which they paid him, as a freeman.

Once we had searched his home, he was allowed out of the manor courtyard. I took him aside. Johannes looked on, his arms folded across his chest.

"John. Look at your apron please, and if you can, tell me if you think it has been used by someone other than you in the past few days."

John looked at me as if I had gone daft.

" 'Tis a new one m'lord. I gave me old one to m'son. 'Tis 'ere somewhere. I ain't used this one at all I was keepin' it, yer see, for the autumn killin'."

"This one, is it?" I held it up. He was still looking at me as if I were moon-struck.

His eyes raked the surface.

"Well...I'll be..."

"Aye, 'tis what *I* thought."

There, high and low, on the apron, which was made of a dark stiff leather, were splashes of dried blood.

"Well it aint me what's done that." He took the apron roughly from my hand. "Well, now, that makes me proper cross."

He turned round, "Hervey Kellog, you bin usin' my apron 'owt my permission?"

"No dad...why would I do that?"

"No, John, I think it's been used for an entirely different purpose than slaughtering beasts for our meat."

"Well, they mighta asked."

I smiled. No, they would not have asked.

"It might be taken by anyone who knows it's there, in the outhouse, when you are not using it?"

"Aye, but folk usually asks me. I never say no."

"And has anyone borrowed it lately?"

"I woulda given 'em an old'un. Not this new'un. Fair makes me boil it does. I were savin' that."

"How many know it's there, John?"

"Oh everyone. They brings their animals to me and they sees me take me apron off the hook and put it on."

I nodded. "Thank you."

***

One more thing came to light as we searched for bloodstained clothing. We had locked Edmund and Edith Brooker in the manor courtyard. Neither of them made any demur and went quietly with the other villagers. I brought them out when we found the hessian apron worn by Meg Poulter the day she died, in their cottage.

Johannes and I took them into their house and up to the loft room.

"Can you explain this please, Edmund?" Edmund took the apron and he blinked a few times as if he was bemused by it.

"Where did you find it, m'lord?"

"It was in your house, stuffed on top of one of the rafters, there. We only saw it because we were searching the loft sleeping place and we could see it poking out from under the thatch."

"I have no idea how it got there."

I ran my eye over the loft space. It was accessed by a ladder from the ground floor and the space underneath was taken up by a goat and the pig. I had seen them moving about through the floor boards as we searched and heard them snuffling. The bed, nothing more than a straw stuffed mattress laid directly on to the wooden floor which when in use would be covered with two good woollen blankets, was tidied away, leaning against the daub wall. The rough curtain which covered the opening of the loft and gave some privacy to Edith, was drawn back against the wall. There was quite a bit of dust and debris on the floor. It must be a never ending task to keep this sort of dwelling clean, though I remembered Edmund saying that his sister was a good housekeeper. We climbed back down the ladder.

"You know who it belonged to?"

"Aye it was Meg's."

"When you last saw her at the stream, was she wearing it?"

"I...I..I can't remember, sir"

I turned to his sister. "Edith, did you see Meg that afternoon, the day she died?"

"I don't remember. I have better things to do than to talk to silly little girls who are besotted with my idiot of a brother."

"Well, try to remember," I said with force. "It's important. Of course you can always go and sit in the lockup for a while, whilst you think."

I stared at her. She stared back. Eventually she said.

"Yes, I saw her. Silly chit. She was in amongst the salleys talking to Edmund."

"Was she wearing the apron then?"

"No."

"No, my lord!" I said forcefully. "Do you know how it managed to hide itself in your rafters?"

"No. My lord."

"Maybe someone put it there, the person who murdered Meg, to make it seem as if we had something to do with it, sir," said Edmund.

"Why would they do that?"

Edmund began to speak then looked away. "My sister is not the most popular person in the village. There's many she's crossed and turned the back up. Maybe one of them thought they'd make mischief for us....for her."

Edith folded her arms across her bosom and scowled.

"Perhaps you stuffed it there, Edmund, when you were busy stuffing your little chicken girl in my loft."

"We never went there to..."

"Well, that's a lie if ever I heard one. When I was up at the field or out in the forest... you..."

"Children!" I cried" You are behaving like children."

They both stopped and looked at me, Edith with a deal of venom.

"Since I cannot get sense out of you, Edmund, and since I have some doubts about you and the poultry girl Meg and how this apron became concealed in your home, I am taking you to the lock up for a while to think about the lies you have told us."

Edmund stiffened, "I've told no lies. I don't know how it got there, or who killed Meg."

"My man at arms will take you up to the manor house lock up and bar you in, Edmund. Come."

Edmund jumped up swiftly and was off out of the door as fast as a hare. I yelled. "HAL! Grab him!"

Johannes and I came back out into the daylight again. There was a scuffle and Hal of Potterne stood with one knee up into the small of Edmund's back and his arm around his neck. The other arm pinned his arms down. Edmund was writhing and wriggling.

"Now there my proud cock. If you want to be able to bend to pull up yer 'ose over yer arse, ever agin, I'd keep mighty still if I were you."

"To the lock up please, Hal. We shall see what a night in our cell can do for his memory."

Hal called for Stephen and Peter, who were lounging close by. The three of them marched Edmund Brooker away.

"And," I turned to Edith Brooker "If you don't wish to go the same way as your brother, I'd seriously think about the death of Meg Poulter and search your memory of that afternoon most thoroughly."

I bundled up the hessian apron under my arm and took it with me back to the manor hall.

Johannes and I followed the arresting party up to the manor and handed them over to Henry. His face was quizzical but I told him nothing, only that he was to lock up Edmund until further notice.

The courtyard had been cleared now of all the manor folk and they had returned to their homes. Only those with a genuine need to be there or who lived or worked in the manor house and buildings, were out and about. Gossip was rife. Curious looks were thrown our way as we ascended the hall stairs and disappeared into the building.

"Do you think he killed her?"

"I don't know, Johannes. His display of grief was real enough when he saw her dead body. There is something he is keeping back, I'm sure, and we may get it out of him eventually."

"Well, there's one thing for sure."

"What's that?"

"Edith Brooker is most definitely not a few weeks pregnant."

I laughed. "You can tell, can you? You're as bad as Agnes."

"I can tell a four month gravid woman when I see one."

I spun on my heel. "What?"

"I saw her when she folded her arms. Her belly is that of a four month....maybe nearer five. She's a small woman. I would say - four, certainly."

"Well, I never," I said. "Some poor man on my demesne has managed to bed that termagant. I was wrong. Somewhere she must have a soft streak running through her, though it's hidden deep."

"Not soft if she wants to blame a man who can no longer defend himself from an accusation of rape."

"Tomorrow," I said, "we shall see what she has to say for herself." I sat down on a hall bench. "We really could do with the church coming up with the answers to the questions in my letter about Swithun. It would help greatly in knowing what we are dealing with."

In a few days we had our answers.

***

The preparations for the wedding were moving on. Lydia was supervising the decoration of the hall for the festivities. There were very few wild flowers now, fewer than there would have been if we were being married in May or June, but Lydia had managed to find other pretty items to decorate the place. In our hedgerows we had some wild hops and these were now harvested to twine around the beams and dangle from the posts of the hall. Berries of woodbine which grew profusely in the forest and hips and haws were cut and Hawise and Lydia had fun making twinings of these, to lay on tables and to hang from the stair posts. There were even some late woodbine, or honeysuckle flowers. Greenery had been hoisted up on thin ropes to loop from beam to beam.

The place looked cheerful and I smiled as I watched my two girls busy ordering the poor menfolk into climbing ladders and nailing the decorations in place. Poor Alfred Woodsmith, the carpenter, had been drafted in to hang these fabulous pieces and was being sent hither and thither, in a flustered frenzy, doing his best to keep all happy.

I nodded to him as I passed and his eyes leapt to Heaven.

"Well, done Alfred. I'm sure they will not need you much longer now."

His face showed me what he thought of that idea.

I was backing out of the hall, into the screens passage, watching the delicate lifting of the ropes by the men on ladders, when a voice behind me instantly took me back to my youth.

"Well, Aumary, my lord. 'Tis a fine thing when such a man as I is welcomed home after years away with such merriment and finery."

No. It could not be. The voice teased at my memory. I turned slowly.

"Crispin!"

The man in front of me bowed.

"You should not have gone to so much trouble for a humble churchman... why, I may have risen in the world but I am still at heart a simple priest!"

"Crispin," I said again, not quite able to believe what I was seeing. "Crispin Darrell... well I never. As I live and breathe. You are most welcome," and I stepped up to embrace him.

Crispin and I were old friends. We had not met, though I had heard news of him, for sixteen years. Not since he went off to Oxford to the university there. I knew that he had been ordained a priest and I knew that he was now working for the Bishop of Salisbury, my Godfather, Herbert Poore, in some capacity.

There were plans afoot, it was said, to move the cathedral at Salisbury, the bishop's residence on the Salisbury plain, stone by stone, to a new site further down in the valley.

The original site was windy, cold and waterless. The cathedral there had suffered damage from storms almost from the day it was consecrated and though a castle had been built on this windy hilltop and a little town grew up around it, old Salisbury had not flourished. Town and castle were often at loggerheads. King Richard had given permission but for some reason the work had stalled. Herbert had not been a popular choice for the role of bishop; there had been quite a deal of trouble, I recalled, in the reign of Richard. Things seemed to have quietened now. The building would actually not begin until 1215 under Herbert's brother Richard. All this information was rolling around in my head as I greeted my boyhood friend. Last I had heard, Salisbury was where he was living and working.

"Crispin, come into my office and we shall be private and quiet."

I closed the door on the comings and goings. Suddenly, it became silent.

"What brings you to Durley? I thought you far too elevated now to allow the Savernake dust to settle on your boots once more."

"Ha! No. Indeed. It's good to be home. You don't know how good. But first things first."

He rifled in his leather pouch and I watched him carefully as he brought out a tubular leather case and handed it to me.

"From the bishop."

"Ah."

I put the letter down on my table and fetched some wine and cups from my pot board. I poured.

"Your health, my friend," I said. Then I broke the seal and read in silence.

We had the usual preamble. My Godfather hoped that I was well and that Durley and the forest flourished. There was a little about the King and his wishes and a sentence or two about the work to be done at Salisbury. He thanked me for returning the body of Swithun to the abbey and lamented his untimely death. He also wrote of his anger and displeasure at events here. He hoped that I would have success in searching out the perpetrator. The King had told him of my uncanny skills in investigating such unnatural deaths, he said.

He was very sad to hear that Swithun had not been the good priest he had hoped. There was some attempt at justification for sending such a man to us.

"I had believed that, once out in your little community he would come to see that he might be able to do the Lord's good works, that it might soften his attitude, for life for simple folk is harsh and difficult and they are in need of succour and aid from God. I had thought that he might be able to bring them that succour and aid. I thought all that was needed was a challenge to his stubborn nature and a sense of achievement in serving God out in the world. I was wrong."

He wrote that Swithun had proved a recalcitrant novice but that he had eventually seen where his duty lay and had, with just a little persuasion, been ordained a priest. The church authorities had thought this would be good for him. As far as he knew there had been no discipline applied to him for any slipping from his vows of chastity, poverty and obedience. He had been reprimanded many times for the sin of pride, (didn't I say that?) He was often disciplined, as a younger man, for his failure to concentrate on the liturgy. For this he had been scourged and he was found truly repentant. Of late he was exemplary in his duties at the cathedral. No, there was nothing for which Swithun might be castigated, the nature of which I had intimated in my letter.

So he did not have a roving eye. He did not enjoy the pleasures of the flesh in a vicarious way. It was unlikely that he had committed rape. He had no history of being a bother to women.

The bishop then went on to say he was sending us a new priest, one he hoped would follow closely in Benedict's footsteps, for we had been too long without proper guidance and he acknowledged that Godfrey, the priest of Bedwyn, could not carry both that place and our own. He was a good servant of God but he was after all, an old man. There was more but I let the parchment roll up.

Crispin was watching me carefully.

"Not what you wanted to read, my friend?"

"No, indeed. It is much as I suspected. It just throws up further questions and tangles the skeins of thought a little more, that's all."

I put that aside. "It is very good to see you Crispin. Tell me everything. Everything you have been doing since you left us here as a callow youth of fourteen."

Crispin laughed. "Callow I never was...but yes...I have had an interesting time this past sixteen years."

"Is it so long...no it cannot be."

"We were both of us fourteen when I went off to Oxford to study and you stayed here to learn how to manage your forest, which I hear tell, you do with inimitable skill and deftness."

"That is most kind of you to say. Whatever you have heard, it's all down to the people who work with and for me. Without them, I should fail miserably."

"Modesty was always your worst fault. Things have not changed, I see."

I laughed. Crispin had not changed much either. I suspect he still had the wit, the quick brain, the ability to sum up a situation swiftly and efficiently and act on his instincts. This must be why the bishop had taken to him so well.

He was a man of middling height; thin, but not gaunt, dark of hair, with dark eyes like a small bird which darted here and there and missed nothing. His features too resembled a small bird; his nose was pointed, his hair was perfect like the plumage of a blackbird. He was tonsured of course but I could see that now his hair was receding. His hands were small and his fingers long and elegant with perfectly formed nails and he used those elegant hands to good effect in speech, with birdlike movements. His clothes were modest but good quality and his smile lit up the whole room, just as it had done when he was a lad.

"Thank you for bringing me a letter from the bishop. Have you left your horse in the stable? Will you stay with us a while? Have you plans to go into Marlborough, to the priory perhaps?"

Crispin held up his hands. "So many questions, Aumary."

I chuckled, "I'm sorry...I just want to know so much."

"Well, you and I will indeed catch up on our sixteen years apart, of that there is no doubt. Yes, I have left my horse in the stable and no, I have no immediate plan to go to the priory."

"Good, then you must rest here a while. In fact, you must come to my wedding."

"I thought that you were married already Aumary. Was she not a local girl? I seem to remember your father made the match when you were but a lad toddling bare arsed around the courtyard."

My face must have grown serious for he looked at me with a more sympathetic eye."

"I see that there is some sad story here."

"Aye, Cecily Congyre was the girl I married. She was murdered a few years ago. I will tell you as much as I am able when we have the time and l the inclination. I had a son too, Geoffrey. Oh, how I miss him. He was killed too, in the same year as his mother. I have a daughter Hawise. You saw her in hall with my fiancée, Lady Lydia Wolvercote."

"Wolvercote near Oxford?"

"The same."

"I know the place."

"We shall be married in three days. Can you stay that long?"

"I can do better than that."

He folded his hands over his middle and leaned back.

"I can stay, forever...and what is more - I can marry you."

"Do not jest old friend," I said, "Life has been...more than unkind these past few years. I could not take another disappointment, should your words prove empty."

"No...no, no empty words." He leaned forward and shook out another piece of parchment from the leather tube I had opened and handed it to me.

I read it. My eyes opened wide in astonishment.

"No...it cannot be true!" I said.

Crispin had resigned his post with the bishop. Why would he do that? It was a post which came with wealth and a certain amount of power, such as a senior clergyman might covet. It was not an onerous role. There seemed little to do except liaise between various church- men, give advice where necessary and travel here and there on the bishop's business.

"Why? Why have you spent all this time and effort climbing the ladder of success only to give it up as you reach the top? Why, you could be the next Bishop of Salisbury!"

Crispin laughed. "Something I have asked myself ever since I told His Grace that I wished to leave him. To answer your question honestly, when you reach the top, there is only one way to go and that is down. I know, you will say that I have not yet achieved all that I can achieve. I say to you that I can smell change in the wind and that change, I fear, doesn't include me."

"Have you fallen foul of someone in authority then?"

Crispin shrugged. "I will forever be associated with Herbert Poore, whatever happens to him and as I say, he is not a popular man. You know of course that he was bastard born? That doesn't sit well with some folk. Lately even he and I have had differences of opinion. I shan't go into those now but suffice it to say, he and I are not working well together now and....oh, I am tired of the bickering of monarch and Mother Church, the picking my way through the glass shards of church business, the politics. I long for a simpler life."

"It may not be as simple as you think here in Durley."

"I was born here, I know this place. I should be honoured to be its priest."

For that was what was written in the second letter.

The bishop had seen fit to appoint Father Crispin Darrell to Durley to act as its priest and confessor.

I was amazed. It was such a very great leap for Crispin. The son of a freeman of Durley, bailiff to the sheriff of Wiltshire, who had been educated in Marlborough town and then at Oxford, he had always been destined for a higher place in the scheme of things and now he wanted to return to his roots and become a humble priest to a hundred or so souls in the middle of Savernake. It didn't seem possible but there was the letter and here was the man.

"Well!"

"Will you have me then? I promise not to scare the children and accost the maidens." Crispin gave a little almost self-conscious smile. I was not fooled.

"We should be very pleased to have you, Father Crispin," I said.

***

We chatted further and I told Crispin of the difficulties we had had and of the murders of Swithun and Meg Poulter.

"Swithun was murdered in the priest's house, in his bed. It's all been changed and cleaned but still, you might not want to lay your head in the same place, Crispin. Oh dear, I feel that his humble cottage will not be good enough for you after your home in the bishop's palace."

"A stable was good enough for our Lord; I'm sure this will suffice. If I remember it a'right, it's a good house, close by the church and near the orchard?"

"But still...."

"Remember from whence I come, Aumary. You have always been used to your manor of stone. You know nothing else. My father's house was a wooden one, a good house of beams and flints and white wash, but a small and humble one nevertheless. The priest's house will suffice."

"You remember Old Joan?"

"Aye she was old even when we were lads."

"Well, she is even older now. She must be sixty if she's a day but she goes about like a woman of thirty. She will tend to your wants I'm sure, as she did for dear Father Benedict."

"I could want for nothing more."

"Have you luggage?"

"Very little. I carry it in two panniers. They are with the horse, which I must send back to Salisbury soon. I am still a monk at heart, Aumary, my needs are few and my wants simple."

I smiled. "I was only thinking earlier of you and a few of the other boys with whom we grew up. It was when I was puzzling about this latest murder, standing on the bank of the stream in the Salley Gardens, where we found the girl Meg."

"Of me...why ever would that be?"

"Oh... just an unbidden image which flashed into my mind...of you and I as lads, learning to swim in the deeper pools."

"Yes, I recall it. Warm summer days for swimming and fishing and catching crayfish."

"Your needs were not so simple in those days..."

"Haha!"

"You always wanted to win. Catch the most fish, swim the furthest and fastest, land the biggest crayfish."

"Ah my lord...I said my needs are few and my wants simple. I did not say that I never needed to *win*!"

***

Crispin was ensconced in the old priest's house, his panniers taken from the stable and the horse returned to Salisbury.

Then began the task of making himself known to the village, something which Swithun had simply not done. Soon, it was the topic of every overheard conversation that Crispin Darrell, famous son of Durley, had come back to us and was to be our priest. That a son of Durley was to oversee Durley matters lay very well with the villagers and forest folk.

Whilst Crispin made himself comfortable in his new home, Fulke and Ralf Sylvestre came up to the hall to seek me out, as requested. I was just making my way to the guest room where Johannes stayed when he visited and the two men shambled in through the gate.

"You two took your time."

"Sorry m'lord, we have been up at..."

"I know where you've been. Come up to the hall now." I turned on my heel and took the steps two at a time. I stood on the dais and towered over them.

"I want to know and I want to know the truth. At about the time of vespers on the night of the murder of Swithun the priest, where were you? Fulke?"

The look which passed between them did not escape me.

"Well, now...." Fulke said, scratching his beard. "I think I were out at Mother Giffard's. Yes, I were. She had some new ale and I had a thought to taste it. I were there all evening."

"And you, Ralf?" Ralf would not catch my eye.

"I was with the wife sir. Did she not tell you?"

"I wanted to hear it from you."

"Yes, sir, well that was where I was. At home with Edwina."

"Do either of you know anything about the death of Swithun the priest?"

They both shook their heads, but I noticed neither would meet my eye.

"It may be your turn next for a spell in the manor lock up. Both of you. I have Edmund Brooker there now, sitting in the foul air next to the privy, thinking about his story."

Both men looked up at me quickly. There was fear in their faces. Fulke recovered first.

"But m'lord, he can't have nothing to do with it. He were at Mother Giffard's too, sampling the ale, with me."

"That is very interesting, Fulke, because by his own admission, Edmund was at home, looking after his sister and entertaining little Meg Poulter. All night."

Fulke's face fell.

"Oh, is that what he says...well it must be right then. I must've thought of another night. You know m'lord, when you have had a skinful of Mother Giffard's ale, you forget what night it is. Damn fine stuff it is."

"Yes, indeed," I said sarcastically and he knew I did not believe him. I let them go. They knew more than they were willing to say and I would just let them stew a little.

I walked back over the courtyard, scratched on the door of Johannes' room and opened it. He was tending a man who had his back to me but I immediately knew who it was, for there was no mistaking the shape of the poor man's head.

Dysig turned quickly. "Ow!" he said.

"Keep still then...." Johannes grasped Dysig by the chin and pulled him round again. I stood by the door.

"There...that will teach you to go banging your head on overhanging branches. Watch where you are going lad. It will be all right in no time. Just let someone know if you begin to feel sick. All right?"

"Sick... yes... Dysig is never sick."

"Well, there's a first time for everything."

Dysig flew past me out of the room, as if the demons he said he had seen on the night of the murder were after him. Once out in the courtyard, he turned and looked at me with round eyes and then was off.

I saw the bruise and abrasion on the side of his head. Johannes had cleansed it and put a salve on it.

"I shall ask Agnes to look to him, Johannes. What did he say happened?"

"A branch struck him on the head."

"Where was he when this happened? Out in the forest?"

Johannes chuckled. "No, he was sitting in front of his cottage, when they had all been let out of the courtyard after our search. He was dozing, he said. A voice woke him."

"What did it say, this voice?"

"Well, as far as I can gather, it warned him to silence, or he would feel the wrath of the angel. Does that make sense to you, Aumary?"

"In a way," and I told him about the strange conversation Agnes and I had had with Dysig.

"He said that he made to rise and to look who it was behind him, but then... wallop. The branch hit him on the side of the head and he was out cold."

"Hmmm. Another warning. Two to date. Hamon and now Dysig. I have just talked to the Sylvestres. They too have been warned, I'm sure."

I chewed my lip. "I can tell you something my friend."

Johannes was wiping his hands and then he folded his arms across his chest.

"And what is that?"

"It cannot have been Edmund, for he is in the lockup and has been all this time."

"Ah yes," he said.

I then related the good news that we had a priest at last at Durley and told him a little of the history of my friend Crispin Darrell.

"I will introduce you at supper."

"I will look forward to it. Intelligent conversation with an urbane man.... Yes, I will definitely look forward to it. We can speak of Oxford."

Johannes had been born in that town.

"I hope you are not to be disappointed then." We laughed together once more, rich and full.

***

I felt that we had to pay a visit to the Widow Giffard. So many had said that they had spent the evening of Swithun's death in her house, sampling her ale. Her house lay by the side of what passed for the village green. It was a fairly large dwelling and I could see that many men might be accommodated there in the summer to drink the night away. The woman was in her yard, scouring a barrel. There were several stacked up around the house wall. She had a small outhouse and there, I saw another half barrel of mash on a pine table ready for the next lot of ale. There was a small bowl of wort just mixed, to be used to take some of the sweetness from the malted ale.

"Mistress Giffard."

She jumped as if she had been prodded with a stick.

"Oh m'lord." She put her hand to her heart, "You gave me such a start."

"I'm sorry. Do you know Dr. Johannes of Salerno, from the town?"

"Aye sir." She smiled. She was still quite an attractive woman, though she was well over forty.

"I have come to ask you a few questions. It's about the night that Swithun the priest was murdered...."

The widow crossed herself.

"Might you be able to tell us who was here with you, drinking your fine ale, on that night?"

"Everyone, sir?"

"Well...yes..."

"All night?"

The poor woman slumped. "Well, I can't rightly remember everyone, all the time. There were so many."

"For example, the elder Sylvestre...was he here much of the time?"

"Aye, Fulke was here. He brought that young lad of his, then he went home. His wife fetched him. Fulke stayed."

"Walter the reeve said he was here."

"Aye sir, he was here. He usually comes to make sure there's no trouble. When some of them have had a bit, they can get a bit frisky ...if you see what I mean."

"I do...I do."

"Was Dysig here?"

"Bless you, no, sir. He don't touch strong ale. He has the watered stuff, small ale or the second runnings. Ain't much power in that, see. My beer is strong stuff. I take him a jug of small ale now and again, when I have a bit left over."

"I see."

"Why do you want to know, sir?" she said, "If you don't mind me asking."

I ruffled my hair. "I am trying to work out who was out and about that night. Who might have seen something, even if they don't know what it was they saw."

"Ah! I see." She leaned against her outhouse wall and wiped her hands on her apron. "Well, there was that Edmund Brooker. He was here some of the time. I kept catching glimpses of him through the door. He's a fine looking lad, that Brooker."

"Glimpses. Out-doors. Why would he be outside, in the dark?"

"He was talking to folk, coming in - going out."

"Do you know what he was talking about?" asked Johannes.

"Oh no sir, I couldn't do eavesdropping. I was far too busy."

"Who did he speak to?"

"Oh Lord...that's hard." She dipped her head and her eyes went from side to side as she tried to picture the evening in question in her head.

"He spoke to the Sylvestres." She squeezed her lips together, "Ummm. He had a word with Henry the steward. He..."

"Henry was here too?"

"For a very short while. He was on his way home to his mother's place I think. Early. Just on dusk."

"He spoke to the wheelwright, the elder one - Phil. He had words with Hamon Deerman. He didn't stay long either."

"Anyone else. Was Matthew Cook here?"

"Oh no, sir. He never comes. His wife is a good brewster. She wouldn't let him sample my wares."

I felt there was a story here but passed it by.

"He talked to Mat Fisher too, late on."

"How long did Edmund stay?"

"Well - that's just it. He didn't stay."

"You said that..."

"No sir, he was here, then he went, then he came back. He stayed outside the whole time. Coming and going. He sampled very little of my ale at all."

"He didn't?"

"No sir. Which is odd because he does...normally. He loves it."

"Hmmm. So, who else?"

"Oh my, well....there was Thomas Miller. He didn't go home. Spent the night on my floor. His wife gave him what for I can tell you. Martyn Carpenter, Martin Forester and his brother Bird. Ummm...yes... the fella what plays that sinformie thingy."

I thought hard.

"Oh yes, the simphony, so you had music?"

"Yessir, some of the time."

"That would be Old Tom."

She nodded. "Aye, Old Tom. He was here till we closed up. And my son Alan played pipe and tabor."

She gave us a few more names.

"Thank you mistress, you have been most accommodating."

"Oh thank you, sir." She flicked a glance at Johannes as she curtsied. "Bye doctor."

He smiled and turned to leave. The smile didn't leave his face till we were back on the road.

"I think we have a word with Edmund again, don't you?"

***

Edmund came out of the lock up surly and dishevelled. We marched him up into the hall where he stood between Hal of Potterne and Johannes.

"So Edmund, have you had any further thoughts about our questions?"

He shrugged. "I can't change the truth. I don't know how that apron got in my house or who killed Meg."

"Well, we have some truths of our own. We have been talking to the Widow Giffard and she tells me that you were in and out of her house the night Swithun died, drinking her ale and talking to folk. You were not, it seems, nursemaiding your sister or pleasuring your girlfriend Meg at home. What do you say to that?"

He shrugged again. "If you had asked I would have told you. Instead you made accusations and threatened me. It was clear you thought I murdered Meg."

"Then why did you run?"

"Because you were going to lock me up. The next thing is the justice and then I'll be dangling from a tree. You'd 'a run."

Hal of Potterne cuffed him around the ear.

"Don' you be disrespectful to 'is lordship you paltry piece o' puttock."

Johannes passed his hand over his mouth and smirked.

"Edmund. You did not pass the night at home did you?"

"Not all night, no."

"You were at Widow Giffard's?"

"Yes."

"She said she saw you talking to folk."

"Since when has it been a crime to talk to folk?"

Hal clapped him again. This time it was harder. "Careful, Brooker!"

"The Widow says she saw you coming and going, that she couldn't see you all the time."

Edmund Brooker sighed, rubbing the side of his head.

"I was outside in the yard much of the night, with people. Ask them. Just because the woman didn't see me, doesn't mean I wasn't there."

"Now to the second thing. I now have knowledge which leads me to believe that Swithun Attwood did not rape your sister at all."

Edmund's chin came up at that but he paled and his eyes narrowed.

Johannes, towering over the young man, drew his attention. "I think that your sister is pregnant, Edmund, and I think that she is a lot further on than a few weeks. Four months perhaps."

Edmund licked his lips. "Maybe the priest lay with my sister before the day he died, as well. You know what she's like. How could I get the truth from her? She hates me. Ask her yourself."

"I do not think that Swithun fathered this child at all, Edmund. There is someone else in the village who is her lover."

"Then you had better ask her."

Hal was about to give him another slap, when I said,

"Rest assured, we shall. Take him home and set Stephen to watch him for a while will you, Hal. I don't want his sister to talk to him at all; is that clear?"

"Right you are, sir," and Hal cuffed him once more round the ear, for good measure.

Chapter Six

A little while later Crispin came in to my office. Alceste was lying at my feet. She lifted her head when he entered.

"Aumary, the church vestments. Walter tells me they were all destroyed in the fire in the priest's room."

"Aye, that's true. I must get some more made. Meanwhile ask Agnes. She might have some spare at home. They won't be the best but they'll suffice. She mends and darns them. She might have some she was looking at before the fire."

"And the rolls?"

"Ah yes, I must get the woodsmith to make a new coffer. We only have four rolls left but we shall need something to put them in."

"We need to enter the deaths of Swithun, Meg and Young Meg into the latest of them."

"Yes indeed."

He turned to leave.

"You have a chapel, don't you, in the manor?"

I beat my brow with the heel of my hand.

"Of course. How stupid of me. There will be some vestments there and altar cloths. We also have a spare set of mass vessels there. I must remember to take the damaged ones to Marlborough to the silver-smith for mending."

I rose. "Come. I'll take you up to the chapel." I patted Alceste on the head as she rose to accompany me and we left the office. I locked the door behind me.

We entered the hall and then made for the small wooden staircase in the corner which rose to the second mezzanine floor, at the opposite end to the solar. Alceste negotiated the steps with ease, despite her lack of sight.

I opened the door and Crispin entered; the dog followed him. He made straight for the shutters, which were closed up.

Light flooded the little space and he genuflected towards the altar.

"My, glass in the windows!"

I smiled. "I promised Cecily that I would use money from the sale of a present which the king had given us to glaze the windows in the solar. There was just enough money to do these four as well. Of course, you know I found the money to glaze the church."

Crispin bowed. "For that I shall be eternally grateful on cold days."

I smiled. How different from Swithun who had been ungrateful and considered the glazing against the cold, unnecessary. Looking round the little chapel brought back painful memories. Here my father had lain in his coffin, a black candle at each corner, before his interment in the churchyard. Here too Cecily my wife and little Geoffrey were laid before the altar prior to their burial. I came here rarely now and preferred to worship with my manor folk in the main church.

Crispin was poking about in the corners. In a chest under the window were the vestments used for this place. He shook them out and slipped the alb over his head.

"A little short for me, but it will do." He looked into the chest again. There's a chasuble. Good. And a stole. And a very nice pectoral cross."

"My grandfather had that made, if I remember rightly. It's fine work. The rest of the vessels are in that aumbry there."

Crispin bent to replace the items in the chest and strode to the little cupboard built into the manor wall. "Locked."

"Oh yes of course. The key is in the office. I'll give it to you. The Belvoir Relic is in there too," I said; the relic upon which I had sworn an oath many years ago. A hair of St. Margaret in a beautiful little decorated box.

Alceste was sniffing around the chest.

"She won't pee on it will she?"

"Of course not. Alceste is a she. She doesn't lift her leg!"

"Ha!"

Alceste suddenly narrowed her milky eyes and growled deep in her throat.

Her lips drew back over her teeth.

"Sorry old girl.. for calling you a boy. Didn't mean it." Crispin put out his hand for her to smell him and she snapped at him. There was no contact but he drew back quickly. "All right ol' girl."

"She's very deaf and can't hear you. She relies on smell."

I went up to the dog and gentled her head. She stopped growling.

"I know what this is. You are wearing vestments last worn by Swithun. She can smell him. She hated the priest. He tried to kick and beat her several times. In fact I know he did make contact for that was why Peter Brenthall...

"John's son?"

"Aye. That is why he and Swithun came to blows. Peter stopped the priest from mistreating Alceste and Swithun struck Peter for it."

Crispin took off the garment and hunkered down. "Come on my old girl...'tis only me."

I led the dog to him and she wagged her tail.

"We shall ask Joan to launder everything for you and I'll order some new vestments when next I go to town. We have two really fine embroiderers in Marlborough, it being a cloth town."

Alceste followed Crispin down the stairs, a little more gingerly than she went up. "Come on girl... let's go and see if we can find you a nice bit o' something to eat." The two of them loped off together in the direction of the kitchen stairs.

***

I waited at the door of the cottage belonging to the two Brookers. Edmund was inside. His sister was out on her strip somewhere up the hill. She would come back when the light began to fade. The goats and the pig were out the back in the fenced off yard.

I chatted to Stephen who I'd set to guard the house. The occupant had been quiet, not a word had been said, was the report.

Eventually, we heard a bucket being put down at the back of the house and a voice spoke quietly to the animals. I put my fingers to my lips to signal silence.

Edith came round the corner of the cottage.

"Are you there Edmund sweetie? I heard you'd been let out?" she said.

Suddenly Edmund erupted in the house, battering the door. "Edith....say nothing...say nothing. We are watched and I am penned in," he yelled.

The woman stopped dead. She put her hands on her hips. "What do you want, my Lord Belvoir?"

"Want? I want to ask you some questions and I want to do it away from your brother." I took hold of her elbow but she shrugged me off.

"Come down to the stream. We can be private there."

I walked through the small garden and out the wicket. The little bell rang as I went through the gate. She did not immediately follow me but I kept walking and I heard at last, the little bell ring again.

I stopped under one of the old sallows. "Swithun did not rape you at all, did he Edith?"

"My brother will have told you that he did and Young Meg also."

"Dr. Johannes of Salerno thinks you are about four months pregnant."

She did not confirm that...

"And Agnes Brenthall, who there is no doubt, is a good judge of such things, thinks this is the truth also. She told me."

In a very small voice, Edith said, " 'Twas not the first time he forced himself on me."

"Now why do I not believe you, Edith?"

She stared into the distance.

"He has no record of such behaviour elsewhere."

"Perhaps he had not yet found one who had stirred his lusts, until he reached Durley."

"So, if he did rape you before, why was this not reported to me? I am your lord. You should have told me."

"Because, just as now...you would not believe me. Who am I? A churl of little value. Who was Swithun Attwood? A nobleman turned cleric. Oh yes, both Edmund and I could see where that would lead."

I leaned against the bent tree trunk. "Who is the father, Edith, and I will arrange that he marry you."

"He cannot marry me."

"He is already married?"

"He is dead and he was a priest!"

I folded my arms. "If the father of your child is named, and if he is able I will make him marry you, Edith. If not, I wonder what the church will think of it?"

"They will make me stand barefoot in the church, in my shift and pour scorn upon me."

I shrugged. "I have no idea what our new priest will make of it."

"I do not care, my lord," she said. "They may do as they wish," and she walked away, holding her head haughtily. I heard the little bell ring again. She stood in front of Stephen.

He looked to me, past her. I nodded and he moved away. She opened the door and walked into the cottage without a backward glance and closed the door.

I beckoned Stephen to me but indicated he stay in the little garden.

Very quietly I said, "Watch them, Stephen, and listen. The walls are not so thick and the door not so well fitting that speech may not be heard through them. I want to know what they say and where they go."

As I turned away a fierce argument broke out inside the cottage. Stephen did not need to put his ear to the wall for the words could be heard clearly a hundred paces away.

"You are the world's worst liar, Edmund Brooker. If you had told the truth about the night Swithun raped me again, then I would be believed. As it is, your stupid story about being here all night with Meg has as many holes in it as a beggar's cloak. Whoever killed her must be laughing themselves stupid!"

"At least I have an alibi... I was at Mother Giffard's with many of the others.

They can ask."

"Good job too or you would be sitting in the lockup still, waiting for your neck to be stretched for you, you stupid bastard."

"Bastard I am not. If I am, then so are you!"

There was a slap. Edith had hit him.

"Don't you ever call me that you venomed shit arse."

Things began to be thrown around the cottage.

I nodded to Stephen and he grinned. He was enjoying this task. I walked away.

I did not need to enrich my vocabulary of insults. I had enough of my own.

***

I was trying to tie up the loose ends of thoughts. I pulled the little list I had made from a pile of parchments on my table top and I sat and I stared at it.

Top of my list was Henry. I acknowledged that I did not want to accuse him outright of the murder of the priest. I had known him all his life. I could not think him capable of murder, but then the genial Matthew Cook, by his own admission, was capable of murdering his own brother in a fit of temper. Who knew what we were able to do if we were pushed?

Ah yes, Matthew. Both Matthew and Henry had, on their oath, said that they had not caused the death of the priest. Matthew had an alibi. He was in the kitchen in full view of all when the deed was done.

The Sylvestres too had alibis, though they were shaky. In law, a wife could not give evidence to help out her husband. So Edwina's assertion that Ralf had been with her all night, after he left the Widow Giffard, was not worth much. If I went to speak to Margaret, Henry's mother, the same would apply. She was a woman and her word was worth very little. Mothers would commit perjury to save their sons' necks from a stretching.

Joan the laundress and her husband Robin, did either of them lose their temper with Swithun? No. This was a planned murder, not a spur of the moment thing.

Hamon Deerman. Now he was guilty of something. The murderer, whoever they were, certainly thought that he knew something and was worried that the man, in his fear, would spill what he knew.

Dysig too knew something but I doubted we would ever make sense of it.

And Edmund, who had had an alibi, first from the poultry girl and then from Widow Giffard and from my own reeve too, was certainly guilty of something, but again, what?

I had forgotten Peter Brenthall. He hated Swithun but he was merely thirteen. Could he overpower him and thrust a knife into him twenty times?

I knew Peter well. He was a gentle lad. I really could not see it.

I had added one more name. He was not a village man but a Marlborough lad. He was apprenticed to the cordwainer in town, for he did not want to follow in his father's footsteps and become a glazier. Harry Glazer. Son of the man who had installed the window glass for me, in the solar and the church.

They did not get on. Harry had accused his father face to face of adultery, in front of me, on this very manor, and Swithun has fixed his ears on the conversation like a flea fixes on a dog.

The sins of a man who lived in Marlborough were not within Swithun's remit. He scarcely sorted the sins of his own flock. They were too small and insignificant for him. An instance of swearing here; a covetous thought about some neighbour's fine pig, there, a failure to say the right prayer at the right time. Then he was interested in the pagan 'goings on' of the village. The harmless festivals, the dancing and the feasting.

Yes, he had found something interesting in the descent rolls, more to his liking but as yet, we were unable to fathom what those sins were, for sins they must be.

Perhaps I'd just trip into town and talk to the lad Harry and maybe I would at the same time, introduce Johannes to the cordwainer, for he needed a pair of soft indoor shoes. I could also take the church plate to be mended and make inquiries about new vestments for the church.

First, I needed to talk to my woodsmith or carpenter, Alfred, about the making of a new chest for the priest's room. This fire in the church had cost me dearly.

I skipped down the hall steps and ran through the rain, splashing in the puddles, of the flagstoned courtyard. I stuck my head through the woodsmith's door. He was there on his hands and knees, searching the floor carefully for something.

"This what you want, Alfred?" I held up a chisel. A wide bladed chisel which had fallen from the bench by the door and was partly concealed by a chest standing there.

Alfred jumped up. "Aye m'lord. Thanks. I felt sure it went under the bench."

I handed it back, handle first, but not before I noticed that the blade had what looked like dried blood at the tip.

"Thanks m'lord. My best chisel for taking off chips of material. Can't do without it, though I don't use it often."

Hmmm. Was the knife belonging to Swithun's brother the only weapon used that night? It set me thinking.

We decided on the sort of chest we needed for the little room in the church and Alfred set to, to make some drawings for me. Off I went once more into the rain.

I ducked as I reached the stable door and at that precise moment, a dribble of rain dripped from the thatch and went straight down the back of my shirt. I shivered.

"Yes, Paul, you are quite right. This always happens. I suppose one must expect it with thatch. One day, you know, someone will make a roof which will collect all the water and funnel it to one place so that it can be disposed of sensibly and not down the shirt neck of a passing innocent. I have seen such things in Normandy.

I admit they are on grand buildings, cathedrals and castles, but there are no rules to say they cannot be made for smaller places, now are there?"

I asked Cedric to saddle my roan gelding Bayard whilst I nipped back to fetch my cloak from my office. Under no circumstances was I going to Marlborough without my best waterproof cloak across my shoulders. No sooner had I passed through the outer door, when I heard a hubbub and turned quickly to the hall door. There was Agnes Brenthall, sitting at the table and she was weeping.

"Agnes?" She turned a tear stained face to me and shakily wiped her eyes on the back of her hand. "Oh sir... 'tis nothing. Don't you fret yourself."

I marched up to her. I noticed that she had a new red bruise around her right eye and grazes on her cheeks and palms.

"What has happened?"

Hal of Potterne leapt up from the table beside her and put an arm around Agnes' shoulders.

"She fell down the stairs, sir. The kitchen stairs. You know how dark it can be in this weather there. Missed 'er footin' she did. Poor chick." He winked at me.

Agnes was inspecting a nasty bruise on her elbow which she was rubbing assiduously and modesty forbade that she look at her knee, in our company. Old Joan appeared from the kitchen stairs with a pot of heated water and a cloth and started to bathe the wounds.

She shooed us away when she reached Agnes' knee.

"What really happened Hal?" We went to stand at the other end of the large table and looked away.

"She was pushed, sir."

"Pushed?"

"Aye... sounds like it. She was going down the stairs to the kitchen. I think we need more light there, sir, for it's as black as buggery jus' there at the top. Easy to lurk, see. Well, someone was a lurkin'. Give 'er a 'elpin' 'and in the back. 'Opin' to break 'er neck I 'spect."

I looked back at Agnes. "No one saw anything?"

"No sir. All the doors were closed."

"Can you take her home Hal? And find someone to look out for her till John comes back? I'm just in my room for a moment then I"m off to Marlborough in a while. I'll be back before nightfall."

"Right you are, sir."

I approached Agnes and thanked Old Joan. "Nothing broken, Joan?"

She shook her head. "Bruises and cuts - she'm were lucky."

"Agnes, go home and rest. Hal will look after you."

Agnes began to snivel again quietly. "Why sir? Why push me?"

"I don't know, but I do know something. We are getting to the truth, events are coming thick and fast now. Whoever has done these things, Agnes, is a very worried person. Very worried indeed."

***

I collected Johannes from his house on Kingsbury Hill and together we took the silver items which needed mending from the church to the silversmith on Silver Street; the road which ran along the side of the hill from Kingsbury Street to the Green. Not too much damage done. Silver, Elias told me, will survive most fires but in extreme heat it might buckle, as our paten had. Elias was a Jew and under the law was not allowed to engage in any trade but usury. However he was a very good silver-smith and the town turned a blind eye to his work. What harm did it do? He took in damaged silver and returned it whole, no questions asked. We walked my horse down the hill and came to Johannes' house from the rear, where he had a small stable for his horse and mule.

"Shall we walk to the cordwainers and leave the beast here? The rain has fair worn him out," I said.

"Aye, why not and I will come with you to the cordwainer's and order myself a pair of indoor shoes. It will be interesting too, to hear what the lad has to say about Swithun, though it might be they met just that once and there's no more than that to it."

We stabled the horse and set off on the higher side of the street, for the rain had made the whole of the wide road a quagmire and the northern-most side was easier to negotiate, for it was a good few feet higher than the southern.

The cordwainer's shop and house was close by the priory gate and on the southern side of the street. The rain was coming down in a steady stream now and Gilbert and his apprentices were looking out of the door, with worried expressions.

"Ah m'lord. Come to aid us with the bailing out, have ye?"

I had known this genial man all my life. He had made my first pair of leather shoes when I was a child and he was but a journeyman. Now he was a master shoemaker, with apprentices and journeymen of his own. His house, workplace and shop were next to the entrance of the Priory of St. Margaret of Antioch and there is no doubt he benefitted from being in such a spot. No pilgrim, visitor secular or clerical - could pass by into the priory without first casting their eyes over his wares.

Master Cordwainer was an avuncular man with a large round red face, thick brown hair and a permanent grin. I smiled at him.

"Oh...surely Gilbert, it won't come to that."

"Damned rain. We need some gullies so that the mud and muck doesn't come straight down from the upper street and through our properties. In the front door and out the back. Third time in three years."

"Speak to Master Barbflet. He is town reeve, maybe he can find the money from the town collections to pay the ditch digger to make a runnel for the water to disappear into." I found myself again, thinking of the water spouts on the cathedral at Rouen that I had seen this time last year and how they channelled the water away from the building.

"May I present my friend Dr. Johannes of Salerno."

"Ah yes, we haven't exactly met but I have seen you about and hear a lot of good things about you, sir." Gilbert bowed and Johannes nodded firmly. "You have a house, do you not, right by St. Mary's?"

"I do and that is where I do my doctoring, if I'm not out in the town, or in the forest."

"Johannes would like some soft indoor shoes, Gilbert. Like mine."

"Ah...those I made you are still good on your feet I take it?" This was Gilbert's favourite phrase.

"Aye, they are. Your young man Harry did well with mending them. Is he about, Gilbert? I'd like a word, if I may?"

Gilbert nodded to another young man whom I recognised as the younger apprentice Felix Castleman, whose father was a man at arms at the castle, which stood at the western most end of the street.

"Run out the back and find Harry, Felix."

Gilbert Cordwainer had a yard at the back of his shop where he kept his skins and stored the awls, marking wheels, sole knives, small hammers, lasts and other tools along with lengths of waxed hemp or linen "cord" that the shoemaker worked with. Harry came ambling in from this yard.

Johannes sat and Gilbert began to take measurements and find out his requirements.

Harry's face lit up when he saw me. "M'lord. Come for some more shoes?" he bowed.

"No, not I, though my friend here has. No, in truth, I've come to talk to you, Harry."

"Me...?"

"Just something I need to know to, how can I put this... tidy up some thoughts I have been having about Swithun, the priest at Durley. You met him when you returned my shoes to me."

"Aye in Durley Manor, I remember."

"You will no doubt have heard that he is dead. He was murdered in his house a few days ago."

Gilbert, Felix and Harry joined in saying, "Aye we heard."

They all looked at each other as if they each suspected the other of the murder.

Gilbert scowled. "Out! Back to work, Felix" he said. "This doesn't concern you lad."

Felix, grumbling at being excluded, passed back into the yard and we heard the outer door close.

"Why do you want to talk to me...? Ah... I see," said Harry. "You heard about the argument we had the day after, when he came to see me... here, sir."

I sat down on the customer's stool and crossed my ankles.

"No, I didn't hear. Tell me."

Gilbert was staring open mouthed at his apprentice. "You never told me he came here."

"No sir, you were out at Gerard the tanner's and when you came back... well..."

"Why did you argue, Harry?" I asked.

"Well 'twas more of a refusal on my part and a disappointment leading to anger on his."

"What did he want?"

"You remember, sir, that my dad and I, we don't see eye to eye." Harry flicked a look at Gilbert, who quickly looked down at his feet, the measuring and consulting with Johannes temporarily abandoned.

"All because you feel that he drove your mother into an early grave with his womanising."

"Yes, that's so. I think she could just about stand the other women Dad went around with, but the woman she considered her best friend and neighbour...well... that was the thing which sent her into the last fit which killed her."

Johannes looked up quickly.

"Harry, Harry Glazer. Your mother was Margery, Margery Glazer. Lived on Kingsbury Street?"

"Aye, sir."

"I treated her, Aumary."

I nodded.

"You realise Harry and I am sorry to have to tell you, that your mother was dying of a wasting disease. There was nothing I could do. I had been treating her for a while for blurred vision and a difficulty in walking, tingling in the limbs and a numbness and some pain. It was all getting worse and there was little anyone could do to help. It is a disease no one knows much about."

"It began with the blurred and double vision, sir, then as time went on, more things began to happen to her. I know you had been helpful to her but the last fit she had, where she took to her bed was after she had seen my father and his doxy at..." He looked away.

"Yes...we see, Harry," I said gently.

"She just gave up."

He drew himself up, "I saw them too, not long after. They had pretended not to like each other for so long. My father always used to call her a saucy wagtail and say she was nothing but a high class drab, and so we thought that he disapproved of her lascivious behaviour, for she encouraged many men in the town to flirt with her. All the time he was playing her game, under the very nose of her husband, Master Pewterer. When her husband's heart gave out, they started to be more brazen about it. Then when my mother died, my father married the woman. She didn't like me being in the house and frankly, I didn't want to be there, so I got myself a place here."

Gilbert got up and put his arm around Harry's shoulder. "And right glad we are to have you, son," he said.

"Why was Swithun so interested in all this? It's nothing to do with him. It's town business," I asked, perplexed.

"I thought he'd come to castigate me again for speaking ill of dad as I did on that day, you remember my lord?"

"I do indeed, Harry. 'Honour thy father and thy mother...' wasn't that what he preached at you?"

"Yessir. I told him to go to Hell."

"Looks like he did, son," said Gilbert with a little giggle. "You didn't send him there did you?"

Even though the subject was no laughing matter, Harry chuckled.

"No sir, I had nothing to do with the death of Swithun the priest."

"So why did he come to see you?"

"He said that he had found an entry in a roll which lay in the church at Durley."

Johannes and I exchanged glances.

"In it, were some words which, he claimed, told of a child born on the manor to one of the women villeins. No one knew the father. The child disappeared shortly after birth but there is no record of their death or burial. I told him that maybe it was missed and that the priest had forgotten to enter the death. That was not likely, he said, for the records at that time were meticulous."

Yes, I thought to myself. They would be, for it was Benedict who had recorded it.

"And moreover, there was a small aside at some other place in the record which said that a boy child had been sent to someone to be brought up by a childless person, as if he were to be given to a wet nurse, though there is no record of who the child was or his parents. It was almost as if it was a secret,"

"Aye, I know this sort of thing happens. And did Swithun think that child was you?"

"I think so sir."

"What made him believe this?"

"The woman who received him, the name was marked as Margery, sir."

"A common enough name."

"Of Kingsbury."

"Ah."

"Did you ever have any suspicion Harry," said Johannes, "that your parents may not have been your true parents?"

"No sir."

I looked at Harry carefully.

"Wait, there is more - I can see it in your face."

"Yes, m'lord. The priest Swithun said that the father I know may actually have been my true father and that he had fornicated with this woman on the manor. I was the result of this coupling. He had been asking questions in the town. No one remembers my mother being with child, all those years ago. I have no siblings. She never conceived again. Well, no, I said, she was ill. But Swithun had an answer for everything. She was barren. My parents took on the bastard from Durley, son of my father and nothing was said. So, my mother was not my mother but in reality, some dirty village slut."

"Have you asked your father about this, Harry?" asked Johannes.

"No sir. I will not speak to him."

I vowed I would.

"How was it left? What did he want you to do?"

"I wasn't sure. He was muttering on about some other wicked people in the village. How the place was rife with sin and depravity."

"Yes, he told me that." I said, smiling.

Johannes chuckled quietly, "And I had no idea that it was such a sinful place."

"I think he wanted to make it public for some reason."

"Did he ask you for money to keep it quiet?"

"I was waiting for that, but no. No, he didn't."

"So what did you do?"

"I told him sir, again, to go to Hell and that if he didn't stop bothering me, I would....."

"Yes?"

"I would make sure he never bothered anyone, ever again."

***

We were walking once more up the High Street. The rain has slackened a little.

"Well, that was interesting," said Johannes. "Do you think he carried out his threat?"

I sighed. "I doubt it, but I could be wrong. Harry just doesn't seem the sort to murder a priest no matter how annoying he was."

"No... I agree with you."

"Yes, we must pay more attention to these descent rolls and to the little notes in the margins."

" 'Tis such a pity you have lost so many."

"But I think the ones to which we need to pay greatest attention are the latest. Harry is only eighteen, nearly nineteen."

Thought of the descent rolls brought the fact to mind, that I needed to talk to one of the seamsters who lived in the town and so I ducked down the alley called Angel Lane to discuss our needs with Master Wyndecraft, who ran a sewing business there. Johannes went on home.

I met him again saddling and fixing panniers to his horse as I entered the back yard of his house some while later.

"Ready for off again Johannes?"

"Aye. Are you done in the town?"

"I think so. Why so much luggage?"

"Unless you have quite forgotten, my Lord Belvoir, you are to marry my niece in two days' time. Here I have everything I need for a prolonged stay." He patted the panniers now in place. "Shall we go? The sooner we get back to Durley, the sooner we can get out those rolls and have a good look at them again."

I looked up at the sky,

"Hmm...better trot on then, for the heavens look as if they are about to upend on us."

***

Upend they did and we were soaked before we reached the turn to Durley, off the Salisbury Road. Luckily, on reaching the hall, Hal of Potterne had a good fire burning in the grate and a jug of warmed spiced ale on the hearth. We stood in front of the flames and steamed. Firstly, I asked Hal about the Lady Lydia and Hawise.

"Ho ho, they's up in the solar sir, gigglin' and fiddlin'. Summat about weddin' clothes I think."

"Good." I smiled.

Then, I asked about Agnes.

"A bit jittery but all right. John and Peter are 'ome now. I went an' asked in the kitchen to see if anyone remembered who was about jus' before Agnes was pitched down the stairs but no one could remember, it being so busy like."

"Were there any folk there who should not have been in the kitchen at the time, Hal?"

"Jus' a few. All of them were doin' things though, in full view."

"And Matthew?"

"In the privy sir...'e came back about an 'undred 'eartbeats later."

"Ah. Can anyone verify this?"

"Aye, sir. Geoff can, Geoffrey Furnier."

"And did anyone pass through here on their way to the kitchen, before Agnes went down the stairs?"

"Ah..." said Hal, stroking his long grey forked beard which shone like silver and was combed to perfection. "That is something I 'ave been keepin' in my 'ead awaitin' for you to return sir."

He lifted his head, stood to attention and pulled down his bright saffron tunic. Hal had a penchant for clothes which were as bright as a May morning. He cleared his throat.

"First Henry. Going from the office to the kitchen, though he coulda gone by the outside door. Jus' afore you turned up an after you 'ad bin to the stables. Ten heartbeats earlier, Peter; he fetched up some soup and sat by the fire and ate it, then went back down. He'd jus' gone when she fell, sir. Then jus' when I put another log on the fire, Hamon Deerman poked his head round the door to see if you were 'ere. He wanted to speak to you. I told 'im you were in yer office. Now that musta bin..." he looked at the newest log burning on the fire, "about a heartbeat or so before Agnes pitched down. 'E went down into the kitchen. His wife was there he said. Then he were followed by that Edith woman."

"Edith Brooker?" My brow furrowed.

"Aye, that wench."

"What on earth was she doing in the hall? This isn't a place you would find her at all."

"Well, sir, she brought a basket o' mushyrums, fer you. Picked 'em in the forest, she said. To say sorry for the way she spoke to you today."

"Never!"

"So she said, sir. An' she looked proper sorry. Like a snotty sneeze, she did."

"She shouldn't be picking those by rights...they belong to me and she needs my permission." But I let it go.

"And she went off down the kitchen stair?"

"Aye, I sent her there, saying they was no good sittin' 'ere an' needed to be in the kitchen.

So off she went."

"And then Agnes fell?"

"Yessir."

"Lord, Hal...get down those stairs and tell Matthew not to cook those mushrooms. We can't trust anything that woman does."

"Right you are, sir."

Hal turned back when I asked, "Is Stephen still watching the Brookers, Hal?"

"Aye...'e's out with Edmund now. 'E told me they separated jus' after you left 'em."

"Pity he didn't follow Edith then...we might have known...oh never mind, it doesn't matter. Recall him before supper will you, Hal."

"Right you are, sir."

Johannes laughed. "You think the woman is trying to poison you, Aumary?"

"Anything is possible with that termagant."

Something was teasing the corners of my mind, something I had heard today. Something that had reminded me of Edith Brooker but I was tired and hungry and could not recall the thing.

"It won't be long till supper. Meanwhile shall we go and look at those rolls again and see if we can find the reference to young Harry?"

"Aye, we shall," I replied.

The screaming started as we crossed the hall passage and began to unlock my office door.

High pitched and incessant, agonised and fearful. We both flew out onto the top step of the hall stairs.

People were coming out of their homes, looking round for the source of the screaming. No one seemed to have any idea from whence it came. Johannes and I ran through the gate-way, into the semi gloom of a mid-October evening. The screaming went on and on.

"This way!" I grabbed Johannes and pulled him around the manor path towards the church; past Old Joan's bothy; past the lych gate, on round the little tower, onto the main village road. Two or three people were ahead of us. John, I could see, was coming towards us thrusting his arms into his cotte, the strings of his shirt undone. He must have been taking his ease at home when the screaming started. Bird the forester, who lived in a house close by, was running up, stuffing a crust of bread into his mouth; he had been at his supper.

Deerman's wife, standing in her doorway, was holding two of her children one, under each arm, the third was behind her, screwing up her dress in her little hand and sucking a thumb.

In front of the bothy occupied by Dysig was Dysig himself, screaming and screaming and stamping his feet and crying inarticulate words in a high pitched wail. John reached him first. He stopped dead a few feet away.

The front of Dysig's tunic was covered in blood but it was not his own. In his hand was a chisel, the broad bladed chisel belonging to Alfred Woodsmith, which I had seen only that day, in the joiner's work shop.

"Dysig...." I cried. John turned, saw me and backed away.

"Dysig put down the ..." I doubted he would know what a chisel was and I sought for another word he would know.

"Put down the knife."

He was now hiccoughing and mewling and he fell to his knees. Johannes stepped up briskly and took the chisel. He handed it to me.

He shook his head, " 'Tis not his blood." John had disappeared into the bothy. He now came out white faced and shaking his head. "No. 'Tis Deerman's."

The house belonging to Hamon Deerman was skewed a little from the road way and the door faced the side of Dysig's bothy. I saw Deerman's wife stiffen and push her children into the house. She stood for a moment holding the door closed.

Agnes came hobbling down the road, her hair flying free, a small shawl over her dress. The bruise on her face had now darkened and her eye was almost closed. I noticed she also had grazes to the side of her face, no doubt sustained as she hit the wall, going down the steps. She ran past me and her husband and stood in the doorway with Deerman's wife, an arm around her shoulder. Johannes had now gone into the bothy but he came out rapidly with a grim expression on his face.

He shook his head at me.

Out of the corner of my eye, I saw Deerman's wife, whose name was Beatrix, gently fall to the floor in a faint.

Johannes was there in an instant. He picked her up and in one fluid movement he opened the door to her house, pushed it with his knee and took her inside, closing the door behind him.

John and I went into Dysig's bothy. I saw Agnes leave Deerman's house and take Dysig into an embrace, regardless of the blood covering him, which would transfer itself to her clothing. "Oh dear," I thought," She will have the devil of a time with the cleaning of that."

"Odd isn't it Paul, that at times of crisis, we think such silly things. I should have been bending my brain to the scene before me but no, I was worrying about poor Agnes and her bloodstained clothes."

On the pallet in Dysig's bothy was Hamon. He was on his back, both arms by the rough pillow as he had raised them as if he had tried to defend himself. His hands were bloodied as if in his death throes he had tried to stem the bleeding from his wounds. As he lost consciousness, they had fallen from his neck.

The chisel had been used to good effect, gouging out huge holes in his neck. The person who had used it as a weapon had not only stabbed, but had ripped and twisted, pushed up and struck sideways. Hamon's throat was a mess.

"Who was set to watch Hamon, John? I asked for him to be watched."

"Ackerman."

"Well, he has done a bad job. Talk to him and ask him to appear at the next manor court please ,John. I will fine him."

"Yessir."

"And take Dysig to the manor and clean him up please," I asked. "I am sure he did not do this thing." John ran to do my bidding.

Hal's words came into my head.

"Hamon Deerman poked his head round the door to see if you were 'ere. 'E wanted to speak to you. I told 'im you were in yer office." But I wasn't. I was in the stables, getting my horse ready to travel to Marlborough and talking to Alfred Woodsmith. I sighed. Oh...for the want of two or three heartbeats, he would have found me and perhaps he would still be alive and I would know more about the terrible deaths happening on my manor.

Bird Forester poked his head round the bothy doorway. "Oh fard!.." he said. "Holy Mother of God..." and he immediately brought up his supper outside.

Chapter Seven

"It's too late to send for the coroner now. Besides I'm fed up of doing it. Leave Hamon where he is and get one of those dense cloths the blacksmith has and cover him. Thank goodness we are not in the season of flies. And find Father Crispin. He needs to be told."

Hal, who had followed me from the hall, nodded and was off on fleet feet.

In the gloom I could see, just ahead of us, John with his arm around Dysig, guiding the shivering, shaking and still wailing, though quieter man to the gateway and the manor house. I trailed them through the gate and took Wyot the gatekeeper aside.

"Leave the curfew tonight, Wyot. Don't lock the door. I think people will be coming and going for quite a while yet."

"What'sa matter sir?" he asked with genuine concern.

"Hamon Deerman has been murdered and I think poor Dysig found him." Wyot crossed himself.

"All the sainted souls....I saw all the blood on him. Why ever would anyone want to murder Hamon? He were a good man."

"Goodness is no bar to the devil's work it seems, Wyot. Keep a wary eye out now."

"Aye, sir. Poor Dysig." He closed the large gate behind me but left the wicket open.

I wearily ascended the hall steps and found John, sheltering Dysig in his arms, waiting for me in the passage. "In my office, I think, John."

Once inside I lit the brazier, found some tinder and piled on some charcoal. Then I took my old winter cloak which always hung on a peg behind the door and wrapped it around Dysig, who was seated on a stool and had stopped chattering.

He ceased to shiver but stared at the flames of the brazier as the tinder took and warmed the charcoal. His eyes were vacant.

"I doubt we shall get much out of him now," I said to John who was lighting a few candles.

"No sir, shall I fetch him something to eat and drink?"

"Aye, and something to wear too. He cannot stay in that state."

John slipped silently from the room and eased the door shut.

"Dysig, can you hear me?" There was no reaction. "Dysig, it's the master, can you tell me what happened to you?" There was no movement. No recognition that anyone had spoken to him.

"Will you let me take your dirty clothes from you?"

I stood over him and leaned to undo the laces of his shirt poking out at the top of his fouled tunic. He shrieked as if the house were falling on his head.

"All right then. I won't try to do that. Will you take off your clothes yourself? John the forester has gone for some new ones for you to wear."

Dysig took up his burbling again. He spoke rubbish as if he had forgotten how to speak and was a baby again.

The door opened and closed. I said, "He won't let me touch him, John. He just goes further into himself if I try to..."

"Let me try then," said a voice.

I looked up. There was Lydia standing by the door, her hands behind her on the latch.

"John has just told me what has happened." She crossed the floor and knelt in front of Dysig. She took his bloodied hands.

"Dysig," she said. "Do you know who I am?"

His eyes focussed. He stared at her.

"Yes. You come from the town, you are the very beautiful Lady."

Lydia smiled gently. "That is very kind of you to say so."

She squeezed his hand. "You have had a terrible shock."

Dysig's eyes widened. "Hamon is dead."

"I know."

"And Hamon was Dysig's friend."

"I know that too, Dysig, and it is a terrible thing to find your best friend dead like that."

The man nodded. "There was all blood."

"Yes, I'm sure there was."

"Dysig went to help him. He wouldn't sit. I pulled him but he felled down."

"Where did you find the knife, Dysig?" I asked.

He ignored me, as if he hadn't heard.

"Was there a knife, Dysig? Did you find it?" asked Lydia.

"Yes...it was one of Alf's knifes. I seen'im afore."

Of course, Dysig would have seen Alfred at work with the chisel.

"Where was it, Dysig?" Lydia again.

"In my cott..." He started to moan again. "But Dysig didn't kill him. Why would Dysig kill him? He were kind to Dysig. Dysig loves Hamon," and he began to cry again.

Lydia got up from her knees and squeezed herself onto the stool with the weeping man.

She took him in her arms and made soothing noises, as one does to a small child.

"There, there. Truly, no one thinks you killed him. You are a good boy and whoever has done this thing is not good at all, Dysig."

"No."

"Did you get all this blood onto yourself when you pulled Hamon up to try to wake him?" she asked after a short while.

He sniffed and wiped his nose on his sleeve.

"Dysig tried to get him out but he wouldn't walk."

"No."

"Then I knowed he was dead and Dysig was angry."

"And that is why you screamed?"

"Dysig screamed and screamed 'cos he were angry."

"Why were you angry?" asked Lydia.

I heard John come back into the room,

He whispered in my ear. "Clothes here sir, food and drink coming."

Dysig's face took on an almost devilish expression.

"Dysig was very, very angry 'cos...'cos...."

He suddenly looked up at us all.

His expression was one of pure hate.

" 'Cos the angel said if we keeped quiet Dysig and Hamon would be saved."

"And you were angry because the angel lied?"

"The angel said we was safe and we never said nothing. Nothing. NOTH-ING!" he screamed.

"This, I think, is about the night that Swithun the priest died," I said in a whisper.

"Come, let's get you into some clean clothes, and there is food and drink coming too, Dysig. You'd like that wouldn't you?"

The mention of food, softened his face. "Aye, Dysig is hungry."

"Good!" Lydia stood and walked to fetch the small bowl of water I always kept, in which to wash my hands, when in the office.

"Let's wash Hamon's blood off, Dysig." She took both his hands and dunked them into my bowl. The water turned brown, red immediately.

I whispered to John as Lydia took charge of taking the clothes from Dysig and dressing him.

"We must handle this very carefully. I can just see the coroner and jury fastening on the fact that Dysig had the chisel in his hand. We cannot have the man caught up in the murder just because he was in his bothy with the bloodied corpse, the weapon used to kill him and no wits to understand his peril."

There was a scratch at the door and Old Joan entered with a bowl of stew and some bread. Immediately, Dysig broke away from Lydia and plunged towards his great aunt. She swiftly put down the food and enveloped him in her arms.

"There, there poor soul, 'tis all right now. Let's get some clothes onto you'm before yer perish and then you can 'ave this nice pottage."

I winked at her.

"John?" I asked. "Is Alfred Woodsmith in the hall?"

"Aye, at meat with the others."

"Tell him to meet me in the buttery next door after he has finished."

It was a matter of heartbeats before Alfred came into the buttery, wiping his crumb filled beard with his hand.

"You wanted to see me, m'lord?"

"Aye." I put the chisel down on the table with a clunk.

"Can you explain why this was in Dysig's bothy?"

"Dysig's….? I would never let him take it or use it. I wouldn't trust him not to..." he then saw the state of the tool.

"Woe sakes! What happened? Has he hurt himself with it?"

"No. Not Dysig. When did you last see this tool?"

"This morning when I knocked it from the bench and you found it by the door."

"I see. I thought when I saw it this morning that it had blood on it then. Did it?"

"Bless you sir, no, 'twas only a bit o' rust. Like I say, I haven't used it in a while and I shall need it in good condition to make the chest we discussed."

"It has been used to murder Hamon Deerman, Alfred."

Alfred's face went pale.

"I...I...Din't"

"No, I don't suppose you did."

"Why sir...why would anyone want to kill him?"

"You are not the first person to ask me that, Alfred. I can only say, that he was wanting to talk to me about something today. I think it was about the death of Swithun the priest and his mouth was stopped before he could get to me."

"Why use my chisel?"

"To implicate you perhaps?"

"But Hamon and I had no quarrel. Why should someone think that I could be blamed?"

"Who did you see around your workshop after I left you, Alfred?"

"No one sir. I was busy drawing, drawing the chest you wanted and working out....."

"With your back to the door?"

"Aye sir."

Does your door creak when it's opened?"

"Sir... I am a woodsmith. I would not let my door creak..."

"Perhaps you should then, because I think someone peeped in, saw the chisel on the bench by the door, where you had left it after you and I had been talking, took it away and used it to kill Hamon. Almost everyone has to pass your place to go through the gate. The chisel was left in Dysig's bothy where Hamon was killed."

"God's wounds sir... I swear... it was not me."

"No, Alfred. I don't think it was. If you were going to murder someone, I doubt you would use one of your own tools. You would not be so foolish."

His colour was beginning to return.

"Dysig wouldn't do it, sir."

"No, I know." I worried my lip with my teeth.

"Oh!" The young man slapped his hand to his forehead. "This means of course..."

"Yes, that your chisel will be taken as deodand."

"Oh noooo!"

***

I returned to my office. Dysig was gulping down the pottage, one swallow after another and stuffing bread into his mouth. His stained clothes were in a heap on the floor. Old Joan and Lydia were encouraging him.

"Best to burn them, I think," I said.

"But sir..." said John. "Won't the coroner want to see...."

"The coroner will see what we want him to see, John."

My chief woodward stared at me for a while.

"Like I said, we must handle this carefully. No one wants to see Dysig hanged for a crime he did not commit."

"He found him - he is the first finder."

"He is, but he will not be able to understand what the crowner requires of him. We shall need to be there to speak for him. Naturally, there will be no blood on his clothes and the weapon will not have been in his hand."

"No sir."

I cocked my head, a gesture which said...."and?"

"Naturally," he affirmed, and smiled.

***

Johannes came in the almost dark, later.

"I have given Beatrix a sleeping draught. She is a strong woman but a little help would not go amiss. She has Agnes and her goodwives with her now. The children have gone to other village families. She has family in Overton she tells me. The children could go there till things become more settled."

"Aye... 'tis a sorry business. Did they find Crispin?"

"Yes. He went straight to the bothy to give conditional absolution and then he talked to Beatrix for a while till she felt sleepy."

"He's a good priest."

"Aye...I think he will be."

"We shall miss our supper if we don't go into the hall now."

"Crispin said he must just return home and then he will be along to the hall."

I smiled at Johannes.

"This was not the meeting of two men of Oxford I had imagined, Johannes. I'm sorry you had to meet in such...such terrible circumstances."

Johannes shrugged.

"We are both men used to death, Aumary. To meet thus is no hard thing. Though I must admit, I would sooner have been introduced over a pint of wine, than a firkin of blood."

***

Supper was a rather restrained affair. Johannes and Crispin talking quietly of Oxford, the town where Johannes had been born and where Crispin had been educated. They discovered they had acquaintances in common. Johannes was the son of an Oxford parchment maker and Crispin had bought parchment, something no student could do without. There seemed no doubt that had things been just a little different, these two men would have met years ago.

"Talking of parchment. Shall we look at these rolls of yours, Aumary?" said Crispin.

"There's enough light here to see by, and it will while away the hour or so before we must take to our beds."

I fetched the four remaining rolls from the chest in my office and we spread them out on the high table.

I pulled the candles closer and asked Hal of Potterne to trim the few lights which burned in wall sconces at night.

Crispin pulled the latest roll to him. "Can we find the reference in which young Harry Glazer is mentioned? The one which Swithun had said indicated that Harry was not the son of his mother?" I asked.

"Why would a Marlborough lad be mentioned in a Durley roll?" asked Crispin.

Johannes and I looked at each other. "Shall you relate the story or shall I?" asked Johannes smiling.

"I shall, for I heard the altercation between father and son on the day Swithun eavesdropped."

I told Crispin of the meeting of the two of them on my manor. How Harry Glazer had taken himself off and had found an apprenticeship with Gilbert Cordwainer. How he had confronted his father and how Perkin Glazer had denied the adultery. I told also how Swithun had listened in at the door and of his castigation of Harry for "bearing false witness."

"Crispin, you read it for your Latin is better than ours and you are used to such work."

"How old is the lad?" asked Crispin.

"Eighteen."

"Then it will be in this roll." He tapped it with a perfect finger. "1180 to 1190."

We began in March the twenty-fifth, the New Year.

Crispin scanned the columns.

"Here…1186, June the twentieth, a reference to a woman giving birth. No father's name. She is Herleva Brooker. In the margin is *ex matrim.*"

"And it means?" I asked.

"Out of wedlock. *Ex matrimonio.*"

"I don't remember any scandal. How old was I? Twelve. No, I wouldn't, would I? Go on."

"The child is baptised four days later."

"Do we have a name?"

"Arnulf."

"But that is the same name as Herleva's father."

"He is taking the mother's name not the father's, Arnulf Herlevason."

"So he is not a Brooker?"

"No, but his mother was."

"Damn, we'll have to con the previous roll for her birth. Who is she? Oh how I wish that Benedict was still with us, he knew all the relationships, all over the forest."

Crispin was moving down the page.

"Here is the reference Swithun found, marked with a straw."

Crispin read the note in the margin and translated it from the abbreviated Latin.

"*Fil bas scorti*. That means, *filius bastardus scorti* - bastard son of a harlot. It says he was given to a woman - not a man - a woman; yes, Margery of Kingsbury. What it doesn't say is if the child was given, let us say, to look after, as for example to wet nurse, or given away completely."

"But the child was Arnulf, not Harold."

Crispin shrugged. "People change names all the time. Besides, how do we know it's the same child? There is no name here. Just the fact that it was a bastard and a boy."

Johannes had opened the earlier roll.1170 to 1180 and was silently mouthing the words he read there.

"Here we have the record of Herleva Brooker. Daughter of Arnulf and Godiva."

I looked up. "No, that can't be, for Godiva died just after her son Benedict in 1187. He was their first born. I remember reading that when I first looked at the rolls."

Johannes turned the roll to face me and pointed.

I read it out loud and the note in the margin.

"Herleva Brooker, daughter of Arnulf. Godiva."

Crispin said, "*Noverca*, that's step mother."

"Ah... Herleva was the child of a first wife. Godiva was Arnulf's second wife."

We were unlikely to find a record of their marriage for the rolls were gone.

"Hal... you have been on this manor a long time." I shouted down the hall at my man at arms who was sitting by the fire whittling a stick into the shape of a deer.

"Do you remember a wife for Arnulf Brooker, before Godiva?"

Hal sucked on his teeth.

"Aye sir... Erm I think she was called... oh something beginning with 'm'... erm... oh now what was 'er name? It was... it was... Millicent... yes Millicent."

"What happened to her?"

Hal got up and laid aside his whittling.

"She disappeared, sir... jus' like that." He walked up the hall.

"Disappeared? When?"

"Jus' after she 'ad her little girl, erm, she were called Herleva, I think. She were about two when the woman jus' walked out and away. Left."

This was becoming really complicated.

"So Arnulf Brooker had a wife who left him. If she was married to Arnulf, she was a tied villein, Hal... how could she just disappear? Did my father make no search for her?"

"Aye, 'e did. But she'd gone into thin air. Brooker... the Arnulf one, said she packed some things and went, leaving 'im with the little girl, sir. 'E were none too 'appy 'bout it I'll say."

I looked at Johannes. "Easy to say in a place like this. Gone away. Easy to disappear into a forest. No questions asked. Either she went or she was eased into the ground somewhere. The forest is a good burial place."

I realised that Hal was now staring up at me from below the dais. I chuckled at him.

"Hal...you have been paying attention to Hawise's reading lessons 'beginning with 'm' indeed."

Hal shuffled his feet..."Ah well...I never 'ad the chance when I were a young'un to learn me letters...but I 'int too old to do it now."

I smiled down at him. "Come up and sit...you may be useful to us with your long memory."

Lydia made room for him beside her, smiling widely

Crispin was frowning at the record Johannes had unearthed. "1186? The record says that Herleva was the daughter of Arnulf. It doesn't mention Millicent at all. It does say in the margin, '*Non accepit*,' not married, but who wasn't married?"

"Wait a minute. I am getting very confused. I'll fetch some parchment and I'll try to write it all down so it makes sense."

I ran to my office for parchment and charcoal. Dysig was fast asleep on my daybed. On my way back I bumped into Old Joan who said she would take him to her bothy, when she left for the night.

"What's that Paul? Oh yes, it must be. Those of you who read and write for a living must have a tough time with all these little shortenings of Latin words and phrases. The rest of us have no chance. Mind you, 'twas a clerk who made them up in the first instance, so you only have yourselves to blame!"

I drew a few lines at the top of my parchment. "So I have Arnulf at the top and his first wife Millicent. We don't know when they married but it must be before 1170 because there is no reference here and the previous roll's gone. Millicent then has a child, Herleva. Do we have a date for that, Crispin?"

"We do. March the thirtieth, 1170, one of the first records in the first roll we have. She is baptised the same day. She would be thirty-four now."

"Millicent then disappears and is heard of no more. She leaves her baby daughter Herleva with her husband. You say, Hal, that she was less than two when her mother left?'

"Aye a littl'un' just toddling about."

"What do we have next?"

Crispin moved his finger down the record again.

"The record of the birth of Benedict Brooker in 1187. This has an added note in the margin, Big."

"Big?" we all said together.

"*Bigamus.*"

"Well, of course, if Arnulf married again then he would be a bigamist for his first wife was not proven dead," I said. "Do we have a record of their marriage?"

This was quite difficult to find for it was in amongst many entries of the deaths from the dock fever which ravaged the county in 1180 and 86 and again in 1187.

"Then we get the details of Benedict's birth and death, and then Godiva's death a short while after in 1187."

"No further information. Nothing."

"Until we see the reference to Herleva and her baby in 1186 in roll two. She was sixteen."

"So Herleva was sixteen when she had the young child who was given away to Margery of Kingsbury. If it's the same child. Why?"

"Hmmm?" murmured Crispin.

"Why give it away?"

"It's a bastard and maybe Arnulf was not happy for it to be brought up in his house."

"That is not for him to say Crispin. The child, bastard or not, is the property of my father at this moment, for he is the son of a tied villein and it is the lord who says what happens to it, not the grandfather."

I thought a moment.

"Crispin, is there no record anywhere of anything else, in the margins maybe, which will help us identify the lad?"

Only what we have read before - 1186 June the twentieth, a woman Herleva Brooker gives birth. No father's name. In the margin is '*ex matri*' which means out of...."

"Wedlock ...yes."

"Wait!" Crispin turned the page sideways, "there's another entry, very tiny and not done at the same time, for the ink is different, and it's written on the slant. Up the page, not across it, '*p.incest part, puer incestuosi partus*'."

"Does this mean what I think it means?" asked Johannes with a shocked look. His Latin was good enough for him to work it out.

"It means my friend... that I think we might have found a reason why Swithun was killed."

Hal took a quick in breath. Something had occurred to him.

"*Puer incestuosi partus*, my friends, means incestuous boy child," said Crispin.

***

We all sat in horrified silence. Lydia broke the silence first. "Are you saying, Crispin, that this child was the result of Arnulf Brooker's liaison with his own daughter and that is why he was given away?"

"It certainly looks like it," he answered "I think Swithun thought so too. Though he did not mention it to Harry, did he, Aumary?"

I shook my head.

"Why did Benedict add this note later, for I suppose this is what happened?"

"The Seal of Confession holds even if the penitent is dead," said Crispin. "It cannot have been revealed to him in confession. He must have learned it in some other way and added it when Arnulf Brooker was dead."

Hal coughed.

"Sir... I think I can throw some light on this now I have had me memory pulled about a bit."

"Speak, Hal."

He fingered his ear and scratched the side of his face. "Well... it were difficult see 'cause the dock fever was getting everyone and even if you didn't die of it, you were very poorly. Benedict had it I remember, and wasn't able to keep up the rolls. We all 'ad to get together, the 'ole village, or them that were left, to test our memories after, so we could write a record of it all, cos it was done afterwards, bit by bit. I 'ad it and recovered, so did Benedict, but it left 'im with a weakness though it got 'im in the end. Poor soul." Hal crossed himself.

"Yes, he did have a liver disease, at the end, did he not, Johannes?"

The doctor nodded, "He did, and this may explain it, for the fever can weaken the organs."

"Arnulf 'ad it and died. Herleva followed. You'll find their burials some-where in the roll I s'pose. Then the boy 'ad to go somewhere."

"And so they farmed him out to a childless couple in Marlborough? A child belonging to the demesne?"

"Oh no, sir."

"What did they do with him?"

A voice from half way down the hall echoed up to us all on the dais. "They gave 'im to my niece, m'lord."

Crispin turned round; I looked around his head. Johannes leaned back, crossed his arms, and smiled, for I swear he had worked it all out. Hal stared down the hall.

"They gave 'im to my niece Margery, who lived at Durley. Margery Kingsbury as was. She's dead now. The child was baptised Arnulf but 'e goes by 'is nickname nowadays."

Old Joan had her arm around Dysig's shoulders. I recalled she was taking him to her home for the night.

" 'E were, it's right, a child born of a father and daughter. Unnatural and against the laws of God and of the land. The sin came out in 'im and he'm ain't right, sir. God touched 'im for the wickedness of the parents.... His name is..."

"Dysig," said Hal of Potterne "That's right. Dysig Herlevason, though he's really a Brooker, m'lord."

Old Joan bowed her head and drew the vacant young man to her side.

"Aye...'tis Dysig, m'lord."

***

We were all shocked into silence. Then something occurred to me.

"But wait... if this is already knowledge which some in the village possess and the perpetrators of the sin are long dead, why would the fact that Dysig is Herleva and her father's son be a threat? What does it really matter?"

"Hmmph," said Crispin, "Swithun obviously thought there was something in it."

"But he was wrong, Crispin. Harry Glazer is not the bastard child."

"And why," said Johannes, "destroy the rolls? If folk knew all this, why bother?"

"Folk did know. It weren't a secret...but then it weren't trumpeted from the roof tops neither," said Hal.

"There must be something else. Something else someone wants to keep quiet that is related to this event... this mortal sin."

I cudgelled my brains but nothing was knocked out.

I yawned. "Ah! Perhaps we should all sleep on it now and see how we feel in the morning. One thing I do know... Arnulf Brooker did not father the Brooker twins on Godiva as we thought."

"Ah yes, indeed." Johannes scratched his head.

"They must be children of the first wife Millicent, born before Herleva."

"We shall have to deal with the coroner tomorrow too," said Johannes, adding to my yawn. "And until we are sure of our facts, all this must be kept quiet."

"It won't be the first time we have kept things from the coroner eh, Johannes?"

"No." he chuckled. "No indeed,"

***

The coroner was not the man we were used to seeing. Here was a younger man, more officious than the last holder of this post, who had been a man over fifty and a local landowner. This one, I thought, would be less willing to bend the rules a little or use his experience and judgement to stare straight ahead when his eye was being drawn aside. He arrived, with his fussy little clerk and called together a jury of twelve men over fourteen.

I brought Dysig to the front of the crowd and pointed out that here, was the first finder.

The coroner, who seemed after all a relatively reasonable sort, looked long and hard at the shaking man in front of him. I kept my hands on Dysig's shoulders and I squeezed lightly, to reassure him that I would help however I could.

"Let it be recorded that ..." the coroner cocked his head.

"Dysig, Dysig Herlevason," I said.

"Is the first finder in this case, the body being found in his house."

The coroner looked down his nose at Dysig. "Was the hue and cry called?"

"If I may be allowed, my lord coroner, to answer for Dysig? You can see that the man is not a whole man, being damaged at birth... he is but a child." I was sticking to this story, even though I now knew that this was not the truth. "He does not understand the importance of the hue and cry and so did not call on the nearest four households when he discovered the body."

"And did no other man perform this duty, knowing the importance of the....?"

"Aye the whole manor was alerted, including myself, who by right of being the warden of the forest, is also the bailiff of the hundred. I eventually called the hue and cry."

"No one was apprehended?"

"No sir. They were long gone."

"The weapon which you say was used...?"

"Was a chisel belonging to my woodsmith, Alfred." I gave him the chisel.

"Is Alfred Woodsmith here?"

"I am sir." He stepped forward.

"You can identify this as your tool?"

"Yes sir."

Then came the long winded process of working out when he had last seen it, how it might have been stolen and how much it was worth. Of course, my word that I was the last person to see it, barring the murderer, that is, was accepted.

Then the body had to be stripped and brought out of the bothy.

"We have preserved it as it was found, m'lord coroner. Nothing has been touched, save the chisel removed from the place where it was lying...just here... outside the bothy, for safe keeping. Is that not so, Dysig?"

I had pointed to the place where Dysig had been standing when we discovered him with the chisel in his hand. So far we had told no lie. Dysig had been told to answer yes to any question I asked him.

Here was his answer. He was so overawed that he simply nodded his head. The coroner grunted.

The twelve men, who included many of Hamon's friends and relations, stood and shuffled their feet. Yes, it was Hamon Deerman and yes he had been foully done to death, they all answered one after the other. No, no one had any idea who had done the thing, or why.

The coroner's eyes narrowed.

"No one knows of any quarrel that the dead man might have had with any other man of the village?"

They all shook their heads.

I felt Dysig take a deep breath, as if he were going to speak, but gave a small shake of his shoulder by way of a warning. It would do us no good to talk of demons and angels, nor for him to try to connect this death with that of Swithun the priest. Leave that to me.

I saw Bird the forester try to step forward but Johannes, standing by him, caught his arm gently and with an infinitesimal shake of his head discouraged him from speaking up. Bird's lips sealed in a hard line.

"Are you certain, my Lord Belvoir, that the death of Hamon Deerman was not caused by the first finder, Dysig Herlevason? It's often the truth that the person who reports the death is the person who caused it."

"I am content with the word of my tied villein, that he had no reason to kill his neighbour. He was seen shortly before the death was discovered and was in a calm and unworried state. A man of his intellect, sir coroner, would show to the world his state of mind and his anger, for there is a deal of anger in the manner of this death."

" 'Twas I who saw him, sir, " said John, bowing low. "He was untroubled."

"You are?"

"Chief woodwarden here, sir, John Brenthall."

"Dysig was angry." I could not stop the man blurting out. I rode over his utterance.

"Yes indeed Dysig you were angry, any man would be at finding the body of his very best friend in his home, killed in so violent a manner."

"There was, if I am not much mistaken, a deal of anger and bitterness in the last death on your manor, sir."

"Yes, master coroner, and several of us here, including Dr. Johannes of Salerno from Marlborough town, are investigating."

"Hmmm. Such anger can be well concealed, m'lord, by some wicked folk. A true villain can smile at your face whilst plunging a dagger into your back."

"Not this man, master coroner, he is too simple for such play acting." I remembered Agnes saying that Dysig could not lie.

"We feel sure we shall apprehend the culprit soon. What is more, we may find that the perpetrator of this crime and the former, are one and the same."

"The *modus occidendum* is the same is it not?"

The jury shuffled their feet. John, I noticed stroked his chin and looked at the sky. Henry who was standing behind me, coughed.

"I am Crispin Darrell sir, late of Salisbury Abbey and latterly, aide to his grace the Bishop there, now in retirement, humble priest of Durley." Crispin bowed. "You are quite right; the way this murderer worked is most similar to the killer of Swithun the priest. His method is the same. I think we are looking at a person with a very troubled mind. One whose fury has overtaken them completely."

"Darrell? Of the Darrells Of Chilton?"

"The very same."

"Pleased to make your acquaintance, sir." The coroner bowed, "I do believe I am married to a cousin."

"Well, well," said Crispin, "You must be Hugo, who married little cousin Marian from Froxfield."

"I am indeed that man," smiled Hugo. "Hugo of Ramsbury," said the coroner puffing out his chest.

"Well, I have been back in my home village merely a day and I discover a relative I have never met. How wonderful. I had no idea. How is Marian? I remember her well. A spirited lass. How long have you been married? Do you live in Ramsbury? I should love to know."

Crispin, all this time, was gently taking the coroner by the arm and turning him from the jury, the body, and from Dysig and myself. As he turned, he winked.

"I have been away many years and must catch up with all the news."

Hugo opened his mouth to answer but Crispin carried on with,

"Then we must take meat and drink together, if we are finished here and discuss family matters. Have you eaten? I have a good pigeon pie, that I was saving for my dinner... "

The coroner nodded at his clerk.

"We record that the forester of Durley, Hamon Deerman, was unlawfully killed by a person or persons unknown. We shall take the tool used as the weapon as deodand. I release the body for burial. I shall withdraw to consider if any further amercements are due."

I heard Crispin say " 'Tis a sorry business, but my Lord Aumary has proven experience in discovering murderous felons. Why, the King was only saying to me a while ago...."

They disappeared around the corner towards the priest's house.

"You must be careful Crispin, I may call you Crispin, since you are family....?" said Hugo of Ramsbury, "This place has already seen off one priest, let us hope...."

And they were gone.

I was unaware how tense I had become but noticed how, when the coroner walked away with Crispin to his house, I blew out a huge sigh of relief.

John whispered in my ear. "A close one, sir."

"Aye, John. Thank you Crispin, Crispin of the Darrells of Chilton..." I chuckled.

Dysig looked up at me. "Are they going to hang Dysig?"

I patted the man on the shoulder. "Not today, Dysig," I said. "Not today."

***

Something the coroner had said niggled at me. Several trains of thought jumbled up in my brain as we walked back to the hall. Old Joan took Dysig as soon as we reached her bothy.

"He is safe from the coroner Joan." I said. "But guard him close. He knows too much."

As we neared the gate, Cedric Groomsman exited slowly and gracefully on my fine stallion Fitzroy, and ducked his head as he met me. "Thank you Cedric," I said. "I had, with all the comings and goings of the past week, forgotten to ask you to exercise the beast. I have not had the time to devote...."

" 'Tis all right sir, no hardship. He's a fine horse to ride but you have to watch him. I've ridden him most days up on the downs. He gets out in the field most days too. But he becomes restless and starts kicking the stall if he isn't taken out. And he can bite too."

"Are you for up the chalk now?"

"Yes sir, I am. Ben is following me on Bayard and a few of the other lads with other horses. We shall give them all a good run."

I smiled, "One so placid and the other, a fiend. One handsome and the other so beautiful."

I watched them go and suddenly, the jumbles in my brain cleared.

"Do you know Johannes...I think a few things people have said over the last two days have suddenly made me think differently about these three murders."

"Such as?"

"Ho, ho...I shall have to do my usual thing and write it all down before I am certain, but yes, it is beginning to make sense."

Johannes laughed. "Then you will have solved it by tomorrow morning and we can all go to a wedding in peace and safety."

"That would be my hope but...."

I saw Henry walking purposefully towards the gate from his duty as a juror. I caught his arm.

"Henry, I need to ask you something."

"Aye, sir," he looked wary and a little put out.

"Answer me this. If the coroner had decided that, by some quirk of fate and God forbid, Dysig was our murderer, of both Deerman and the priest, would you have told what you know in order to save him from the noose?"

"What I know, sir?"

"Yes...that is what I said for I know that you, and you are not the only one, do know something about these matters which I hope you would tell to save an innocent man from hanging."

Henry looked away.

"I would tell the truth to save an innocent... yes sir."

"And when I spoke to you about the murder of Swithun you swore on your immortal soul, did you not, that you did not cause the priest's death."

"I did,"

"You did not lie?"

"No sir."

"No, you did not. I am beginning to see that now. However, you are not entirely blameless, for I think you were there when he was attacked. I just need to work out how to prove it now."

Henry went very pale. "Excuse me sir...I must go. I have so much work to do for the wedding." And he ran off speedily.

"Well!" exclaimed Johannes, "There goes a guilty man."

"But guilty of what, my friend? The answer to that is as yet, locked in my brain. I must put pen to parchment and set it free."

***

Johannes had gone to rest in his room. I wrote and wrote in my office, with the door open. My parchment was full of scribbles. I drew lines connecting names and events and gradually a pattern emerged.

Agnes came from the hall, still limping from her fall. I called her as she passed the open door.

"Agnes, a word."

"Yessir."

"Can you ask Dysig for me, about the demons and the angel? Do you think you might be able to get him to describe them somehow?"

"Oh that's easy, sir. I couldn't stop him later that day when we questioned him. He went on and on about it. They were all black, he said with, black heads and bright little eyes...or something like that."

"Thank you. And the angel?"

"It was white, with a white head and eyes the same."

"No wings then?"

"Well, he didn't talk about wings...no."

"Thank you."

"Is that significant, sir?"

"Yes Agnes...I think so. Dysig didn't know it, but he saw the murderers of Swithun the priest gathering outside his house to do the deed. I think Hamon saw them too."

"Murderers sir?"

I nodded. "I think so,"

Agnes crossed herself. "Saints Almighty, protect us. Who would've thought the lad was right? Demons!"

"Oh no, Agnes, these weren't demons."

Her eyes grew as round as berries.

"Unless you think that several people out for revenge are demons."

"You've lost me, sir."

I smiled. "I'm floundering around myself, good lady, but I can see the bank and I am swimming towards it as fast as I can."

***

Wherever I wrote on my paper, a Brooker would turn up on a line. The Father Arnulf.

The daughter Herleva. The son Dysig. Edmund and Edith.

This family was the key to the whole thing, I was sure. One thing did leap out at me from the page as I wrote. I recovered the rolls from the chest and searched them again.

Arnulf died in 1187 therefore he really could not have been the father of Edmund and Edith for he had no wife at the date the twins were born. Millicent was missing and he had not yet married Godiva. So who was their mother?

And more to the point, who was their father?

I sat in my office and I conjured up the faces of both Edmund and Edith.

One, so dark and the other so fair. Both of them were very good to look at. One so amiable, the other so frosty. Both of them had a look of Harry Glazer.

I thought about their little cottage on the bank of the stream. I saw in my mind's eye, the garden, the little wattle gate with its bell. I saw again the cottage as I had seen it the day we searched and found young Meg's apron. There was something fundamentally wrong with that cottage and for the life of me, I could not fathom it. I would go again and see if anything jogged my memory.

Johannes was lying dozing on his bed, with his ankles crossed and his hands across his belly, when I looked through the door.

"I need some help. I have an idea....are you game for a walk to the Salley Gardens?"

He stretched out his long frame. "So of what does this idea consist, Aumary?" He pulled on his boots. "Have your scribblings borne fruit?"

"They have...and they haven't, but let us go and see."

Before we entered the small garden I held the little bell in my hand so that it could not ring and gently opened the wattle gate. I left the bell hooked over the fence. I put my fingers to my lips to signal silence but the cottage was deserted and the door open.

Johannes leaned against the doorpost and folded his arms. "What are we looking for Aumary?" he whispered.

"There is something here which tells me that what we are led to believe, what we see here, is not the truth, though I cannot as yet tease it out. I got a glimpse of it the other day, but it was like trying to catch a bat, too quick and not enough light on it."

Johannes chuckled at my image.

"Two people, brother and sister. Twins. Yes...They are brother and sister for they look alike do you not think?"

"Well, apart from the hair, yes they do. The same nose, the same eyes."

"They even have the same way of talking." I added, "and some gestures in common though that can happen when two people live in close proximity to each other for such a long time. One can take on the characteristics of the other."

"Oh God forbid...."

"Hmmm ?" I was looking round bemused.

"You and Lydia."

"What of us?"

"When you are man and wife at last and can sleep in the same bed," he chuckled "I hope you take on Lydia's characteristics and not she yours!"

"Johannes! You are a genius! "

"I am?"

I bounded up the little ladder which led to the upper room.

"Tell me what you see here Johannes?"

My friend ascended the ladder slowly and poked his head over the floor's edge.

"A small sleeping space, with a curtain for privacy. One tiny window. Erm... a pallet against the wall, two blankets folded....."

I bent to the floor and ran my hand along it. A cloud of dust lifted and Johannes sneezed.

"Not kept very clean....Ah."

"I think, my friend, the answer along with the dust, has just entered your head, has it not?"

He sneezed again and made his way back down the ladder.

I reached the third rung and jumped down.

Johannes pulled the pallet which Edmund used as a bed from its keeping place behind the main door. Four blankets were folded neatly on a chest in the corner. This floor was kept spotlessly clean.

He laid it down on that floor.

"Big enough for two?

"Aye, it is."

"The upper floor is never used is it?"

"I think," I said, "that we have now discovered what it was that Swithun was really looking at when he was found those many times, here by the brook. He wasn't watching Joan the laundress, he wasn't peeping at the girls at their ablutions. He wasn't going in and out of the forest. Neither was he following Edith Brooker around like a lovelorn puppy."

"He was watching these two."

"He knew their history, or part of the history of the family and I think he became suspicious."

"They killed him for it?"

"Oh my friend..." I said. "I think it is much more complicated than that."

***

We left the cottage.

There, just entered in the gate, a hoe in his hand, was Edmund Brooker. His face was stony. He had heard us. Of that there was no doubt. He stared at us a heartbeat, threw down the hoe, then as nimble as a deer, he vaulted the fence and was off up the field. We could not hope to catch him and I put a hand out for Johannes to wait.

"He cannot go anywhere that way for the deer fence prevents him. Besides, I think he will find his sister first and then they will attempt to flee."

We both ran back to the manor and collected a few folk together. Hal, Stephen and Peter, who had been playing jacks in the hall, immediately jumped up and followed us out.

I called for Henry as I passed his office and all those men who worked in the courtyard, the woodsmith, wheelwright and blacksmith, and a few others.

I told Wyot to bar the door to Edith and Edmund and let none pass into or out of the manor without my word.

John and Peter Brenthall would be out in the forest at this time of day. Where had they gone? They would be at the Balliwick of West Baily where work was still being done.

It was too far from us here to fetch them. Time was not on our side.

I ran back and hammered on the door. Wyot let me in with a rather startled expression. I pelted for the manor steps, fumbled with my key, opened both the office door and my chest and took out the Belvoir horn.

With the horn to my lips I stood on the top step of the manor stair and blew for all I was worth. It took me three tries but at the third attempt, I made a good noise which carried. Practice made me better and better and I blew it a further eight times.

Lydia had come down the solar steps, alerted by the comings and goings and naturally by my blowing of the horn.

"What on earth....?"

I thrust the horn into her hands. "Stay here, blow it if you can. If not, find someone who can. Johannes and I are off to catch a murderer."

Off I ran at full tilt and as I turned at the gate, left open for me by Wyot, Lydia shouted. "Take care my love."

With those words ringing in my ears, I ran towards the main village road and into the forest.

Chapter Eight

We could see Edmund running along the perimeter of the deer fence, up on the manor fields. We kept pace with him along the road. If he got ahead of us, he might be able to get into the forest and over the Salisbury Road to evade us. However, I felt sure he would go nowhere without Edith and she was somewhere here, out in the field.

She appeared a moment later from the trees at the edge of the forest. There was some hurried discussion, then Edmund took her hand and they ran. We saw them dipping in and out of the trees at the top of the slope and then in an instant, they were gone.

"Where'd they go?" shouted Hal, his eyes raking the hillside.

"I think they have ducked into the ditch by the paling of the fence," said Hubert Alder the blacksmith. "They hope to gain on us whilst we cannot see them."

We loped along the lane getting ever closer to the road to Salisbury. I heard a tentative blow on the Belvoir horn, echoing through the trees, then a better attempt. Well done Lydia, I thought.

Suddenly the Brookers broke from the trees ahead of us and ran along the side of the lane. Here the trees began to be denser and the underbrush thicker with dry, brown docks and rusty bracken.

"Shall I sprint on ahead sir?" asked Alfred, whom I knew was a good runner.

"No, Alfred, for he has killed several times and I would not have you on my conscience should he decide to fight." I scanned the forest, "We should stay together, until we have no choice."

Before we knew it, we had reached the main road to Salisbury which bisected the Bailiwicks of La Verme and West Baily. Coming down the road on foot at a trot, was a party of men led by John. The Brookers were trapped between us.

I signalled for John to stop them but before he could work out what I meant, the fugitives had plunged into the forest again.

Our two groups merged where Edith and Edmund had disappeared.

"We heard the horn, sir, and knew something was amiss."

"The Brookers," I said quickly, "No time to explain. We must catch them. I think they are trying to reach the downs at the other side of West Baily."

We flung ourselves into the trees and fanned out. The Brookers were not following any particular path but just darting between the trees, wherever they could find a space.

John knew every inch of this forest, every track and short cut, every lane and animal trail.

He signalled to me that we should move north and try to reach the lane which ran from Cadley to East Kennet. This lane eventually led to the Shaftesbury Road. It would be much quicker than zigzagging through the forest, as the Brookers were forced to do, and we should be out of the trees faster than our quarry. I nodded and whistled the company to follow. The forest here was dense and difficult to negotiate. We were snagged by brambles, tripped by writhing roots and hindered by impenetrable clumps of prickly holly. A shout on our left flank said that one of our number had seen the Brookers and we forged forward. Then suddenly there was a yelling and neighing of horses. Voices, angry and insistent, floated back to us. We heard the trampling of hooves through undergrowth. Ahead was the small path which led from Cadley to East Kennet.

Through the trees we could see shapes coming and going, disappearing and reappearing. Our line reached the lane and when we turned into the open space, we signalled to each other that the two pursuing groups were all present and correct. I saw a shape disappear around the bend in the road ahead.

A little way along the lane was a party of horses. These were my stable lads and grooms returning from exercising the beasts out on the downs. Five horses milled around, their riders trying to calm them. I saw Bayard with Ben, Bill his brother on Fenrir, leaning at his neck, whispering in his ear, trying to pull him away from a man on the floor. Another lad was leaning over the stricken groom.

Cedric moaned and writhed on the flinty floor of the lane and Johannes was there in an instant.

The lad Ben, looked down at him. I heard him say, "No, no knife sir. He was pushed off and has wrenched his shoulder." Ben saw me running up and dismounted.

"Sir, take Bayard, take him, Brooker has taken Fitzroy!"

"Go, Aumary," said Johannes. "The lad has dislocated his shoulder. He will be all right in a moment."

I vaulted into the saddle, turned Bayard's head and was off up the road. John and some of the other search party followed me on the other horses and on foot.

I heard Cedric yell as Johannes pulled his shoulder back into place and a sigh of relief escaped from my lips. Cedric would be sore for a while, but he would not die of it.

"What happened, Bill?" I shouted, over the noise of several hooves pounding on the chalky surface.

"We were riding back to the manor m'lord, when, on the road in front of us, we saw Edith Brooker waving and yelling at us. As we slowed and came level with her, her brother leapt out from the bushes and lifted Cedric from the saddle by his stirrup. He fell over the other side of the horse, off Fitzroy, and Brooker jumped up onto Fitz, grabbed his sister and they rode off. It was all so quick, we had no idea what was happening."

"Brooker cannot ride. He has never learned. He will be floundering before long, especially with his sister riding pillion," I said. "Fitz will not be an easy horse to control, not for one who does not know what he is doing."

"No sir... we can only hope they fall off. Fitz is a very fast horse though. Not easy to outpace."

"Yes, that is so Bill, but he is a horse for short bursts of speed, for racing. Bayard here..." and I patted my horse's neck, "can outrun him over a distance, as long as Fitz is not too far ahead."

No, they were not too far ahead. We could see them urging the horse on. They were slithering and sliding in the saddle. Edmund had lost a foot from a stirrup. Edith was clinging onto him. Neither of them had ever sat upon a horse before. They had no idea how to make him go where they wished. Fitz would run where he wanted. He did just that. Fitz ran back into a gap between the trees, pulling on his head. He wasn't used to two riders, moreover two who gave him no instruction at all. We lost them for a short while in the undergrowth and then they reappeared in a mossy clearing at the edge of the trees.

Here the downs met the forest in a series of small coppices, glades and meadows. Ahead was a gradual but steep slope; a grassy bank of dips and mounds, an ancient hillside of ridge and furrow. The water ran off this hillside into the trees where it collected in small pools formed by the flint and clay capping on the chalk. There were several such pools in Savernake. Time had gouged some of them deep and centuries of fallen leaves and debris had made them muddy and in some cases, dangerous, boggy quagmires.

There was one such quagmire here. Forest folk called it The Hungry Pool, for it swallowed any animal unlucky enough to wander into it. I had lost sheep to it in the past and had prohibited my shepherds from allowing the flocks, pastured on the nearby hill, anywhere near it. Occasionally the drowned carcass of an unlucky beast would surface in a welter of bubbles and foul smelling fog, often perfectly preserved, as if the devil had coughed up one of his own, from Hell.

We could see Fitz heading for the part of the forest where lay The Hungry Pool.

Our quarry disappeared in the trees. We drew up and listened. Then plunged on again, but more carefully lest we suddenly find ourselves in the bog.

The afternoon was drawing on. Shortly, the light would begin to fade and we would need to be on firm ground if we were to stay safe. John, who had taken one of the horses from a groom to ride with me, pointed ahead. "The horse has stopped sir."

We could see Fitz pawing the ground and backing away snorting, his head tossing, the muscles under his coat rippling. As we drew closer we could see the whites of his eyes. He was afraid. I jumped down from Bayard and pushed my way through the bushes. Catching hold of Fitz' loose reins I looked round. No sign of the Brookers; then I heard the wailing.

A few feet ahead, Edith was on the ground screaming and yelling, frantically calling Edmund's name and on God to help him.

I drew level with her and could see that she was attempting to hold out her hand to her unfortunate brother who had gone head first into the mud of The Hungry Pool. Fitz had thrown Edmund over his head and Edith had fallen from his back as the horse had stopped abruptly.

Edmund floundered in the water, then sank and surfaced again. Edith was screaming "Help him... Oh help him. God, he will drown."

"Can he not swim?"

I was throwing off my cotte and looking round for a sturdy branch with which to reach the man in the black water.

I lay on my belly, testing the ground as I inched forward. John reached me and grabbed my boots.

"I've got you sir...you just reach for him."

Reach I did. I strained every muscle as I squirmed forward holding the branch out. Edmund patted the water, trying to catch the branch. Each attempt took him further out it seemed and further into the black slime. I leaned into the water, I ducked under the surface and came up spluttering. Shaking the water and mud from my eyes I tried again to reach him. He caught the very end of the branch but it broke off and he sank in the water again.

"Another better branch..." I cried turning my head over my shoulder. One was handed to me, I turned back to the pool. The man had gone.

Edith too had found a branch, but rather than use it to help her brother, she made for me, prone and helpless on the ground and hit me several times over the head with it. She was swinging for another swipe when John pushed her away and took the log from her and dropped it close to me.

Edith Brooker stumbled and starting to scream again, she waded into the pool. Several pairs of hands brought her back. Edmund surfaced again. The look on his face was one of pure horror. He saw his sister straining against the hands which held her. With the breath that was left in him, he cried out to her.

"Edith...say nothing, plead your belly...you must plead your belly! They cannot hang you...plead your belly. Say nothing! Edith, I love you."

And then he was gone for the last time, slowly inch by inch, terribly in the back mud and water of The Hungry Pool.

I stretched out once more with the longer and more sturdy branch used to hit me but it was futile. I just stirred up the black water and began to sink into the mud myself.

John and Bill pulled me back. I lay for a while on the tufty grass at the edge of the pool, staring up at the sky, breathing hard and listening to the hysterical screaming of Edith Brooker, calling Edmund over and over. She was past caring about anything now. There was no doubt, if we had allowed it, she would have followed her lover into the pool. John grabbed her roughly and pulled her towards his horse. He mounted and one of the grooms handed her up to him. He sat her before him and pinioned her with his two arms. She slumped, sobbing but passive now, all fight spent for the moment.

We abandoned Edmund to the belly of The Hungry Pool and made for home.

***

My head was throbbing by the time we reached Durley and I was seeing double. John secured the sobbing girl in the lockup whilst we sorted the horses and regrouped to exchange information. Johannes came striding across the courtyard, "Cedric is fine, dislocated shoulder. It will be painful for a while but he'll live." He took one look at me. "Oh...what happened to you?"

"Never mind. Get Walter and Henry up here. I want to talk to them."

Lydia came running down the steps. "Oh, Aumary....what is happening? I can't get any sense....." Her eyes widened as she saw the damage to the side of my head, made by two swipes of a large and heavy branch and the mud and blood caking my tunic.

"Oh... no."

"Don't worry, Lydia," said Johannes, "I can patch him up."

I was wet, cold and dizzy, and had to be helped up the manor steps. There sitting at the top table of the hall, I succumbed to the ministrations of my beloved and my friend the doctor with little complaint. I eased a new shirt and tunic over my damaged head.

I was wincing at the pain of Johannes binding my head when Henry the steward and Walter Reeve came into the hall and bowed.

"I want you to call everyone to the hall...I don't care where they are, or what the time is. EVERYONE... do you hear me? NOW! Village, nearer forest and manor. Everyone. And the gate is to be locked"

Walter and Henry looked at each other and turned on their heels.

***

In the two hours or so it took to marshall everyone into the hall, I went to the lock up with Johannes and Hal and asked the doctor to look over our captive to make sure that she was all right. She may have been a felon, but her unborn child was not and she had taken a tumble from Fitz. This was what Edmund had cried out to her as he sank into the mud, that she was to 'plead her belly.' A woman who was found guilty of a crime and was destined to hang, could stave off the day of reckoning by pleading the fact that she was pregnant. It was a crime to kill an unborn child, even that of a self-confessed criminal. Edith sat staring into space and would not answer any question put to her. In the end Johannes shrugged and bent over her to pick up her wrist to feel the throb of her pulse.

As quick as a darting minnow, she slashed out at him with her other hand, raking his cheek with her nails and drawing blood.

Hal, who was guarding the door, leapt forward. "Now then you little strumpet, you keep yer 'ands to yerself!" Edith turned her attentions to him. Hal was having none of it and he pivoted her quickly with a gentle swipe and pinned her to the bench on which she had been sitting.

"Can we ask Agnes to get some clean, dry and warmer clothing for Edith please, Hal?"

"Aye, sir. Though she don't deserve it. She'd send a bolt right through yer with 'er eyes she would, jus' by lookin' at yer, if she could."

I waited a heartbeat or two. Johannes held his hand to his face.

"Go and see to that, Johannes. Hal and I will manage." I shifted my feet and folded my arms.

"You struck your lord in the forest, Edith; just for that you can hang."

"I don't care."

"No, I know you don't. You cared about nothing but Edmund, did you?"

Her tear stained face came up to look at me at that.

"He was my brother. I loved him."

"He was more than your brother, Edith. He was your lover and the father of the child you carry."

Her eyes filled with tears and she sobbed quietly again.

"Edith. I have to know. Do you know that Dysig is your brother?"

She almost laughed at that. She swiped her nose on her sleeve.

"Aye, my brother. My half-brother. One so ugly and stupid and the other so beautiful and clever. Why is it that the beautiful, clever one is dead?"

"Did you kill Meg the poultry girl?"

"Why would I do that?"

"Because she was, as you said yourself, besotted with your brother, and you could not bear it that I might make Edmund marry her because he had been tupping her all along."

She laughed then, "Marry her? Never!"

"As your lord I could command it. She admitted that they had slept together on several occasions."

"He would have denied it. You would never have made him marry her."

"It was good ruse, a clever cover to have Edmund fall in love with the girl, whilst you two were..."

Edith sniggered. "Stupid little bitch."

"And your play acting, how you hated your brother, how you would, in everyone's hearing, belabour him and argue with him, throw things at him and call him from hill to burn."

Her eyes watched me under fair brows, like a feral cat. She tossed back her long fair hair, which had come loose from its plait.

Into my head came Harry Glazer's words, words he'd spoken to me the day we saw him in town and he told us about his father and his new wife.

"They had pretended not to like each other for so long. My father always used to call her a saucy wagtail...."

No wonder I had felt uncomfortable when I heard this tale.

"But all the time you were lovers and lived together as man and wife in that little cottage of yours. All the while sleeping together in one bed. The upstairs loft was not used, was it?"

Edith shrugged.

"You tell me...you are so clever. Where is your evidence?"

"The little bell on the garden gate. That was to alert you when someone approached too closely. It was a cue for you to start to argue and fight, when all the time you were embracing and caressing. You make me sick, Edith."

She smiled, showing perfect white teeth.

"Show me your boot."

"What?"

"Right foot."

She blinked then. Hal bent down and tore the small boot from her foot, almost without her realising he had done it.

"I shall take this and compare it to the print of mud I found on the back of Meg the poulterer's dress, when she was held down in the mud at the Salley Gardens to choke and die. I think we'll find it will match this boot."

Edith shrugged again. "I don't care."

"Now we come to the night the priest died."

"I was asleep in my bed, after he had brutally..."

"No, Edith, that is a lie. You were at his house organising his death with your brother. Swithun knew that you and Edmund were lovers. He had been spying on you both for quite a while. It was easy for you to put into the heads of simple folk like the washer woman that he was watching them. All the time he was watching you. Not because he wanted carnal knowledge of you, as you say. No. Swithun was true to his vows on that score. He did not rape you... ever. That night you were not recovering as Edmund claimed. You were murdering Swithun."

Hal's face was ashy white with shock. His mouth opened and shut like a landed fish and his long grey beard wagged.

"What... this little shrew? Kill the priest?"

"With her brother's help... yes."

"Well, me brain must be soft fer I never ever thought... Edmund... maybe but...."

"No, Hal, not Edmund. Edith." I sighed. "Lock her up again. We shall have more speech with her later. Let Agnes in to see her but watch her carefully, please. Remove anything she can use as a weapon."

As we crossed the manor courtyard, the starlings were massing for their evening display, wheeling over the forest and dropping one by one into the trees below. I looked up at the sky; it was dark, grey and forbidding.

Everyone was now crowded into the manor hall. Some sitting on the floor, others leaning against the walls. The benches were full of the old and infirm. The children were kept close and quiet by anxious parents. Even the dais had been called into use as a bench, for folk sat on the edge and dangled their feet.

Lydia; Johannes, now cleansed and salved, Walter, Henry, Crispin and John were sitting on the chairs and stools on the dais.

I walked into the hall with Hal at my heels and all who could, rose to their feet. I saw Cedric by the hall door, his arm in a sling and called to him. He bowed carefully

"I am fine m'lord...really."

I smiled at him then stood on the dais and filled my lungs.

"Sit!" Those who could, sat. It seemed like just one movement. There was silence.

"I have called you all here today, to bear witness to the crimes committed on this, my Manor of Durley. This evening I will show you all how the murder of Swithun the priest, Meg the poultry girl, Hamon Deerman the forester, the attempted murder of Agnes Brenthall, the attack on Dysig and the death of one other; how all these things were achieved and I will ask many of you, on oath, to tell me your part in the story, for I know that some of you are involved and I will have the truth."

I saw several people shifting their feet and looking at the floor. No, I thought, I do not have this wrong. I am right. Plough on.

"Crispin, will you please fetch the Belvoir Bible from its box in the chapel."

Crispin jumped up and threaded his way through the throng, to the chapel stairs. He had to step around the folk who were using them as sitting places.

"Many of you disliked the priest. A few of you hated him. I, for one, did not see eye to eye with him and before his murder, had asked the bishop, that he be removed from the village and another priest be sent in his place. I did not intend that he be killed."

I moved my eyes slowly over the assembly. Some would not meet my gaze. Others looked at me and then at their feet. Some looked blank. A few of them glanced at their neighbour or family member with a worried expression.

"However, he was not killed because the person who murdered him, hated him. This is what we were led to believe." There was a muttering at that.

"Silence!" shouted Walter Reeve. "Listen to the lord."

"The fact that he was so despised was very fortuitous and was useful to the murderer, for it muddied the water sufficiently to send us off on false trails and lead us astray nicely. So firstly, we have the fire in the priest's room. This was caused deliberately to destroy the descent rolls kept there. What was there in those rolls which was so awful that it must be kept a secret? Who would kill to keep the information contained in those pages, from becoming well known? Swithun had looked through those rolls and had discovered something, in fact several somethings, which he thought was so wicked; wicked enough to be brought out into the open and punishment meted out. We did not know that this was why he was killed. To keep him quiet." I stopped and watched as folk looked at each other and shook their heads or muttered to their neighbours.

"I want a show of hands. Who knew that Dysig was the bastard son of Arnulf Brooker and his own daughter Herleva?"

The question caught many people unawares. They gasped, sighed or blinked; they looked up, they glanced at their neighbours, some mouthed the word 'incest'. A few fought to keep their hands down.

"A show of hands NOW!" Six people put up their hands. Another three followed them until, I counted quickly, about thirteen people had hands in the air, including Hal of Potterne and Old Joan.

"Thank you. So, this was not common knowledge but it was known to some. It was not known to me and I am the law in the forest. It was known to Benedict the priest obviously, for it was he who wrote in the descent roll almost as an after-thought, once Arnulf and Herleva were dead, the fact that they had produced an incestuous child."

I saw Old Joan draw Dysig close to her as some villagers and forest folk, who were obviously unaware of this fact until this moment, made the sign against the evil eye and gave Dysig strange looks.

"The fact must have been a secret for quite a while, for Benedict, who knew much of what went on in the village, seemed unaware for years that Herleva and Arnulf were living in an incestuous relationship, years after her mother disappeared." Again there was a rustle of whispers.

"How many of you knew at the time, that this was so?"

No one put up their hands.

"No one?"

They just stared up at me blankly.

"It was thought, was it not, that Herleva had become pregnant by a village man who would not, or could not, own up?"

There were several noddings of heads.

"Or that it was another man from the town perhaps?"

More noddings and blank looks.

"I have a suspicion that Herleva also, shall we say, entertained another man from Marlborough and in that Swithun was correct. When I look at the Brookers, I also see Harry Glazer, the cordwainer's apprentice of Marlborough town. That is why Swithun thought as he did, that Harry was the bastard mentioned in the descent rolls. He was wrong. It was Dysig. He believed Herleva was mother and sister to Dysig and mother to Edmund and Edith. Dysig's father was Herleva's own, Arnulf. The Brooker twins were I think however, fathered by Perkin Glazer on Arnulf's daughter Herleva when she was but thirteen. Even in such a small place as Durley, there can be secrets."

I vowed to myself I would go to Marlborough and have words with Perkin Glazer and I would tell Harry that his despised father was just that, and his beloved mother was indeed, as he had hoped, his birth mother.

The crowd in front of me grew silent and wary.

"So now we come to the murder of the priest."

I cleared my throat.

"Swithun had made enemies of several people."

I turned to the steward of my manor who was sitting on a stool behind me.

"You, Henry, you truly hated the priest and cursed him with twenty knife blows." Henry paled and shuffled his feet. My eyes sought out his mother on a bench at the long table.

"You, Margaret, hated him for he caused the death of your younger son." She looked away.

"You, Matthew, you threatened to kill him for the secret he had discovered about your past." Matthew opened his mouth and was about to speak but Walter Reeve put up a hand and he fell silent. I saw Matthew's wife, Edgiva, sitting some way away, their small son on her knee, turn on her bench and look at him.

My eyes roamed around the hall. "You, Fulke, and you Ralf, had reason to hate Swithun, for he would not bury your grandchild and child in hallowed ground in Durley, and had refused her baptism."

Fulke's head came up to confront me. "Aye, 'tis so. We did. I cannot deny it."

My gaze swung to Mat Fisher, sitting with his wife and their three children.

"And you, Mat you too had reason to dislike him for the information he discovered, or thought he had discovered, in the manor roll."

Mat was the confident sort. "That is true, but it don't mean I killed him for it."

"No..it's true, it doesn't." He nodded as if my agreement was the end of it all.

"And then there was you, Joan...you disliked Swithun for you thought that he was peeping at you and your friends when you were at your work by the stream, in the Salley Gardens. He frightened you. Your husband Robin threatened him with violence, I believe."

"Aye, but he never...."

"Robin, where are you?" The man detached himself from the wall under the hall windows.

"Here m'lord." He walked forward.

"Did you make good your threat; did you kill Swithun the priest?"

The man licked his lips.

"No sir. I did not kill him."

Crispin jumped back up onto the dais with the Bible in his hand and laid it reverently on the table in front of me.

"How many others had a grievance against Swithun…even you Agnes?"

She had just returned from the lock up and ministering to Edith Brooker, with my two men at arms and was standing almost in the passage at the back of the hall.

"Even you had a reason to dislike him, for he refused your mother burial in the churchyard here."

" 'Twas your intervention put that right, sir, so there was no need to be killing him because of it."

People craned their neck to see Agnes, raising her voice to reach me at the dais end of the hall.

I sought out Peter Brenthall who was sitting with his back to me on the edge of the dais, swinging his feet. He jumped as I called his name. "Even you, Peter, fell foul of the man and must have felt a grudge against him, for the way he treated you when you tried to protect my old hound Alceste from a kicking." Peter turned with an open mouth and blinked. "He beat you, did he not, and humiliated you?" Peter nodded.

"How many others would have liked to have killed the man, or at the very least give him a beating? Come…be honest. How many of you had fallen into his clutches? How many of you did he annoy with his uncompromising attitude and his nastiness?"

Folk looked round at their neighbours. They saw Hal of Potterne put up his hand immediately. "I 'ated the bugger," he said. "Coulda' given him a slap or two…but murder…no."

More people began to put up their hands. In the end, there were forty or so hands in the air.

"Good. Thank you for your honesty." I paused and looked at the sea of faces in front of me.

"You are good people. In the main you are loyal folk, faithful to your families and friends and to me, your lord. You are kind, tolerant people who respect the church and its representatives, who confess your sins freely and accept your penances with good grace. However, you have not taken lightly those miscarriages of justice, as you see them, those slights and hurts meted out to you all by Swithun the priest."

Many folk now were becoming visibly worried by my words and the looks they exchanged told several stories.

"Who have I left out of the list of people who were bothered by Swithun the priest? Who was it who conceived this little charade connected with his death? Whose idea was it that vengeance might be taken but that no one person might be responsible for his death, as you see it?"

I turned to Hal and called my two men at arms.

"Hal, Stephen, Peter, fetch the Brooker girl here but make sure you bind her."

I leaned over the chair to Johannes.

"Can you fetch Meg's dress from my chest in the office, Johannes? Here are the keys. I have the shoe here." It lay on the table before me.

I turned back to the hall. "I will now tell you all, what happened."

"Step forward John Kellog," I said.

John the butcher, looking bemused and a little self-conscious, stepped to the dais from his place at the fireside and looked up at me.

"John, you have a new apron, do you not? A leather one. You use this to protect your clothes when you slaughter our beasts here in Durley, a task you do about this time of year, every year?"

"And at other times too sir. But yes, I do, at this time of year, so that we might salt down the meat, or smoke it, for the winter."

"Where do you keep this apron?"

"Everyone knows that I keep it on a peg in my outhouse."

"You have not used it this year?"

"No sir, as you said, 'tis a new'un and..."

"And yet, it's bloodstained. Can you explain that?"

"In a word sir, no."

"Thank you, John."

He wandered back to the fire place.

Once more, I addressed the room.

"We searched the village for bloodstained clothes, for when Swithun was murdered there was much blood and whoever killed him would have been covered in gore. John the butcher's apron was used by the killer to protect their clothing and so we did not and will not find any clothing which will point us towards one man or woman." There was a general shuffling and murmuring and I heard John say to his son, "Well I'll be damned, 'twas the priest's blood." When the noise had died down, I raised my voice again.

"Dysig...Dysig... can you come up here to me. Don't be afraid. Agnes will come with you."

Agnes led the quaking man to the dais and I gave him a hand and pulled him up beside me. With my arm around his shoulder I carried on.

"Dysig is a very brave man." People looked at each other as if to say, "the Lord has gone mad." I saw Johannes return with Meg's dress.

"Dysig saw the murdererer of Swithun the priest from outside the door of his cottage. Hamon Deerman also saw the murderer, but unlike Dysig, he recognised them properly. The murderer saw both Dysig and Hamon and frightened them both into keeping quiet.

Dysig has kept faith, haven't you, my boy?"

"Aye. Aye, Dysig have."

"Hamon was killed because the murderer thought that he was getting too jittery, that he was about to tell me everything. That is so, isn't it Beatrix?"

Beatrix, Hamon's wife, was sitting on the large bench with her older children either side and the smallest on her knee.

"He told me he had seen something but that he was going to say nothing, for what was the priest to us anyway and the village was better off without him."

"He was warned with an arrow fired at him from the forest, by Edmund Brooker. An arrow which purposely missed its mark. However, it just served to make Hamon more worried. Was he coming to speak to me that day, the day he died, to tell me what he knew, Beatrix?"

"Aye sir he was. He said that you would protect him...us." She began to weep. "He was going to bring Dysig too and make him tell what he knew. I think that is why he was in his bothy."

"I am truly sorry I was not able to protect you all, Beatrix. Do you know what he was going to tell me?" Beatrix sobbed into her apron. Her eldest, Gerald, put his arm around her shoulder.

"No sir..." she said. "He said if we didn't know anything, we couldn't be in danger."

Out of the corner of my eye I saw Ackerman, the man I had set to watch Hamon, shifting his feet and looking very guilty.

"So Dysig, tell everyone what you saw. You are the only one now who knows."

Dysig looked up at me. I was a good head taller than the man. "Oh no... no..."

I whispered in his ear. He nodded.

"Dysig has given me permission to tell you all that he saw and that if I am wrong, he will shout out and put me right."

There was a laugh. Whenever was a half-wit allowed to 'put' right' the lord of the manor?

I strengthened my grip on his shoulder.

"Outside the priest's cottage when it was very dark... it was very dark, wasn't it Dysig, and no moon?"

"No, no moon."

"Outside were some shapes which Dysig thinks were demons." A small snigger went around part of the room and died.

"Dysig thought this because they were dressed from head to foot in black, or at the very least in dark colours and they were hooded. You couldn't see any faces could you Dysig?"

"No, no faces but eyes..."

"Yes, shiny eyes."

I could see people looking at each other. Some were becoming really worried now.

"Yes... yes..."

"One of the shapes was dressed differently, wasn't it Dysig?"

"Yes... it was an angel."

"And it was this angel which told you to keep quiet and that you would be safe."

"It whispered to Dysig... yes. It was all white."

There was a commotion at the door and Edith Brooker was brought in by Hal. Everyone moved out of the way to allow her to walk up the hall. Her hands were tied before her and she wore clean and dry clothes. A pale blue dress faded somewhat to pale grey and a pale grey cloak. I had instructed Agnes to fetch the lightest coloured clothes the woman possessed.

Dysig dived behind me and shivered as he whispered, "It's the angel."

The light in the hall was good. We had lit every rushlight in the sconces on the walls. Some light, but very little, was filtering through the windows, the firelight flickered and candles had been lit on every table and surface. Above the high table was a wheel in which were several beeswax candles. The woman who had just entered, although she was not wearing white, seemed pale in the candlelight. Her hair which was blonde white, had been plaited again and hung down her back. I heard Lydia gasp as she saw Edith walking up the hall.

I turned to her, "Was it her?"

"Yes, it was, I think."

I nodded. Lydia had just identified the woman she has seen in the Salley Gardens committing incest with her brother Edmund.

"Edmund Brooker is dead."

The room rippled with astonishment. Few people as yet knew the story of the pursuit of the Brookers into the forest and Edmund's death in The Hungry Pool.

"He died accidentally, by drowning in The Hungry Pool in the forest, trying to escape with this woman, his sister." People shifted about, whispering.

Edith walked to the dais and stared ahead.

"Edith, tell me if this is true. You and your brother were living in your cottage as man and wife."

The room erupted. Some laughed in disbelief, knowing that the woman was a veritable virago and that she hated her brother vehemently.

"I will say nothing."

"Then I will, for I do have evidence and can prove what I say."

I handed the quivering Dysig back to Agnes.

"For many years, the Brookers, in their isolated little cottage by the stream, had been carrying on an incestuous relationship. The shouting and the scream-ing, the fights which we all heard, all over the village, were but a clever ruse to make us all think that they hated one another. They had a small bell fitted to the gate which would warn them when someone was close and they could set up their bickering again."

"Aye… aye they did," said my blacksmith… "I made it for them."

"And cease their… well whatever it was they were doing.

Swithun had his suspicions, because he had read in the descent rolls, that the family had indulged in incest before. Dysig's mother and father were father and daughter. Edith and Edmund themselves, were the product of a relationship between a man not of this village, and this incestuous and immoral woman."

The hall became a seething mass of moving people talking to each other, gesturing, appalled, disbelieving.

"Quiet!" Walter banged the floor with his staff and all became silent again.

"Swithun began to watch the pair down by the Salley Gardens. You, Joan, thought that he was watching you. In fact, he was hiding himself so he could spy on the Brookers."

Joan's hand flew to her mouth and her eyes locked with her husband's. He visibly paled.

"Edith Brooker is about four months with child; a child fathered by her own brother."

Whispering set up again and was stilled by a bang from Walter's staff.

"Agnes knew this. Edith and Edmund had to do something and so were claiming that this child was the result of a rape by Swithun the priest. We knew this could not be so. Agnes was pushed down the kitchen stairs by Edith who was angry with her for knowing the truth and for telling me. Nothing more complicated. Anger. That is so, isn't it, Edith?"

The woman was silent.

"Edmund carried on an affair with the poultry girl Meg. This was to throw any suspicion away from the brother - sister relationship. If Edmund was courting Meg... then all was well, was it not? Meg loved Edmund, and trusted him and gave him an alibi for the night of the murder of the priest. Sadly, this woman in front of me here, became jealous. I also think that she began to be concerned that Meg was getting worried about the lies she had told and so, Edith Brooker lured Meg to the bank of the stream and pushed her face into the mud and killed her. She then hid the apron which Meg had left in the Brooker cottage, in the thatch of her loft."

Those closest to Edith drew away, and there was an indrawn breath from many mouths.

"Here I have Meg's dress, the dress she wore that day. This is Edith's boot." I held up the two and fitted one onto the other.

"They match. Edith held Meg down with two hands and there were bruises on her upper arms. They too would match the small hands of Edith Brooker." I threw the boot back to her. "Put it on, Edith. You can manage that even if you are tied."

Edith smiled as I watched her put on the boot. She is mad, I thought. We cannot hang her anyway for she is not in her right mind.

I lifted Meg's cap and showed the room.

"The poultry girl went into the water by the Brooker's cottage and she floated down- stream. Her cap became caught much nearer to her point of entry into the river. I found it there. Edmund told me that he had just been talking to Meg a moment before we found the body. That cannot have been the whole truth, for he was fishing at the other end of the stream and her body must have passed him as he fished. Is it likely he did not see it?"

I shook my head.

"He was genuinely upset about Meg. I saw that. It was then, I think, that he realised his sister had killed her. Edmund was the one, I suspect, who poured oil into the church window to destroy the manor rolls. He did not want anyone working out what had happened in his family - was still happening in his family. Swithun had seen the pages. He had seen the Brooker's behaviour and had come to his own conclusion. He had to die."

Chapter Nine

"What Edmund did not know, was that I myself had removed four of the rolls from the priest's room. I took them to my office for safe keeping before the fire. What made me do that, I have no idea. It was just a feeling I had, that they were important."

I noticed that I had Edith's attention now. "Yes Edith, you failed, after all, to conceal the facts about your family you so wanted to keep quiet, for I read the rolls. I called in Crispin the priest who read them and interpreted the Latin for us, for Dr. Johannes, Lady Lydia and myself. Naturally you could not read, so you did not actually know what was in those pages, but, perhaps in the past Benedict the priest had intimated that there was something important in them and so you knew that anyone who could read, might discover your sordid history, as Swithun did. That is why you searched his coffin. Just in case he had anything with him which might incriminate you. This might have been found when Swithun was lowered into his grave at Salisbury. Maybe if Benedict had not been as ill as he was, he too would have gone the same way as Swithun. A knife to the heart. As it was he slipped away from you and died of a liver disease. He was the only person who knew where the evidence of your family's sins lay... until Swithun."

People were pressing together now, away from the woman before me as if close contact with her might taint them in some way.

"Widow Giffard, can you step forward please?"

Emilia Giffard pushed through the throng on the floor in front of me and stood beside Edith.

"On the evening of the murder of Swithun, you had brewed some new ale and were selling it to manor folk, were you not?"

"Yessir, that's right. I did."

"Can you describe to me the people coming and going from your house at that time? Just as you told me a day or so ago. Those people we discussed before."

The widow swallowed and looked round at her neighbours.

"There will be no repercussions, Emilia, I promise."

The woman bobbed a curtsy and began her tale.

"Walter the Reeve came before it was fully dark and stayed till after supper, until the ale ran out."

I smiled. "Yes, I know that. He was there as a peacekeeper, just in case of drunken trouble."

The widow Giffard smiled and nodded.

"Early on, Henry the steward came. He spoke to Edmund Brooker outside the cottage. He drank a pot and was gone."

"Step forward Henry, stand here please." I gestured to the floor in front of me, below the dais. Henry reluctantly jumped down from the dais and stood dangling his hands uselessly.

"Then when it was fully dark, the two Sylvestres came. Father and son. They stayed a while. The son went first, as his wife came to fetch him." The room smiled at that for it was known that Edwina ruled her husband wholly, in thought and deed.

"Then the elder one went for a while. I thought he had gone to the privy. He came back a while later and he drank till he could drink no more."

"Step up here please, Fulke and Ralf. And Edwina and Mistress Sylvestre too. Stand here by Henry."

The Widow Giffard tucked a stray curl back under her wimple. "Yes, then Mat Fisher came in and he too talked to Edmund and they disappeared. Edmund stayed in the garden I think, for I could not see him and he didn't enter the house, and folk got him drink for I filled his cup just a couple of times. I know that one, see... a wooden one with the mark of a little river round the rim."

"Here too please, Mat Fisher." I gestured to the man to come and stand with Henry.

"Go on."

"Fisher came back too. He was very shaky and I thought he had had too much to drink already but 'twas not so when I think about it now. He was just shaking. Joan's Robin. He talked to Edmund outside too. They seemed to be arguing but after a while, he too came back into the cottage for more ale. He looked very pleased with himself."

I did not ask Robin to come forward for he was already walking towards the group I had collected under the dais.

"Thank you, Emilia. You are most observant. I see you have been thinking hard since our conversation of the other day."

"Aye, sir. Then there was Hamon..."

"Hamon was with you for a while?"

"He was, sir, though he too argued with the Brooker boy and after a sip or two of his ale was gone."

I heard Beatrix say.

"If it please you m'lord...." I looked over the sea of heads at her.

"Hamon came home without really sampling the Mistress Giffard's ale. He said then that he would not stay a moment longer. I think it was when he was coming home that he saw what was happening at the priest's house."

I nodded.

"I think you are right, Beatrix. And I also think that Brooker approached your husband with evil in his heart and Hamon rebuffed him."

I lifted my voice a notch. "Now we come to the part played by Edmund Brooker."

I saw Edith's eyes narrow. She would be listening very carefully to this.

"We have already established that the Brookers did not wish their relationship to become common knowledge, for incest is a mortal sin and it is also against the law of the land. For this you can be hanged.

Brooker borrowed the apron that night from the butcher. He knew it would not be discovered for quite a while. A little while earlier when he knew that Swithun was out by the Salley Gardens, he stole a knife from the priest's house, a broad bladed knife which had belonged to Swithun's brother who is a knight. The priest Swithun himself, had stolen this knife from his despised brother many years ago and he had secreted it away somewhere. How Brooker knew it was there I do not know... Edith?"

She remained silent.

"Very well. Now we have the weapon and the apron to protect the murderers from the blood. When it was almost dark, Edmund hid the two items near to Swithun's house. He then went to the Widow Giffard's ale tasting and was seen there in the yard, talking and drinking ale with others in the village."

I looked down at Henry. "Henry Steward, come up here."

Henry looked at me under his fine pale brows and then jumped up.

"I asked you, when first investigating this murder, for you had the most urgent need of revenge upon Swithun, if you murdered the priest or if you had seen the knife before. Your answer was?"

"No sir, I did not kill the priest."

I nodded to Crispin who said in a clear voice.

"Please place your hand upon the Bible and tell the truth to your lord, at the peril of losing your immortal soul."

Henry had done this before and it did not bother him.

His hand went down quickly. What he did not expect was the next question nor the form of it. I spoke loud and clear.

"Henry Pierson, had you seen the knife depicted in my drawing before and did you strike the priest Swithun of Attwood with that knife on the night he died?"

Henry looked up. His face filled with blood. His hand came up from the book, it hovered over the Bible, then he lowered it and said,

"Yes I had. Aye, I did." Margaret Manton jumped up from her seat. Hands pulled her down again.

"Did you strike the priest twice on the right breast?"

Henry took a deep breath. "Yes, I did. One for me and one for my mother."

I saw Margaret lower her face into her hands.

The whole room erupted into cries and wails. Walter had difficulty bringing order to the gathering but at last it was quiet.

"It was all a matter of the form of the words, wasn't it, Henry? You did not lie. You did not kill Swithun. You had not seen the drawing of the knife before. You may stand down now."

"Fulke Silvestre - come up here."

The man walked slowly and silently around the people crowding the dais and up the side steps. Crispin repeated his form of words.

Fulke placed his hand on the Bible and in a loud voice which carried right to the back of the room and beyond, said, "I too struck Swithun the priest with a knife, on the right breast but I did not kill him."

His son was already beside him and the moment his father's hand went from the Bible, his own slapped down upon the cover.

"I struck Swithun the priest with the knife. He was alive when I left him, upon the word of God."

Ralf's wife came running up the steps and grabbed his arm.

"I too struck him, though I was sore afraid and I did but pierce his belly a little."

People were looking round now to see who else was moving towards the dais. Ralf's mother came to the front of the crowd.

"The man was an ogre and suffered for his sins. Yes, I too struck him with the same knife. He was alive when I left him."

Mat Fisher, did not move but shouted,

"I too donned the butcher's apron and struck the priest. I wished that I had given him his death blow, but no. I made him suffer."

I looked over the crowd. Peter remained silent, standing by his mother and between John and Dysig.

"Peter, did you strike the priest with a knife?"

"No sir."

"Agnes....did you?"

"No sir."

"Matthew?"

"On my oath, no m'lord."

"I did sir," said Robin, Joan the laundress' husband. "Now I feel terrible for it was not as we thought. He was not trying to hurt my Joan. Oh God help me."

"Thank you Robin. There were twenty blows. Henry struck two, each of the others, one.

We have so far, seven blows. Will anyone else own up to striking a blow? Not a mortal blow, but a hurtful stab by way of revenge on a hateful priest?"

Mat Fisher folded his arms over his belly. "I struck twice, one for me and one for my wife, sir." Matt's wife was sitting absolutely still, her mouth open in shock. Then she shook herself and said, "Mat Fisher, why ever did you do that? Can I not do my own dirty work?"

Mat didn't turn to face her but said, "I struck him, that filthy canker of a man for what he said about you, my sweetheart. I would not have him say such things. Wicked things." He cleared his throat as if he were about to burst into tears.

"Anyone else? I do not need to know what it was that Swithun had done to you. I just need to know who struck him."

Four more folk put up their hands One of my grooms; Plum, my dog man who was also a huntsman and two foresters.

A ripple went around the room and then, as if by common consent, one after another, folk raised their hands, admitted they had struck him. One after another, after another. There were many more blows struck than Swithun had sustained that night.

I rubbed my aching forehead. On went the confessions.

"ENOUGH!"

I sat down heavily on my chair.

"I can see what you are all doing."

The room slipped into silence.

"The final blows, two of them, were struck by Edmund and his sister and these two are the blows which killed the priest. Am I right, Edith?"

She chuckled then, an inhuman laugh, low and merry.

"I struck him several times. I enjoyed every blow. Then I slipped the knife up into his black heart. I gave the knife to Edmund and he made sure the priest was dead."

"Does this sound to you, Johannes, the sort of series of events which led to the death of Swithun?"

Johannes cleared his throat. "It does. He was struck several times, none of them were immediately mortal blows but they would have killed him naturally, had he been allowed to bleed to death as he most certainly would have done. No, he was finished by a blow to the heart just as Edith has said. She most certainly killed him."

I stood up again I don't mind admitting, a little shakily.

"Edmund Brooker planned this murder. He approached, in secret, every person who had a grudge against the priest. He asked if each one would like to strike a blow for the hurt done to them but these would not be killing blows and they would be struck in secret. Each person would be hooded and cloaked and would wear, for the short time they were in the room, the butcher's apron so that no blood would spurt onto them.

Their hands would be easy enough to cleanse, in the stream perhaps or a bowl of water, which could be thrown out onto the earth and no one would ever know." I saw in my mind's eye, Agnes with the overflowing pot in Dysig's bothy and knew that this was indeed how each person had purged their hands of the blood of the priest.

"The attack was secret, except in the case of the Sylvestres, who knew each other had struck a blow and kept silent.

"Dysig saw the attackers collecting, coming and going by the door. Each one hiding their face from their fellow attackers, probably with a cloth tied around the face so that only the eyes were visible. Only Edmund and Edith knew who the attackers were."

I looked down at Edith who was staring into space again.

"Edith, when the first blow was struck, Swithun was drunk, asleep on his bed. Did you strike the first blow and then realise that he would have to be bound for he would struggle against his attackers?"

Edith lifted her face as if she were dreaming.

"I struck the first and then Edmund the second blow. The bastard was writhing and yelling and we knew he would have to be bound should the rest of them be able to strike. We found some rope and tied him to the bed. We gagged him so his screams were lessened. Then in came Henry. Two blows. The noise of the music at Widow Giffard's masked the screams. Oh how I enjoyed those screams."

"And Hamon Deerman?"

"He was weak. I followed him into Dysig's bothy. Dysig was missing. I pushed him down onto the bed and I killed him with the chisel I took from the woodsmith, for Deerman said that he was going to explain to you how the killing had been done. We could not have that."

"Why did you use the chisel? Could you not have struck him with something else or..."

"I wanted the woodsmith to suffer for it."

"Why?"

Edith looked coyly at Alfred, who was standing by the kitchen door in full view of those in the body of the room.

"He rebuffed me... said I was an unnatural woman, too forward, too ardent. I was going to blame him for the child, once you had discovered that I could not have been raped by Swithun... but then, it came to me... I could blame him for the murder."

I watched a few of the manor folk, not involved in this fracas, make the sign of the cross, for they could not believe in such wickedness. Alfred Wood-smith simply shook his head.

"And Agnes... you pushed her down the stairs?"

"A pity she did not break her filthy neck, the witch!"

"And Dysig... you struck him with a branch?"

"Aye, to warn him to keep quiet."

Crispin, sat down heavily on the cushioned chair. "By God's Bones, Aumary, I have never heard anything like it."

"No one is guilty of murder, except the Brookers and Edmund has already gone to pay for his sins," said Johannes shaking his head. "Edith is guilty of murder but will plead her belly...what are we to do?"

I sighed and shook my head "Crispin?"

He blinked several times.

"We have several confessions, not to murder, but to wounding. We have the murderess who can stand trial when she has had her child. We have a whole village admitting to... God knows what." Crispin ran his hands through his hair. "I know not what to do for the best."

"Nor I..." I said wearily.

"Let us all depart now. Go to your homes, all of you. I will think on this and on the punishment I should by rights mete out to you all. Let Edith Brooker be confined to her house, under guard, until she gives birth then she will be transferred to the castle to await the justices, who will no doubt wish to hang her. Her child will stay here on the manor and I will have it cared for. It will be, after all, one of my villeins.

"However, I do think that the woman is not in control of herself. I think that her mind is damaged and has been for a very long time. I cannot say if the justices will hang her or find her mad and confine her somewhere for the rest of her natural days."

I saw Edith's eyes narrow at this. This was something she had not bargained for. I could see it was something she would have difficulty accepting.

"I am to be married tomorrow." I said.

I stretched out my hand to Lydia and she grasped it tightly as if I were going to float away from her.

"Let the village forget this for the day. After that....we shall see."

***

It was the strangest wedding you ever did see. The bridegroom, in his finery, was bound about the head and bruised in the face. One of the witnesses and family to the bride, Johannes, was scratched and his cheek was covered with a salve. There were several injuries, for Edith Brooker did not go to her cottage quietly that night, and bit Hal on the arm, tripped poor Crispin as, once in the house, he tried to take her confession, and he sprained his ankle trying to get away from her. She bit him too when he was helpless on the ground. I truly think the woman was deranged. Poor Cedric was bound in a sling from his fall from Fitz, and Peter of Devizes, who had gone to Hal's rescue, was hit on the head by Edith, two handed, bound as she was, with the old iron pot which had lain concealed in the cottage and he too was bandaged about the head. Agnes was still limping from her fall down the stairs and her bruises were as colourful as the forest trees.

Only Lydia looked radiant in a dress of dark blue silk sewn with seed pearls about the neck. My daughter Hawise wore a tawny gown with sleeves turned back with green and comported herself as a little lady, happy and smiling and full of fun.

The wedding took place at the church door and then in we all went to Mass. The village was quiet and somewhat contrite but they entered into the day well enough and all the planning made for a good day with food and drink for us all.

Towards the end of the day, tired and hurting from the beating I had taken the day before, I sat in my chair on the dais and beckoned to Henry to approach.

"Can you take some food from the feast to Edith, Henry? Take men with you. She has already brained a couple and bitten others. Arms' length... all right?"

"Aye sir."

He was back, very soon after. "She is gone, sir."

"Gone!"

Whilst the village was at the wedding, and the guards posted had been outside the gate watching the procession to and from the church, Edith had dug a hole in the back wall of her daub cottage with a sharp stone, had enlarged the hole up towards the thatch, pulled it out and had slipped through without anyone knowing. No one had seen her go, for we were all in the church. She could be anywhere in the village or in the forest, waiting to take revenge and folk crossed themselves in case she was lurking ready to do them harm.

***

She was in neither the village nor the forest. That evening, she was found by Stephen Dunn, my man at arms, partly submerged in the stream, in one of the larger pools. She wore the pale clothes in which she had dressed to murder Swithun, and which Dysig had said made her look like the angel from the painting in the church. Her fair hair was unbound and floated about her like weed.

We eventually pulled her out but she had been long gone. Life without her brother was too much to bear, it seems and I did not think she would take kindly to incarceration, somewhere the justices would decree, for the rest of her natural life. There was no doubt she had taken her own life and that of her unborn child, for she had found some ropes about the village, tied them around her to make pockets and filled her clothes with stones; those flinty rocks which lay about the field everywhere in Durley and the wider forest. She was a self-murderer, a suicide and as such was not allowed burial in the churchyard.

Our wedding night feast was a little marred by this event for everyone was jumpy and disturbed by her death. Some folk said she would walk for she was a troubled soul and had gone not to God in God's good time but had been taken by the Devil for his own ends.

A short while later, once the body of Edith Brooker had been recovered and the stones removed, a few of us were still milling about the bank of the stream by the old willows. Suddenly, there was a cracking sound and one of the old leaning sallows toppled gently over the bank and into the river, splitting in two. This was no doubt due to the disturbance of the bank. So many feet had trodden the mud that day. So many people had leaned out over the river and caught hold of the branches to anchor themselves, whilst the stone heavy body of Edith was reeled in. It was no surprise the tree had protested and had lost its hold on the shifting soil of the bank.

We watched as the river began to gouge a new course and buffet the lower branches of the fallen sallow.

Slowly and eerily a decaying bundle of materials disengaged itself from the remaining roots of the sallow still anchored to the soil. We peered into the bank. There, under the roots of the old willow, was a space which had been created some while ago, by the undercutting of the bank. Here the package had lain undisturbed, preserved in part by the dampness of the soil of the bank and the protecting cage of the tree roots.

The bundle floated out, turning and twisting. As it turned, the cloths wrapped around it began to unravel.

The men who had recovered the body of Edith Brooker and were now soaked to the skin, had a second soaking.

John Brenthall manhandled the strange bundle to the bank and it was gently lifted from the water and placed on the grass.

There was little left of Millicent Brooker, for Millicent it was. Hal peered carefully at the decayed corpse. Her hair was bright and still blonde, though as it dried it shrivelled and lost colour. He identified our missing villein from her hair and what was left of her clothes.

You remember that clothes were a passion for Hal of Potterne and he would remember such things. She always wore, said Hal, a little St. James of Compostella cockle shell, which someone had given her. It was a pilgrim's badge, though she had never been on pilgrimage; she had, in life, never left her village. It was a tawdry thing of base metal and she had pinned it to her dress. He unpinned it and gave the very rusty thing to me.

She had not packed up and left. The right hand side of her skull was caved in from a heavy blow. Johannes hunkered down and in the fading light, examined the skull. Yes, she had been murdered.

Another corpse for our little mortuary. Another corpse for the coroner to examine, another day. This time, we would not be able to discover the felon who committed this crime.

"Yes, Paul, I suspect it was Arnulf Brooker, but he was long gone and there was nothing to be gained by raking it all up like muck from a midden. We buried our little corpse, we consigned Edith to a lonely grave in the forest and Crispin wrote all of it in our descent roll for October 1204.

What's that?

Oh yes, you do like a ghost story, don't you? You think that the deranged Edith Brooker haunts the forest looking for her drowned lover? Remember that you have to go back through the forest to the priory in the fading light this evening. We mustn't frighten you. Hooooo. Ah well then. Write on young man."

Before we retired, as was our habit, Lydia and I stood on the top step of the manor house stairs, looking up at the sky. This was how the whole episode had begun. Lydia snuggled up to me.

"It was Edmund and Edith that Hawise and I stumbled upon the day we went blackberrying, Aumary. Had I known who they were I might have been able to tell you and then..."

"It would not have prevented the priest's death."

"No, but perhaps others."

"We cannot turn back time, Lydia. If that was the case, then I should turn back the wheel of time to the day I first saw you singing at Johannes' house. That was such a good moment for me."

Lydia smiled.

"For me too. Except when you burned your hand."

I laughed, "oh yes, silly man."

"You wouldn't want to go back to that."

"No, we must forge forward and do the very best we can, mustn't we?"

I turned to open the door more fully so that Lydia could precede me into the screens passage.

"Oh." Her hand tightened on my arm. "See... over there by the salleys," she whispered.

Turning back I followed her gaze, over the wall of the manor. In a gap between the buildings, the gatehouse and the barn could just be seen, in the moonlight, the stream and the nearer trees of the Salley Gardens, now almost denuded of their leaves. Hand in hand, what looked like two people, absorbed in themselves, floated over the grass. One was fair, the other dark. There was a certain luminous quality to them both. Whether that was the moonlight or something else, I could not say. I blinked. Yes, there was no doubt. Two people.

Lydia crossed herself quickly. I rubbed my eyes and looked again. They had gone but Lydia was still watching with an intensity born of disbelief.

"It's them... it is."

"Maybe..."

"They have gone into the water...into the stream together. I saw them go."

"Aye... they did. Both of them ended in water."

"Oh, Aumary....." She pressed herself up to me and buried her face. "Oh that I could be so out of love with the world that I would risk eternal damnation to be with the man I loved, even unto death."

"Would you not?" I jested.

But the moment was not really for jesting. We hastily closed and locked the door. Then we made our way slowly to bed for the first time as man and wife. I am ashamed to say, I fell fast asleep.

"Is it true? True, young man? Naturally it's true, we were all exhausted and we had all had a very trying few days and I had been bopped on the......

Oh...the ghost? Well... there you will just have to accept that in these tales of mine, I do not lie. No, Paul. I most certainly do not. Never."

GLOSSARY

Aumbry - A small cupboard in the wall of a church.

Benefit of Clergy - A provision by which clergymen could claim that they were outside the jurisdiction of the secular courts and be tried instead in an ecclesiastical court, where penalties were less harsh. Some other non-ecclesiastical folk took advantage of this ruling.

Bliaut - A roomy over garment worn by both sexes (but mostly women) and pleated to the waist or under the bosom in women.

Bothy - Small simple building often of daub and wattle, roofed with thatch and with a beaten earth floor.

Breeks - Type of trousers.

Buttery - Place where food is prepared when it comes from the kitchen prior to being served at the High table.

Chausses - Protective trousers often of mail but often referring to long 'stockings' made of fabric. These were tied at the waist.

Coppicing - The cutting back of trees, almost to the ground to produce new straight stems.

Cordwainer - A master shoemaker.

Coroner - The man appointed by the crown to deal with unexpected deaths. The coroner was the man who drew up the jury of twelve men to decide the cause of death and if need be, impose fines. Sometimes known as the crowner.

Cotte - A long sleeved or sometimes sleeveless shift or tunic. A coat.

Crucks house - A timber framed house built by bending two trees into an upended 'v'shape.

Deer Fence - A barrier erected around a plot of land in a forest to prevent deer from straying.

Demense - (Pronounced domain) Land belonging to and adjoining a manor house. Lord's estate.

Deodand - Some personal property, such as a horse or a spade, was considered a deodand whenever a coroner's jury decided that it had caused the death of a human being. In theory, deodands were forfeit to the crown, which was supposed to sell the chattel and then apply the profits to some pious use.

Farced - Stuffed

Firkin - A small cask formerly used for liquids, butter, or fish. A unit of liquid volume, usually 9 imperial gallons or about 41 litres

Fox and Geese - A medieval board game.

Freeman - A person not beholden to a Lord for his living. Not a tied peasant.

Journeyman - A man who has completed his training as an apprentice but has not yet achieved master state, by creating his masterwork. He works for a master.

Limner - A painter

Liturgy - Elaborate ritual of the church.

Lytch - Small gate often with a roof allowing access to the churchyard and where coffins might be rested.

Masterless Man - An outlaw

Matins - The first of seven Canonical hours of prayer often recited at midnight.

Minnows - Tiny little freshwater fish.

Oblate - A child given to the church as an offering, to become a novice

Pattens - wooden overshoes which elevate the foot above the muck and mud

Pollarding - A pollarded tree was pruned back drastically at the top, above the browse line, in order to protect the crop from grazing animals in areas where livestock had access to the trees.

Potage - A thick soup of grain and pulses and vegetables mostly.

Privy - Rudimentary toilet.

Reeve - An official elected annually by the serfs to supervise lands for a lord.

Rouncey - Ordinary all purpose horse.

Scrip - A purse worn on the belt.

Simfony - A musical instrument rather like a hurdy gurdy.

Solar - Generally on an upper storey, a room designed as the noble family's private living and sleeping quarters. The room was usually situated so that sunlight would be caught for the maximum amount of time in the day.

Strip - The small piece of land farmed by a peasant.

Supertunic - A short dress which goes over another often to show off the hem of the garment beneath worn by both sexes.

Surcoat - A sleeveless or sleeved garment which goes over another and often over mail.

Termagant - A violent, overbearing, turbulent, brawling, quarrelsome woman; a virago, shrew

Undercroft - Lower part of a building used as a storehouse.

Vespers - Sunset, evening prayer service.

Wicket - Smaller gate in a large one for pedestrian access.

Woodbine - Honeysuckle.

AUTHOR'S NOTE

Marlborough was an established settlement by 1204 but began to expand with the rebuilding of the castle, at both ends of the wide, long High Street. The charter was indeed granted to Marlborough in 1204 by King John. The fair continues to this day but it has moved to October and is now a Mop Fair - once a hiring fair. There are still two markets a week - much shrunken, but still operating, as John intended.

Savernake Forest lies at the southern edge of Marlborough town in Wiltshire and can still be visited today. Access is along the A4 to Newbury or the A346 to Salisbury. It is much smaller now (forty-six square miles) than in the thirteenth century when it was at its most extensive, covering some one hundred and fifty square miles. Today the Forestry Commission manage it, but there is still a hereditary warden, the Marquess of Ailesbury and it is Britain's only privately owned forest.

Today Savernake is a forest of mixed woodland but in the thirteenth century, it had for example, few of the large beech trees, we see today. They were planted, in the seventeenth century, and sadly are coming to the end of their lives now. The oaks though, are of considerable age. Big Belly (ied) Oak, is one of the oldest, already being about two hundred years old when King John rode past it! I have mentioned a few beech trees growing in West Baily simply because I wished to have a glass making industry in the forest.

There were many different people and officers in the Mediaeval forest; agisters, verderers and regarders to name but a few. Understanding the individual roles of these men and sometimes women, is quite a feat, even with years of study, so I have kept things simple and given the different roles names which are easily understood. Likewise, although surnames were not common in the early

13th century, for ease of reading, my characters have two names in the main.

In the days of John, the L'Estourmi family were the wardens of the forest. Geoffrey L'Estourmi fell foul of King Richard, having to pay a huge fine for supporting Count John in his uprising against the King. In my tale I have changed the family's name. Unless we know who they really were and what they actually did, I'm loath to make them do anything, so I'd rather make it up and have fictional characters, though the names of some of the minor players are to be found in the annals, if you look. The name Belvoir IS pronounced Bell voir and not 'Beaver' as it is nowadays. The English pronunciation 'Beaver' was built up over many centuries through the inability of the Anglo-Saxons to master the French tongue. It's the name of a small town of eastern France and there is still a castle there which was once owned by a noble family of the same name. Aumary is from the Norman branch of the family.

Now to Aumary (pronounced Aymery). He is a minor lord, not terribly wealthy and more a business-man than pure aristocracy. As warden of the forest he has quite a practical job and needs to know about the forest and its trades. He is a knight - yes; but first and foremost, a forester. I have made him a sympathetic character as so many folk of his class in novels are portrayed as proud, haughty and nasty. I fail to see how many of them could be so. They were dependent upon their peasants for their livelihood. If the peasant didn't prosper, neither did they at this level of society. Grander folk perhaps could be less amenable. Aumary takes every man as he finds him and isn't averse to rolling up his sleeves and getting on with it. His job as warden means he is very in touch with the lesser people who work with and under him.

Durley, now a small hamlet on the edge of the forest was once well hidden in the trees. The manor can no longer be seen but there is a farm and a house called Durley House, though this manor wasn't founded until the fourteen hundreds. The manor most people know about of course, is the one in Hilary Mantel's book, Wolfhall, (originally Ulfhall) a timbered building very near Burbage. The manor belonged to the Seymour family in the sixteenth century (who were also the hereditary wardens of the forest) and was the childhood home of Jane Seymour. With archeological exploration, Wolfhall is proving to be a grand Tudor palace. I didn't want to go anywhere near there.

The Regalia existed. It was extant until the seventeenth century when it disappeared. It was very likely broken up and melted down in the Civil War. However the ivory and silver horn is in The British Museum but is not on display.

The manor I have 'invented' is a walled courtyard house with a stone hall of two storeys and a mezzanine floor, accessed by a staircase of stone and an undercroft below, very much like Boothby Hall in Lincolnshire, the finest surviving mediaeval house of its type in the country.

The village around it owes much to Sheila Sancha's portrayal of Gerneham (Irnham near Grantham) village, again in Lincolnshire, in her wonderful children's book The Luttrell Village - Country Life in the Early Fourteenth Century.

This is a depiction of the home of Sir Geoffrey Luttrell in the thirteen hundreds, so wonderfully documented in the Luttrell Psalter (now in the British Library) considered one of the richest sources for visual depictions of everyday rural life in mediaeval England.

Salerno in Sicily was one of the finest medical schools in the known world from the tenth to the thirteenth centuries. It was the most important source of medical knowledge in Western Europe, both of the Arab and ancient world and people of both sexes flocked from all over to study there. Books were the mainstay of the school, hundreds being translated from Arabic, Greek and other languages. As a result, the medical practitioners of Salerno, both men and women, were unrivalled in knowledge and practicality.

Sadly the school declined in favour of Montpellier later in the thirteenth century and then as the church tightened its grip, medical research came to a grinding halt, not to be resurrected until the seventeenth century.

Many manors chose their own priests. Those who did not have the luxury of a pool of educated boys whom they could send to a larger town for ordination, relied on the bishop of the diocese to help out.

Villeins were tied to their manor and had to have the permission of their lord, amongst other things, to travel, marry and extend property. Freemen could do as they pleased within reason, though they too had to stay on the right side of their lord.

Little is known about the thirteenth century castle and town of Marlborough. Most historical research concentrates on the period of the later Middle Ages and tells us that the castle was an extremely large and important one even early in its history. The original market place of Marlborough town may have been on what is now the Green. The castle I speak about in my book, consists of just the inner, kidney shaped bailey. There may have been a huge outer bailey extending to the middle of the High Street, but nothing now remains. The motte of the castle keep is behind some buildings in the Marlborough College grounds and is a re-used prehistoric mound not unlike Silbury Hill, its big sister a few miles to the west. The town of Marlborough must have been important enough to have a charter and I have made it perhaps a little bigger and grander than it really was.

The Gilbertine Priory of St Margaret of Antioch; the only completely English ecclesiastical foundation, was actually situated up the hill to the south. I have placed them on the High Street for ease of storytelling. The order whose buildings actually lay on the High Street were the Carmelites, founded in 1316, and too late for our tales.

I have also straightened the river Kennet to make it easier to follow on my fanciful map and shortened the (present) High Street a little.

ABOUT THE AUTHOR

Susanna, like Aumary Belvoir has known the Forest of Savernake all her life. After a period at the University of Wales studying Speech Therapy, she returned to Wiltshire and then moved to Hampshire to work, not so very far from her forest. Susanna developed an interest in English history, particularly that of the 12th and 13th centuries, early in life and began to write about it in her twenties. She now lives in Northamptonshire with her husband and a small wire haired fox terrrier called Delphi.

TITLES IN THIS SERIES:

Belvoir's Promise
She Moved Through the Fair
Down by the Salley Gardens

Please visit the website for further information.
www.susannamnewstead.co.uk

or the Facebook page
The Savernake Novels.